Directions for

Stephanie Sowden grew up in Manchester and studied History and Politics at Durham University. After a brief foray into magazine journalism, she retrained in another love of hers – food – and now runs her own catering company. Stephanie took part in Curtis Brown Creative's selective novel writing course, during which she completed her first novel. She lives in South Manchester with her partner, Dave, and their little mad staffy, Butter.

Also by Stephanie Sowden

DIRECTIONS FOR
DARK
THINGS

STEPHANIE SOWDEN

CANELOCRIME

First published in the United Kingdom in 2024 by

Canelo
Unit 9, 5th Floor
Cargo Works, 1–2 Hatfields
London SE1 9PG
United Kingdom

A CIP catalogue record for this book is available from the British Library.

Print ISBN 978 1 80032 771 9
Ebook ISBN 978 1 80032 772 6

This book is a work of fiction. Names, characters, businesses, organizations, places and events are either the product of the author's imagination or are used fictitiously. Any resemblance to actual persons, living or dead, events or locales is entirely coincidental.

Cover design by The Brewster Project

Cover images © Shutterstock

Look for more great books at www.canelo.co

Printed and bound in Great Britain by Clays Ltd, Elcograf S.p.A.

1

For Dave

(and Butter – you are the very best dog)

One

The driveway up to the Lloyd Estate was as long as a cliché. It wound through the California scrub with overgrown dogwoods encroaching on the path, their grand potential long lost to years of neglect. Terri raced through those dogged dogwoods, far and away from the main road turn-off, its ratty wire fence and signs threatening trespassers. She didn't have a company car, but her red Ford Maverick made easy work of the unkempt drive, loose clay rubble skittering out from under its tyres. She couldn't help a twinge of a satisfied smile as she skated around the winding track, moving the gears effortlessly as she swung around a hairpin bend.

She pulled the car to a halt on the turning circle at the top of the driveway, as above the orange terracotta steps, the front door pulled open. Audrey Lloyd greeted her with an expression of omniscient expectation, though Terri had not warned her she was coming. No one had known where she was intending to head when she'd faked a headache and abandoned the office. 'Menstrual migraines,' she'd muttered conspiratorially to

I

Glenn, who'd pulled a face and told her not to be so gross at work.

'Miss Lloyd.' Terri introduced herself with her brightest smile, but felt the nerves tug at its corners. 'I'm Terri Nicholls. I've come to see you today with a proposition from Thornton Kendal.' Audrey Lloyd made no movement to suggest she either understood or cared what Terri had said, and so Terri elaborated, weakly. 'The property development firm. In West Hollywood. I'm an acquisitions broker there.' She added these extraneous facts in staccato sentences, each one losing its tone of hope in the face of Audrey's blank expression.

Audrey's eyes flicked beyond Terri toward the top of the driveway. 'You're alone, I take it?' she said finally, as if expecting a cavalry to be following her up.

Terri gave a stiff nod and thought it an odd question.

Audrey scrutinised her for a moment longer before evidently deciding this was the answer she'd wanted. She stepped back from the large oak door, its ostentatious stained-glass frontage flashing disco lights to the floor inside. Terri locked the Maverick and trotted up the steps, heels clacking on the smooth stone.

In contrast to its surrounding three hundred acres of private land, Lloyd House itself did not appear desolate or abandoned in any way. It had just the one resident, but was packed with possessions, memorabilia, and trash alike. Having greeted Terri from the steps, Audrey strode into the entrance hall, leaving Terri to close the front door behind her. Terri turned back into the hallway, illuminated only by an electric chandelier with less than half the bulbs in working order, and made an effort not to pull a face at the surroundings.

She followed Audrey through the narrow path between towering stacks of papers and boxes. They were piled high on an antique sideboard and overflowed with once glamourous bric-a-brac – a tarnished old Oscar, a stuffed Persian cat, a gold-edged mirror. Terri picked her feet over a decaying mound of what she thought might be racoon faeces and stifled a shudder.

Audrey herself appeared as eclectic as her environment: a navy Hermès scarf wrapped around her head, a tumble of black curls emerging from beneath, emerald hoop earrings glistening at the sides of her cheeks. Her skin was withered yet somehow alive, as if the markings of age couldn't suffocate her spirit. Amber yellow eyes flicked a glance over the old woman's shoulder as they journeyed through the hallway, bright against her dark olive colouring – both features inherited from her Dominican mother.

As if on cue, they passed by a portrait of Estella Lloyd – that infamous beauty forever captured in oil on canvas. Audrey gave a vague wave of her hand in the direction of the gilded framed painting where it rested listlessly on the floor – half-hidden by the wheel of a rusty bicycle.

She led Terri through the entrance hall and out into the main living room. The wall to the right was a curved semi-circle of smudged windows from floor to ceiling. When the house had been built in the midst of the First World War, Arnold Lloyd had hired an artist rather than an architect to design a home that would allow the family good luck and a prosperous future. This artist included glass and curves at almost every turn, features which the architect later hired to bring the vision to life cursed at and argued against. But Arnold Lloyd was firm. And if you offer someone enough money, they'll do just about anything.

Audrey gestured for Terri to take a seat on a crowded couch piled with pillows, blankets and cat hair, which Terri managed to navigate and find a small patch on which to settle. Audrey herself remained standing, just to Terri's right. The glass wall looked out across the vast Lloyd Estate, the undeveloped goldmine Terri knew would get her not just a sizeable bonus, but a promotion and respect at the office too. The early afternoon LA sun cast into the living room in golden strands, illuminating highways of dust. Terri gazed for a moment out at the marble cenotaph that ruptured the vacant scrubland, still gleaming an impossible white for a monument left abandoned for over sixty years. Audrey caught the direction of her gaze.

'A cenotaph is meant to stand in memorial for a body laid elsewhere,' Audrey said in her soft, girlish voice. 'But Daddy didn't care about rules like that. He paid, gosh, hundreds of thousands of dollars to get Mama moved from Westwood Memorial Park to be buried again here, right underneath that monument.' She extended a knobbled finger to point out of the window.

'It's quite a memorial,' Terri replied politely. 'I'm sure your mother would have loved it.'

'Oh yes,' Audrey agreed. 'Mama did enjoy an ostentatious display of affection. That was why she and Daddy were so perfect for each other.' She looked at Terri with her deep amber eyes, ringed in what looked like days-old, smudged kohl. 'You'll probably be wanting to rip it up.'

A thick swallow stretched painfully down Terri's throat at the unexpectedly abrupt turn to business.

'Well, ah...' It took a moment for Terri to find her words, as she blinked around the vast, overstuffed living room, feeling overwhelmed. She turned back to Audrey, letting her professional instincts take over. She could do this.

'That's not strictly the case,' she began, straightening herself up and flashing the smile she saved for the toughest business negotiations. 'We would want to honour your family's history here. We could make arrangements to set aside a portion of land for a memorial garden around your mother's grave. A place for residents to walk and meet up and—'

'Let their dogs shit on my mother's corpse?' Audrey interrupted. But Terri was surprised by the air of lightness in her tone. A humour she hadn't expected. Audrey laughed at her expression and moved to sit down on the equally crowded couch opposite her. 'I'm sorry,' she said with a gentle titter, adjusting her flowing satin robe around the loose-fitting slacks and shirt underneath. It was patterned with fleur-de-lis outlined in gold thread. 'I don't mean to make you uncomfortable, Miss Nicholls.'

'Please,' Terri replied smoothly. 'Call me Terri.'

Audrey gave her a deft nod. 'I really don't mean to make you uncomfortable, but sometimes an old woman can't help but get her kicks where she must.' She gave a small smile and it occurred to Terri that Audrey's voice wasn't girlish at all, but delicate. It was a sound Terri was not used to hearing in her world of men – and the women that mimic their hard, loud tones to gain respect. If you want to get on in a man's world, there's no use speaking like a woman. But Audrey Lloyd had never had to get on in a man's world. She had her own world, right up here.

Terri cringed as her own voice sounded crassly tough in response, delivering the hollow promises she knew the old woman would want. 'You haven't made me uncomfortable. But I *do* want to assure you that your family's connection to this property will not simply be thrown by the wayside. Your history here is legendary. Your mother was an icon, your father a figurehead. The Lloyd Estate will not just be turned into cheap condos and flashy apartment blocks.'

'No, of course not,' Audrey replied, sitting back on the sofa. 'This land is worth far more than that. Let me guess – you're thinking a hundred homes, each with a few acres of their own land. Private swimming pools for popstars to drown in, sweeping staircases for starlets to fall down.' Terri didn't know what her face did in response to this, but it made Audrey laugh. The truth was of course that that would be exactly what Thornton Kendal had in mind for the Lloyd Estate, although Terri wouldn't have put it quite so morbidly.

Audrey levered an arm out across the back of the sofa that had visible marks of soiling. Cat pee, possibly. Although Terri had seen no cat that wasn't stuffed.

'It's not a bad ploy, sending you up here,' Audrey said with a conciliatory nod. 'Who better to persuade the mysterious old woman to sign on the dotted line than the only female working in the office?' One carefully painted eyebrow twitched upwards. 'Oh, you didn't need to tell me that. I've had property developers coming up here for years trying to buy this land off me or trying to figure out who it's left to in my will when I finally croak.' She leaned forward, resting her elbows on her knees. 'And not one of them has been a woman.'

Terri felt her bottom lip fall just a little, her eyes widen a fraction.

'No, it's not a bad ploy, sending you up here,' Audrey repeated after a beat. 'But we all know who's pulling your little marionette strings back at the office. Who'll actually get the juicy bonus, the corner office, the promotion.'

'They don't know I'm here,' Terri blurted, surprising herself with the admission. The old woman had riled her into defending herself, into proving herself worthy. She couldn't read Audrey's expression, but it lingered somewhere between surprise and approval. 'I told them I had a headache so I could leave the office early.' She made a rash decision to continue her confessional. 'They wouldn't have let me come on my own, you're right – they don't trust a woman with an acquisition this big. But' – she inhaled deeply, steadying the trembles in her hands by shoving them tightly between her thighs – 'I decided to take things into my own hands.'

Terri hoped the confession would warm Audrey up to her, and from the slight tug at the edge of the old woman's lips, she dared to hope it might be working.

'So you'll listen to my demands?' Audrey asked. 'Put forward to your bosses what *my* vision of this estate is?' She gestured out of the vast windows behind her. 'I want my mother's grave to remain sacred. Fenced off. I want a statue of my father at the entrance gate.' She sat back again, keeping her eyes laser focused on Terri. 'I want my name written in ten-foot lights down the driveway.'

Terri blinked in surprise and Audrey held her for a beat before tipping her head back with a wide laugh, yellowed teeth with blackened roots gnashing in the air. 'Oh, you are easy,' she said and Terri felt the marionette strings Audrey spoke of earlier, twitching from Audrey's hands to her own limbs.

Terri swallowed stiffly, unnerved. Audrey laughed at her serious expression, but it was warmer this time and

Terri couldn't help but think that despite it all, the old woman was starting to like her.

She didn't know why.

'I tell you what.' Audrey cocked her head to one side and Terri felt the marionette strings tighten. 'I'll give you what you want. I'll sell to your bosses.' Terri frowned in surprise. 'But,' Audrey continued, taking an evident enjoyment from her shock, 'I'll only sign on Friday.'

'On… Friday,' Terri repeated slowly, trying to understand what Audrey was getting at.

'Yes.' Audrey nodded. 'On Friday.' She smiled at her again, baring those yellow teeth. 'If you spend the week with me.'

Terri's frown burrowed deeper. 'You want me to spend the week with you?'

'Old ladies can get so bored. Especially up here all alone,' she replied gently. 'Keep me company for a week and I'll sign whatever papers you want.'

'I–I don't know if I have enough vacation days to take a week off,' Terri stumbled, thinking hard. It wasn't just the vacation days, although it was true she'd already used up her measly allowance going back home for her niece's christening. Did she *have* a week to spare? She'd promised Ethan this would be sorted by tonight; she knew they were running out of time. Her fingers went agitatedly to twist the diamond ring on her left hand, as a small prickle of embarrassment stung her cheeks. Who had she thought she was to make promises like that?

'Well, they already believe you to be ill today.' Audrey batted her concerns easily away. 'Who's to say your ailment won't progress throughout the next four days?'

Terri inhaled and then looked at Audrey with interest. 'I'm sorry, but can I ask why you want me to spend the week here?'

She was surprised to see Audrey look sad for a moment before answering. 'It's been a while since an intelligent young lady sought out my company. Forgive an old woman for wanting to indulge in being desired for just one last week.'

'OK,' Terri said slowly. She looked up at the crowded living room, taking in the stacks of boxes, the overflowing piles of books, sheets of paper haphazardly discarded. She could use this week. She *needed* this week – surely Ethan would understand that. Finally, she nodded and gave her new companion a broad smile. 'OK. I can come visit you this week.'

A cautious relief slowly settled on the tattoo of her heart. She had a whole week now.

But no longer.

Two

Don
Friday

Detective Don Vernon accepted the polystyrene cup of coffee Rose handed him from the machine hidden away at the back of the nurses' station.

'Don't go telling everyone about this now,' she said with a faux-stern expression and a wink. 'Don't need all your guys expecting our secret coffee supplies whenever they're hanging around waiting for a victim or suspect. They can head down to the cafeteria like everyone else.'

Don mimed locking his lips with an imaginary key and Rose laughed. 'This old codger thanks you from the bottom of his aching old man feet.' He jerked his head down the industrial lit corridor, turning to business. 'So which do you think she is? Vic or suspect?'

'It's your job to tell me that, Detective,' Rose answered.

'I've not seen her yet.'

Rose considered and seemed to accept the explanation. 'She's pretty beat up. Not as bad as the other one, so I hear' – she paused for Don to raise his eyebrows pointedly – 'but she's been through it.'

'Find anything on her person?'

'Couple of bits – a pen, some notepaper, pair of earrings, compact mirror.' Rose shrugged and gestured behind her. 'I've got them in a box somewhere if you want me to dig them out?'

Don shook his head. 'Maybe later. How long will the doc be?' he asked, turning to face the corridor, itching to get started.

'Shouldn't be long now,' Rose said, her attention dropping down to the brown paper files on the desk. 'Take a seat and be patient like I'm sure your mom taught you.'

Don gave another gruff laugh and held his cup aloft in thanks before turning away toward the cracked vinyl seating. He took a sip of the hot coffee and picked up the copy of the *LA Times* on the seat next to him. It was a few weeks old – the front page still full of Reagan captured mid-statement talking about Israel and Beirut, a smiling Jimmy Connors underneath giving an interview ahead of the US Open. But Don couldn't focus on this old news. His foot tapped agitatedly against the metal pole of his chair. He'd waited his whole career for this, and now it was so close the thought of these last few minutes sparked his childish impatience.

He'd trudged into the station that morning, on the cusp of lateness but uncaring. He stared into the elevator's large rectangular mirror as it took him up to the fourth floor, marvelling at the old man who stared back. Silver temples and not much on top, heavier jowls than when he'd first walked into that place thirty-five years earlier. Dried yolk from the fried egg sandwich Jill had made him for breakfast still clung in curling yellow crusts at the corner of his lips. He'd jabbed his tongue out to try and push the remnants of his breakfast back into his mouth.

The doors had dinged open to the morning briefing already underway in the centre of the open-plan office space. The captain – Ray Glover – was perched against a desk going through the roll call of cases for that day.

'Nice of you to join us, Detective Vernon,' Ray said, without glancing up from the file in his hands.

Don gave a half-hearted nod, but took no notice of the reprimand. He was the longest-standing member of the squad, his gold watch almost in sight. He'd mentored Ray when he had first joined from the academy, five years Don's junior. Don had never had ambitions of rising through the ranks further than detective, his passion firmly cemented in boots-on-the-ground investigation. But he had supported and cheerleaded his friend as he'd climbed higher and higher, even, eventually, over and above Don himself.

'Alright, we have an abandoned car down on Sycamore, reported stolen in the early hours of the morning from the Quick Stop Motel parking lot in San Bernardino. Mitchell.' Ray raised a chubby finger to the red-headed junior detective at the front of the encircled group. 'Liaise with the guys down there, they want witness statements and prints from our end, and transport of the vehicle back.' Mitchell grunted. 'Problem, Detective?'

'No, sir,' Mitchell said quietly. Don knew what the grunt was about. It was a boring case, unlikely to go anywhere, bureaucracy and admin work to burn up the day.

Ray handed a file over, before turning to the next one and nodding deeply, a small frown puckering across his forehead as he thought.

'Don,' he said, turning for the first time to his old friend. 'You're gonna want this one.'

Don looked up, intrigued, as he shrugged off his jacket and hung it on the back of his desk chair. 'What have we got?'

Ray glanced back down at the folder before holding it out. 'Body down at the Lloyd Estate.'

Don had stilled and checked his friend's face for any sign this was a ruse, a prank for the sake of old times. But Ray remained as serious as ever, the folder still held out in front of him. Don stepped forward and took the proffered file, as Ray started speaking again. 'Be careful with this one, Don. Could be press attention. Do it properly, and do it discreetly.'

'Always, boss,' Don replied, flipping open the cardboard cover of the file. 'Details?'

'Most of it's in there, what we know. Which isn't much. Call came in about four a.m. from a payphone down by the Double Tree strip mall. Deceased appears to have fallen down a flight of stone steps in the garden. Likely killed instantly, but the guys from the coroner's office will confirm that when they get to the postmortem.'

Don frowned and looked back up at Ray. 'So what's our involvement?'

'There's a witness. Woman who called it in. Claiming it was an accident.'

'You suspect foul play?'

Ray shook his head. 'Hard to say. She's not in such a great state herself. She's down at Sacred Heart being treated for several injuries.' He paused to gesture at the file in Don's hand before shrugging. 'Details should be in there. Whatever happened, looks like she got caught in some kind of crossfire, or got back nearly as much as she dished out. Just find out if it was a tragic accident, or if we're gonna have to fend off a load of suddenly interested hacks.'

'Alright,' Don said again, nodding. He pulled back his chair and sat down, spreading the thin file across his desk. The morning briefing carried on around him while he read, feeling adrenaline seep slowly through his veins as he took in the scant details.

Don had always known of the Lloyd Estate – it existed in a state of semi-permanent infamy. Growing up during the golden age of Hollywood in LA, it was almost impossible not to develop some kind of fanboy obsession with the movie industry. He could remember seeing grainy images of the grand house set against its surrounding three hundred acres in early issues of the *Hollywood Reporter*, with Arnold Lloyd, the legendary writer, producer and director, posing against the vast landscape of his home. Since his death nearly fifty years ago, the property had been owned by his reclusive daughter, Audrey, hidden behind chain-link fences among grounds patrolled by wild dogs, a brief stop on the celebrity bus tours that trawled through those gilded hills.

It had been a long time since Don had stood at the base of that driveway, staring up at the tall iron gate, nervous energy shivering through his hands as he reached forward to push them open. If someone was dead at the house now, Don knew he would not be the only person intrigued by the case. It would make headlines, just for the mysterious property itself.

'The Lloyd Estate,' he murmured to himself, picking up the cover sheet in the file. 'Here you are again, old friend.' Because Don was not just a fan. He had a professional interest in the Lloyd Estate. An interest that now seemed to be book-ending his career.

He took in the few details they had. Name of deceased. Name of witness. Time of call. Location of call. Then he flipped over the paper to reveal a photograph of the body in situ, limbs askew and a pool of deep scarlet that suggested, as Ray had pointed out, instant death.

He read through the rest of the short file while the morning briefing continued, waiting, out of politeness, for Ray to wrap up before getting to his feet again and pulling his jacket back on across the brown leather shoulder straps of his gun holster. Ray came over as he was fitting his notebook into the inside pocket.

'You got a good scope of the Lloyd case?' Ray asked.

'Reckon so.' Don gave a nod. 'No previous connection between deceased and witness, no obvious motive for anything untoward. Witness called it in herself.' He gave a shrug. 'No one else is going up to that old house, would have been easy enough to get away with. Likelihood is an unfortunate accident, but I'll get an answer about the witness's injuries too.'

'Thanks, Don,' Ray answered, before speaking again after a brief pause, eyeing his friend carefully. 'I'm trusting you to do this properly, Don. I could've given it to any of the other guys.'

'I know.'

'Stick with the facts of *this* case. Don't...' Ray paused again as if trying to work out the order of his next words. 'Don't get carried away. Look for horses, not zebras.' That was something Don himself had taught Ray in the very early days of his career. *If you hear hooves in Griffith Park, you think horses not zebras.* Usually, with police work, the least interesting answer is the solve. 'Don't make me look like an old fool indulging his friend's whims.'

Don took the warning with a solemn nod. 'I know what I'm doing, Ray.'

'I know you do.' Ray clapped a hand on his bicep.

'But there *is* a history up there.'

'Doesn't make it zebras, Don.'

And when Rose finally called to him from behind the nurses' station, one hand raised to catch his attention, it was that history of Lloyd House Don had to forcibly pull himself out of. He knew Ray was right. He had to focus on this case. But if he could use the opportunity to resolve a couple of unanswered questions from years gone by, then he would grab it with both hands.

Three

Audrey
Monday

Audrey watched carefully, scrutinising the young woman as she made her decision.

'OK,' Terri said finally with a small, satisfied nod, and a bright smile. 'OK'.

And Audrey knew she had her.

Audrey had never been lonely, exactly. She'd always found comfort in her memories, in her loved ones. But real-world companionship was something quite different. And this intelligent young woman, with a mass of thick dark hair, curly bangs falling just shy of her eyebrows, felt familiar in some way. As if time had reset itself, and Audrey had been delivered another chance. Audrey smiled at her new companion, feeling her face split into a grin of genuine satisfaction.

'Wonderful,' she said, clapping her hands together softly. 'Now then, I'm going to make some tea.'

'Oh, really, you don't have to.' Terri raised one hand in a futile attempt to halt her. 'Please don't go to any trouble on my part.'

Audrey felt the skin beneath her eyes twitch a little at Terri's refusal. 'It's no trouble. The tea is delicious; you'll enjoy it.'

Terri gave a shallow laugh. 'More of a coffee person myself.'

'You'll like the tea better.' Audrey heard the sentence come out as hard as the marble surface of the coffee table. It had been a long time since she'd had company. She corrected herself, remembering the old golden cafetière that was gathering dust in a kitchen cupboard.

'For tomorrow, I'll find some coffee,' she conceded with a small smile. Terri gave a twitched, awkward nod of acceptance, and Audrey turned to the kitchen.

'Thank you,' she heard her new guest say in a small voice, and Audrey felt a swell of warmth blossom somewhere in her cold chest. 'Oh.' The small voice stopped her again just as Audrey reached the kitchen door. 'Which way is the bathroom?'

Audrey directed her down the corridor out of the living room before pushing into the kitchen and making her way to the far corner by the sink. She pulled open a cupboard that clung on by only one of its rusty old hinges and retrieved Mama's tea set.

As ever, when she brought out her mother's tea set, Audrey felt rather than heard her small sigh escape into the room. They'd played tea parties when Audrey was small, out on the veranda in the stuffy Floridian heat of their old home. Then when they'd moved here, they'd set up on the terrace just outside the kitchen and watch the workmen build the rest of their magnificent home around them.

'Oh, Mama,' Audrey said softly to herself, one finger encircling the gold embossed lid of the teapot, feeling the memories of her long life form a current pulling her back into the past, dragging and swirling her as if they were a flood disappearing down a drain.

As always, she allowed herself to drown.

It would be a quiet funeral thanks to the influenza outbreak. Audrey had been shoved into a black velvet dress with long, puffed sleeves and a white sash around her middle. Mrs Hackton, her father's secretary, tugged at her curls with a brush, muttering under her breath while jamming pins painfully into the young girl's scalp. But Audrey barely noticed. She had been numb ever since last week when the doctor had shut the door to her mother's room behind him and crouched down to his knees.

Audrey had taken to sitting outside the room, legs stretched out into the corridor, tripping up the staff as they went about their daily work. She would bury her hands in the carpet and draw pictures by moving the fibres in different directions.

'I'm afraid you're the lady of the house, now,' the doctor had said with a soft voice. It was interrupted by a wail of anguish from her father, who was still inside the room. *The lady of the house.* Audrey had ruminated over the words. She was just ten years old.

Today Audrey walked next to her father, her small hand gripped in his shaking fist, stoically silent while Arnold mourned visibly enough for the both of them. Group gatherings were banned to protect the city from the deadly Spanish flu that had taken Mama, but the church still had a collection of mourners – friends and colleagues, their wet faces swaddled in white cloth masks.

'They'll scare the girl.' Mrs Hackton tutted as they entered the church, eyeing the faceless people suspiciously. But Audrey wasn't scared. She preferred people like this. Like she preferred the silent dancing figures of Daddy's films. They always disappointed her when they stepped off screen to come to their house, only to shriek and laugh and sing at the top of their voices.

In the week since Mama had died, Audrey had felt, quite literally, nothing. Hollowed out, like a soft-boiled egg at the end of her teaspoon – the shell polished clean inside as if it had never contained anything at all.

'It's not right, Arnold,' Mrs Hackton had hissed to Daddy the morning the coroner had taken Mama away. A lump on a stretcher covered in a white sheet secured tightly with ropes. 'The girl's not cried once.'

Arnold had not replied but sobbed louder than before and returned to his office to weep into the night. Of course Audrey couldn't cry, she'd thought to herself with a small frown. Daddy was using all the tears up.

Audrey slid onto the pew next to her father and squeezed his hand tightly while she lowered her head to listen to the priest's prayers. The service went by quickly – or slowly, Audrey couldn't really tell which. She spent the duration counting the manicured tiles on the back wall behind the altar, working out different methods and calculations to find out how many tiles there were without counting each one individually. Numbers and patterns always soothed her. She could spend hours in her room coming up with new patterns, designing rules and building sequences that could grow and grow forever. But she'd learned not to tell the grown-ups about this. Whenever she did it would be met with a furrowed brow and pursed lips and she would be sent to play outside, or a playdate would be set up with the child of a family friend.

There were no other children at the funeral, Audrey was grateful to see. As they filed out of the church and toward the graveyard where Mama would be laid to rest, Audrey nodded politely at the whispered condolences from the faceless people. She knew Mrs Hackton's eyes would be on her, even more closely today of all days. Audrey knew she disconcerted other people. She was told off for asking too many questions. She was called precocious for beating adults at chess. She was told not to take life so seriously, to go and be a *child* for Christ's sake. Most of these rebukes came from Mrs Hackton, who seemed perplexed by the very notion of Audrey's existence. Mama had always smiled blandly at Audrey's observations on the world, with never much else to add, and Daddy would tell her she was a clever little thing and then go back to work. But Audrey had learned to navigate life around Mrs Hackton. She had learned to recognise when something she was doing or saying would result in what Audrey deemed punishment. The grown-ups never seemed to think them punishments, but for Audrey to be sent off to dance class with little Melissa Gerritsen was a tedium so great that Audrey could feel her very soul drift from her body. Avoiding these situations had become something of a game, and Audrey did like to play with Mrs Hackton. To watch the woman scrutinise her closely, waiting to pounce on any opportunity to 'socialise' her better, only for Audrey to thwart it at the last moment. And so, when Audrey had heard Mrs Hackton's words of concern about Audrey's lack of tears for Mama, she began experimenting with ways to allay those concerns – lest she be sent to singing lessons next.

She could feel Mrs Hackton's eyes on her from across the brown rectangle in the ground where Mama would soon be deposited. The six besuited pallbearers came to a stop at the head of the grave, Mama's gleaming white coffin resting elegantly on their shoulders, the solid gold fixtures glinting in the autumn sunlight. Audrey bent her arm back to the taffeta white bow of her sash and slipped her fingertips into the folds of heavy material. Earlier that morning, once Mrs Hackton had finally pinned her hair into a satisfactory enough style, Audrey had made her escape while Hackton was distracted with the catering plans. She'd snuck down the corridor lined with mannequins showcasing Mama's favourite dresses, into her parents' bedroom and the en-suite bathroom attached, knowing exactly what she was looking for. She'd spent a lot of time sitting on the chaise longue in that bathroom watching her parents get ready for galas and balls, spraying Mama's perfume into her face to taste it, and drawing ruby red lines on her arms in rouge. Mama had loved dressing up, and Audrey loved it with her. Although, since moving to California, those occasions had become fewer and fewer.

She'd flipped open Daddy's bathroom cabinet and pilfered one small blade from his razor set. She pulled the blade from where it was now stowed in her bow and let it fall into the palm of her hand. She squeezed tightly and felt a warm wetness erupt in her palm, the edges of the blade digging easily into the soft skin inside of her hand. She'd spent her nights experimenting with a knife stolen from underneath Mrs Doyle, the cook's, nose, but knew she would never be able to smuggle something of that size into the church. Her hand and thigh were decorated with small red nicks from her experiments, and she felt the healing skin split painfully open once again. As she'd practised, the tears streamed from her eyes, running fast and free down her cheeks. She stared into Mrs Hackton's face, vision blurred and disorientated, but she saw the small, accepting nod Mrs Hackton gave her before lowering her head to the sight of the white coffin now framed by mud.

Audrey released her grasp on the blade, letting it drop into the grass behind her, and wiped her palm on the back of her thigh, the bloodied smear hiding among black velvet.

Audrey flexed open her hand above the now perfectly laid tea-tray. Sixty-four years had passed by, and the scar from her mother's funeral now blended seamlessly among other cracks and wrinkles of age. But it was there. The reminder nestled forever, deep in her skin, of the things you had to do to deal with other people. The wrong sort of people. Audrey picked up the tea-tray and smiled to herself. She supposed she would find out soon what sort of people her new friend would turn out to be.

Four

Today hadn't exactly gone as expected. A whole week in Lloyd House with this strange old woman was not what Terri and Ethan had been planning. She recognised now how naive they'd been – driven by panic, surging on the adrenaline of unfamiliar hope. It was meant to be simple, quick – get in and get out. But now she knew, in the formidable presence of Audrey Lloyd, in her overflowing living room, that that had never been an option.

Glenn had outright laughed in her face when she'd first asked around the office about Lloyd House.

'Ridiculous plan,' he'd said, shaking his head. 'Folk have been going up there for years trying to make a bid for that land. The mad old bitch is having none of it.'

The whole office had laughed, and Terri had bristled. Her time with Thornton Kendal had been two years of unfulfilled promises – of being told to keep her head down and do her job well and then maybe, just maybe, she'd be allowed to take the lead on an acquisition. But she had since learned to expect nothing from her firm. She'd once heard Matthew, the Dartmouth graduate who still had his college bumper stickers on proud display, suggest trying to buy a section of Griffith Park from the city for Christ's sake, and Glenn had just patted him on the back and told him that he liked his spirit, but Griffith might be 'just a bit out of reach'. Matthew had laughed harder than anyone at Terri's questions about the Lloyd Estate.

'Fuck what they think,' Ethan had told her that night, shaking his head in dismissal at her colleagues' reaction to her proposal. Her fiancé had never had much time for the boys' club at her office, something that had been obvious after the first awkward Christmas party where Ethan had got drunk and called her boss, Mr Thornton, a *dirty fucking hawk* for supporting nuclear progress. Terri had not brought him to any other work events. 'Call in sick,' he'd continued, 'and go up on your own. The old woman doesn't need to know the bosses are in the dark. All you need is to get through the front door.' His blue eyes had darkened then, brow furrowing seriously. 'You've got to do this, Terri. We don't have anything else.'

And now she *was* up there alone, and Audrey Lloyd was a force she could never have expected. Terri didn't quite know how to describe it, but she seemed to influence even the very molecules of air around her. And up in this house – her *lair* – it was almost impossible not to gift your entire agency over to her.

Once she had agreed to visit with Audrey every day for the week, the old woman smiled. It was an odd smile, with her bottom lip stretched straight, but her eyes shone with it like a little girl at the fair. She offered tea, which Terri had accepted after an ill-received comment about preferring coffee, before asking her way to the bathroom. Audrey directed her down a corridor off the living room, in the opposite direction to where Audrey disappeared off into the kitchen.

The hallway, like everywhere else, was crammed with possessions, although the route through was a little less crowded. She passed by a mannequin draped in an extravagant emerald ball gown, spangled with small stones Terri knew would not be worthless crystals. She'd seen an old black and white photograph of Estella Lloyd wearing this dress to some state dinner, but the greyscale had not done the colours justice. Even more than sixty years later, coated in a thin layer of grey dust, it sparkled.

Terri moved on and gazed up at a movie poster hung on the wall – *In the Clouds Above* – Arnold Lloyd's classic war epic about a fighter pilot in the First World War, which had secured him his first golden statue. His genius had come from his easy transition from silent film to the talkies, embracing rather than shunning any new and wonderous idea the industry could throw at him. A beautiful blonde in a dramatic black dress stood in one corner of the poster, gazing up at a plane surrounded by bubbly illustrated clouds, with a handsome, square-jawed pilot reaching down toward her.

Terri found the bathroom and, after peeing, stood before a large worn mirror, dark pockmarks marring her reflection. She stared dead into her own dark eyes and gave herself a silent pep talk before running a finger underneath each eye to catch the dried flakes of fallen mascara. Next, she fluffed up her hair with her fingertips, pleased that it still held its bounce from her work that morning with the blow-dryer. She straightened her jacket so the broad shoulder pads sat back evenly on her frame, oddly embarrassed that she'd sat in front of Audrey for so long with her body at such a strange, twisted angle.

Exiting the bathroom, Terri noticed another door opposite, slightly ajar, the light from the hallway illuminating an inviting path inside. She hesitated for a moment before softly kicking it wider and staring into the room, which looked to be some sort of office. Hope dared to bounce in her chest; perhaps this would be easier than she'd first thought. There were the usual piles of debris she'd already become accustomed to seeing around this house – some valuable-looking trinkets among battered old playbills and notebooks. It would take a whole team of people to rid this house of its junk. A small, unexpected shudder of something like guilt rippled through her at the thought. But then Ethan pushed his way into her mind, the last few difficult months prying a monumental wedge between them – and her own selfish needs smothered any guilt for the gilded life of Audrey Lloyd.

'If you just let me look at the accounts,' she'd said for thousandth time, legginged legs folded up under herself as she sat on the floor of their once-proud condo. Ethan was already slurring at only five p.m. and she'd winced to think he'd driven home in that state. What must the people at the office have thought?

'*You* won't understand the accounts, Terri,' he'd said with a note of derision she'd only really heard creep into his voice over the last year of financial woes. The Ethan she'd moved to California with would want to hit the asshole she was now being forced to cohabit with. The ex-hippy forced into a suit and tie for dreams that were never really his – continuing the legacy of his father's business, his hand forced by grief and loyalty. 'Can't you just stay in your goddamned fucking lane for once in your life and let me *sort it*.'

The first time they'd had this argument she'd railed and fought back. Stupidly made the fight about his rudeness like he wanted her to, to shift the focus away from their dire financial straits. But she'd learned to stay focused. She no longer had the luxury of principled rage at her fiancé's terse tone with her.

'Well, it doesn't exactly seem like you do, either.' She hadn't meant it as a dig. Not entirely. But he'd responded with a flinch as if she'd slapped him all the same. She continued talking before he could formulate words from his outrage. 'But *I* was the business major at college, while you spent four years reading Tolstoy. I *do* understand accounts; I might be able to—'

But like all the other times it had been no use. He'd been frozen on the edge of vocal outrage, only to realise he had nothing of merit to say. His eyes had fallen, and he'd taken a step back before swinging around and escaping into the kitchen for the bottle of gin that was still on the counter next to plates of last night's barely eaten dinner. He'd got drunk, passed out on the sofa in front of the flickering TV while Terri had worked diligently on the latest project Thornton had had her assist on. Back then, she'd still naively believed that if she could just prove herself, she'd get her due. And maybe, just maybe, if she got a promotion, a decent chunk of commission from a new development – maybe they could start to crawl their way out of Ethan's mess.

Naive indeed.

Shaking loose the memories, she stepped further into the office. There was only one window, tangled by the shadows of overgrown trees outside, so only thin streams of daylight illuminated the room. There was a desk pushed up underneath it, drowning in boxes split at their corners so old pages creased out, yellowed and wrinkled from years of storage. Terri felt the boxes call for her, felt her fingers flex instinctively toward them in return – but then she heard Audrey's footsteps back on the tiled floor of the living room.

It was OK. Terri had a week now – she had time. It would be here somewhere. She'd find it, she had to. And now at least she had a place to start.

She escaped the office and when she got back to the sitting room, Audrey had laid the marble coffee table with a golden tray, a tall gold-lidded teapot with a long china spout and two elegant cups and saucers wrapped in what Terri was certain was real gold leaf embossed with flowers. Terri approached, but Audrey didn't seem to hear her at first, lips murmuring unheard words to herself.

Terri cleared her throat awkwardly to make her presence known again and Audrey blinked up, something almost like blank surprise clearing her features. As if she'd entirely forgotten Terri was there. Another beat and the confident expression from before settled back into place, eyes seeming to twinkle again as she smiled at her guest.

'My mama collected this set,' Audrey told Terri as she retook her seat, perched on the edge of the filthy couch. 'From Vienna. Daddy wouldn't even let her get it out during the war – some of his friends were *that* pedantic about their patriotism.' Audrey picked up the teapot and poured a long stream of brewed brown liquid into the cup nearest Terri. 'I had a British tutor when I was younger. Obsessive' – Audrey looked at her earnestly – '*obsessive* about her tea.' She blinked and shook her head lightly while she turned her attention to her own teacup. 'Well, I've just never been able to shake the habit. English breakfast tea with a splash of milk.' She gave a firm nod. 'You know I even get Twinings imported over from Fortnum and Mason in London. It just tastes different to the stuff they have over here. Every six months they send a huge package and charge me handsomely for it.' She sat back and considered Terri with an indulgent smile before giving a little half-hearted sigh. 'You must think what a waste of money that is. That for what I spend on buying tea from England, you could no doubt have a new car.' She shrugged. 'But money is a funny old thing, and you lose track of its power when you're accustomed to it.'

Terri thought for a moment before replying, feeling a jolt of sickness at what she could do with the money Audrey spent on a hot beverage. 'It's not my job to police how you spend your money,' she said instead, before taking a sip of the tea once Audrey had splashed a white cloud of milk into it.

'Well, I'll have even more of it by the end of this week if you get your way I suppose.'

'So you will,' Terri said, feeling suddenly uncomfortable again.

'Now then.' Audrey eyed her carefully. 'You'll need to be getting off soon, won't you?' She drank her tea in inelegant gulps that juxtaposed the small teacups. Terri had resisted looking at her watch so far, but the sun streaming in through the curved glass window had taken on the golden hue of evening. 'You'll need enough time to call the office and tell them you won't be making it in for the rest of the week.' She smiled kindly. 'Little do they know the sacrifice of missing you for a week will reap them dividends.'

Terri nodded and felt herself relax just a little. Everything would have changed by Friday. She'd make sure she did this right – she'd make sure she'd find it.

But as she climbed into the car and made her way back down the driveway, there was an odd contraction in her stomach. A floating threat she didn't want to acknowledge.

Five

Don
Friday

'Room eighteen,' Rose said, when he'd hauled himself back up to the nurses' station, tossing his now empty cup into the trash can just behind it. She directed him down the linoleum corridor, with its strip lighting and strong stench of disinfectant.

'Thanks, Rose.' Don nodded. 'Any details I need to know?'

Rose tilted her head to one side. 'She's OK, but drowsy. Bad ankle sprain, cuts to her hands, broken finger and a bad hit on the back of her head.'

'She said anything to you?'

'Not a peep.'

Don raised his hand in a silent gesture of thanks and set off down the corridor, looking for room eighteen.

He gave a small knock on the door before opening it wide to find his witness propped up in bed, drinking dazedly from a plastic cup of orange juice while a flickering TV played an old episode of *Magnum, P.I.* in one corner. Her dark hair was pulled to one side with an elastic band, a thick white padded dressing covering the base of her skull, just above the nape of her neck. She looked up as he entered, cavernously dark bags slung from her eyes.

'Theresa Nicholls?' he said gently, as if he was approaching an easily spooked fawn.

She nodded and tried to speak, before coughing to clear her throat and trying again. 'How can I help you?'

'I'm Detective Don Vernon with the LAPD.' He flashed his badge from his pocket. 'I just wanted to ask you some questions about what happened last night and this morning – if you're feeling up to it?'

She gave a nod and gestured vaguely to the plastic seat next to her bed. 'They've given me something for the pain,' she said. 'So it's all a bit fuzzy.'

'That's alright,' Don said with a kind smile as he settled into the chair, pulling out his notebook. 'We can go slowly and stop if you feel it's getting too much.'

Theresa nodded again in understanding.

'OK. Well, shall we start with the basics? Your full name?' Don already had the information, as collected by the first responders, but he always found it settled a witness into talking to first ask them something they could answer confidently.

'Theresa Nicholls.' She paused to swallow. 'But everyone calls me Terri.'

'May I call you Terri?' She nodded in response. 'OK, Terri.' He smiled warmly. 'And your address?'

'125 Slater Drive.'

'And that's West Hollywood?' She nodded in confirmation. 'And your occupation?'

'I'm a broker at Thornton Kendal. They're a property development firm.'

Don nodded and noted it down. He'd seen their signs outside plenty of new condo and apartment developments around town. 'OK, so...' He adjusted his position to lean forward, keeping his voice steady and gentle. 'Do you want to tell me what happened?'

'She slipped,' Terri said, wide-eyed in obvious alarm at reliving the events of the previous few hours. She shook her head as if she was trying to settle something inside of it. 'I – I tried to reach out for her as she fell, but my footing wasn't firm and, and I think she must have knocked me off balance.'

He raised a hand to gesture at the gauze at the back of her head. 'Is that how you hit it?'

She nodded. 'I think so. I was out for... a bit.' She stopped, trying to recall. 'I don't know how long, but I don't think it could have been more than a few minutes.'

'OK,' Don said, scratching some notes in his book. 'And what happened when you came to?'

'I went to see her, at the bottom on the stairs. She was stirring, muttering something.'

'She was still alive?' Don interrupted, surprised, thinking of the photograph of the body he'd seen at the station.

Terri nodded again, but there was something stiff and awkward in the gesture, her brow furrowed desperately above her eyes. 'Yes, I... I told her I was going to get help.' Terri's face creased as she remembered this, the soft hiccough of a sob interrupting her words for a moment. When she spoke again her voice was raspy. 'I didn't know if there was a phone in the house. It's so big and...' She looked up at Don with wide eyes, as if working out how to describe it. 'It's a maze,' she settled on. 'So I had to walk. To find a payphone. But my ankle... it took forever.'

The Lloyd Estate was deep into the hills; it would take someone in decent shape well over an hour to walk up to the gate from the nearest civilisation at the strip mall, and then there was that long winding driveway to get up to the house itself. With her injury, it wasn't impossible to believe she didn't reach payphone until gone four a.m. Four nineteen a.m., to be precise. The logistics of her story fit, but Don was adept enough at his job to know when something was off. The way she avoided his direct gaze, only darting strained glances toward him, checking to see if her tale had landed. She was hiding something.

'And what happened to your ankle?'

'An accident.' She dismissed the question too quickly.

Don made a note to come back to it. Get the easy details first, keep her talking. Then press for the complicated ones.

'And why were you there? What's your relationship to the deceased?'

'I don't have a relationship to the deceased!' she wailed in reply.

Don blinked. Startled at this explosion of emotion that didn't quite fit with the professed lack of relationship. He watched her carefully as she visibly collected herself after her outburst.

'I was there for work, only for work. You can call them, they'll tell you. I wanted to purchase the land for development.'

Don made another note to call the offices of Thornton Kendal. And to follow up why she was there, apparently working, close to midnight.

'I was only up there for work, I didn't want, I don't want anything—' She broke off with a dazed expression, eyelids slinging low. She blinked up at him. 'Sorry,' she said, 'let me get it straight. I don't know her.' She looked down and shook her head, a stifled yawn stretching against her jaw. 'Only for work,' she repeated.

'OK,' Don said calmy, watching the painkillers take effect and stifle the young woman's evident panic. He made another note. Could just be shock. Could be something else. But worth remembering all the same. 'It's alright, I can check on that. Do you have a next of kin?'

His questions weren't over, not by a long shot. But he could sense this interview was. He wasn't going to get any better answers out of her right now. Best to gather his own opinion on what happened, and then get her to fill in any blanks.

'My family's in Connecticut,' she said limply.

'Husband? Partner?' he asked.

'Fiancé,' she corrected. 'He's out of town.'

'I'm sure if he knew you were in the hospital, he—' But she was shaking her head so vigorously he felt the interruption as loud as if she had screamed right over his words.

'Alright.' He got to his feet and placed a hand gently on her shoulder. 'You get some rest. I'll be back in a little while to check on your progress.' *And to get some real answers*, he didn't add.

He shut the door behind him as he headed back down the corridor.

'Get everything you need?' Rose asked cheerfully from behind the nurses' station.

Don gave a bark of laughter. 'I never do.'

He bid farewell to the nurse and took the elevator down to the parking lot where his shining blue sedan was waiting.

It was time for him to go back up to Lloyd House. He wondered if the place had changed much in thirty-four years.

Six

Terri
Monday

Terri knew as soon as the door closed behind her that the condo was empty. She exhaled into the lonely air and dropped her handbag on the couch, shrugging off her jacket and loosening the top few shirt buttons that seemed to have tightened around her throat on the drive home.

She kicked off her heels and padded into the bedroom, where she undressed with stiff mechanical movements. She changed into sweats and her old, faded Barnard T-shirt from her short-lived days running track for the university. She'd done it only for her freshman year and had failed to win anything memorable. By the time sophomore year rolled around, she'd had Ethan by her side and extracurriculars seemed like a waste of attention. Terri moved back into the kitchen and picked the receiver off the base of the grey plastic phone that hung on the wall and dialled the office. It was only just past six; someone would be there for a little while yet. As predicted, Glenn answered after only a couple of rings, sounding disappointed when she told him who it was.

'It's progressing,' she said in a weak voice. 'That's the way with menstrual migraines, sometimes. It might take me out all week.'

She took a moment to enjoy the disgust in Glenn's voice on the other end of the phone. 'Do you really need to be so graphic about it?' he said. 'Well, if you think your career can afford a week off, I guess you gotta do what you gotta do.'

He hung up on her without a word of well-wishes for his supposedly ill colleague, and she retrieved a green bottle of wine from the fridge, shaking off a still-damp glass from the drying rack. She grabbed a fork and bottle opener and, carefully arranging her cargo in a firm grip under her armpit, she slid a half-eaten casserole off the counter, resting it on her forearms. The casserole had appeared on the doorstep yesterday afternoon from Mrs Washington next door. Ever since she'd seen them unloading their U-Haul two years ago and learned that Ethan was without both his parents and Terri's were across the country, Mrs Washington had taken it upon herself to mother them almost as fussily as she did her brood of three teenage boys. Ethan had been out most of the day, supposedly at the office, and Terri had dug half-heartedly into the food as the sun had set, standing over the counter taking uncomfortable mouthfuls that settled like undigested rocks in her stomach. She'd pushed back the aluminium foil and not even bothered to refrigerate it.

She walked toward the sliding door at the back of the kitchen, and, resting the wine bottle momentarily on the side, jimmied it open. Ten years spent working in her parents' restaurant, from moody middle-school student to clueless college graduate, had trained her for life in the art of balancing an awkward selection of objects.

The garden smelled sweetly of the wildflowers they'd planted when they'd first moved in, the vines wrapped around the trellis above her head flourishing this summer – big, thick leaves she'd chop down and stuff with her dad's famous dolma recipe if she had the inclination or company to feed. Perhaps she should make them and drop them off next door to repay the favour of the endless casseroles. Maybe next week. Terri had enough to worry about this week.

She dumped everything on the square table, the frosted glass top murky with splodges of mildew creeping in from the edges, and expertly extracted the cork from the wine bottle. She poured herself a large, crisp glass and felt the sharpness slide down her jaw with satisfaction as she sat back in her chair, closing her eyes into the still-warm evening sun.

She'd met Ethan at a freshman mixer for Barnard and Columbia – the women's and men's colleges coming together for a night of drinks and socialising. Both had been young and awkward, faking a confidence neither had really had. He'd had long messy hair back then, a hangover from the hippy fashion that had died out a few years before. It had straggled down his back, dandy blonde from what she later learned was Sun-In and flecked with ginger. Up in the cold winter of the northeast, there weren't many people maintaining the soft glow of a tan, but somehow Ethan had managed it. It seemed inevitable that in that grey world of drab academia this misplaced surfer would catch her eye. They were both idealistic and opiniated and spent the youth of their courtship attending protests and rallies, fighting for the rights of their generation, clashing with the cops and generally enjoying pissing off their parents. But somewhere in the ten years since graduation, they'd grown up, mellowed out and lost the heat.

And now they had other things to eat away at their attention. How she longed to still have some far-away war to worry about, rather than the battle that raged within her very home.

It had been an adjustment moving to California. After his dad had died almost three years ago, Ethan had spent a tricky six months traversing the country trying to keep things afloat before deciding he had no choice but to take over his dad's business himself – even if he had no idea what he was doing.

At first it had been idyllic. In the vast space of California, they could afford a real house – a condo of their own that their New York studio could fit in four times over. The property industry was different but more vibrant than the small firm Terri had worked for in New York, and the jitterbug excitement at her landing an interview – and then a job – with the infamous Thornton Kendal had kept them high on the utopia of their move for weeks.

But utopia could never last forever.

It soon became apparent that Ethan, who until that point had harboured dreams of writing science fiction novels, had no idea how to run a thriving logistics firm. His days in the office got longer, his face became more drawn, his tone snappier. And Terri was lonely. She had no friends beyond a few acquaintances at aerobics who, if she was lucky, would be free for a quick coffee after class before rushing off to continue their busy lives, always assuming that she, too, had somewhere else to be in this City of Angels. She missed her family – busy and shouting, the wails of her nieces and nephews, the strained but loving bickering of her brothers and sisters-in-law. The smell of the charcoal grill that curled through her parents' restaurant, the salty bite of her mom's creamy taramasalata on her tongue.

Ethan's family was sparse in comparison. His mom had died in his infancy, and his dad's girlfriend, Paula, was sweet but distant. Aside from one remaining grandfather who lived over in Arizona, there was no one else.

And now she felt like she was losing Ethan as well.

Terri pulled open her eyes and sat forward, peeling a corner of the tin foil back across the casserole dish. She plunged her fork into the white, creamy meal and pulled up a chunk of ham with strands of leek decorating it like ribbons. The casserole was delicious even cold – Mrs Washington never disappointed.

Dusk fell without her notice, and she ate and drank in dull blue illumination, by now more than tipsy from the rapidly emptying bottle of wine, the sounds of cicadas keeping her company. Terri hadn't realised the doze that had crept up on her until she was snapped awake by the sound of the front door slamming shut. The wine bottle was empty, only dregs left in the bottom of her glass, flies flitting around her abandoned casserole.

'What are you doing out here?' Ethan asked from the kitchen door, frowning into what Terri now realised was deep, dark night.

'Oh,' she said, sitting forward. 'I must have dozed off. You're back late.' She didn't ask where he'd been, because far too often these days the scent of bourbon and beer answered the question for her. But this time, as she twisted around in her chair to face him, she didn't smell that tell-tale booze, and his eyes seemed fresher than they had in months.

'I stayed in the office,' he said, stepping into the garden and dragging another chair out from under the table so it scraped across the patio. 'Getting stuff ready, making plans for how to pull the business out of this.'

Terri smiled and felt a well of emotion rise in her chest. For the first time since everything had turned to shit, Ethan had hope.

'Ethan, that's gr—'

'So,' he cut her off, sitting forward urgently, excitedly, grabbing at her hands across the table with his own sweaty palms. 'You got it, right?'

In her drowsiness, it took her a moment to understand. 'Oh, yes, right… today.' She forced herself back to the present, back to Lloyd House. 'No, no I didn't, not yet. But it'll be OK—'

'Jesus fucking Christ.' He cut her off again, pulling back as if her touch burned. His expression changed at once, jaw tightening, hands clenching in and out of frustrated fists. 'You had one job today, Terri — for fuck's sake. We *need* it! Don't you fucking understand how bad this shit is?' Panic tremored his voice and she felt the guilt of failure slick greasily down her oesophagus.

'I do, I do,' she pleaded, hearing the wail in her voice. She got clumsily up from her chair and kneeled down in front of him, grasping at his clenching hands, trying to soothe them in her own. 'It'll be fine, I'll get it, I will. I have all week.'

'What?' he snapped, turning to her as a drop of spittle landed on her cheek. She didn't wipe it away.

'The old woman asked me to visit her for the week. She's lonely or something, I don't know.' She tried to dismiss this request as if it were nothing out of the ordinary. No point throwing fuel onto the fire of their worries by placing credence on the unnerving chill that Audrey Lloyd seemed to project.

Ethan creased his eyebrows together. 'What do you mean she's asked you to visit for the week? Why the fuck does she want *you* around for so long?'

Terri flinched inwardly at his words. At one time *Ethan* had wanted her around for so long.

'Like I said, I think she's lonely. She – she seemed impressed that I was a woman.' Terri stuttered over the explanation, trying to recall what else Audrey had said in her invitation. 'Men have been going up there for years; she liked my initiative at going up on my own,' she finished weakly. 'The house is *huge*, Ethan,' she continued, trying to salvage some dignity in her failure. 'It's sprawling and it's packed, *packed* with stuff. Just everywhere. I found one office – it was overflowing with boxes. And she barely let me out of her sight except to use the bathroom. This is a good thing – I need this week. I can do it with this week.'

'You'll find it?'

'I promise. I'll find it.'

'You better,' he said, pushing himself up off his chair so she fell back, her butt cracking painfully on the patio. 'Because we've run out of any other fucking options.'

Seven

Audrey
Tuesday

Audrey was an early riser. She always had been, as if her brain didn't quite understand how to turn off. And on a day like today – with the prospect of new company arriving in just a few short hours – she certainly couldn't crave the peace of sleep. She finished her morning tea on the terrace outside the kitchen, watching the newly risen sun spill slowly over her land.

She tidied away her things and started to set up for the day. Terri had said she preferred coffee to tea, but just as Audrey had been about to dust off the cafetière and hunt in the pantry for some old beans to grind, a voice had stopped her.

'The tea is much better,' Mama said, draped in an elegant, beaded gold gown. It had always been one of Audrey's favourites. 'You know that, *mi amor.*'

'I know, Mama. But she likes coffee.'

Mama gave her a stern look. 'Not everyone knows what's best for them.'

Audrey could not argue with that, and so returned the cafetière to its spot in the cupboard. She brewed a fresh pot of tea instead. And as she poured it over thick-cut slices of lemon in her Tupperware jug, Audrey thought that Mama was right, it was best to wait to decide whether her new companion was indeed worth retrieving the cafetière for. She topped the plastic jug off with ice cubes and cold water and set it in the refrigerator for later.

Audrey moved into the living room and decided on chess for the day. There was no better way in the world to get to know someone. She found her old, polished mahogany box of chess pieces, where they sat atop the mother-of-pearl inlaid board she'd played on in her youth. But as the years had whittled away her strength, she'd been forced to turn instead to a cheap cardboard replica that she could at least carry down the steps to the staggered terraces outside. She ran her hand across the beautiful board from her past, the grooves of her withered fingertips collecting layers of dust and grime.

1926

'Checkmate!' she declared, sweeping her bishop down a free run on the side of the board to the corner spot where her father had been forced to retreat his king from her attacks. He stared at the board for a moment, his grey-pink bottom lip falling open a little underneath his heavy moustaches.

'Well, I'll be damned.' He chuckled after a moment and gazed up at his daughter with two black, twinkling eyes. 'I don't even remember the last time I beat you.' He grinned with pride and shook a chubby finger at her. 'Come on, rematch!' he declared delightedly, and Audrey rolled her eyes with a playful smile.

'Daddy, is your plan to just keep playing me until the odds fall in your favour?'

'One of these times, my darling,' he said, laying his pieces before him again. 'One of these times I'll have you again.'

'Alright, Daddy,' she said, reaching to replace her own pieces, 'but I must warn you odds don't work when you're pitting intellect against intellect.'

Arnold sat back with a mock blow, cupping his hands around his heart in mimic of a gunshot wound. 'Intellect, my darling,' he said, sitting forward again with a smile, 'is something I am proud to lose to you on.' He cast conspiratorially around the sitting room, although there was no one else there, just the sounds of Mrs Doyle in the kitchen. 'But don't go telling any of my business partners that. They'll think I've lost my touch, and we'll be out on our ear!'

Audrey laughed and sat back in her chair, feeling the satin skirt of her dress crease into folds. It was a pale blue column dress with intricate beading in the shape of peacock feathers running from the bust down each side of her hips. She'd bought it from one of Mama's favourite boutiques, but in a rare oversight had not predicted it would prompt Mrs Hackton to accept an invitation to Melissa Gerritsen's birthday party on Audrey's behalf.

'Well, where else were you planning on wearing it?' Mrs Hackton had asked with half a raised eyebrow.

'Beautiful things can still be beautiful even without the eyes of the world on them,' Audrey had snapped back. But it was too late to back out of the party; Melissa's father was an important business contact for Daddy – he owned half the lighting and camera rigs in Hollywood – and Audrey couldn't risk putting Lloyd Productions on the back foot with an important supplier like that. She had fifteen minutes before Daddy's driver would come to take her to the party, but Audrey was confident she could easily beat her father again in that time.

'Don't forget you can't just sit here and play that game all night.' Mrs Hackton bustled into the living room from Arnold's study, her arms full of contracts. 'You've got the Gerritsen girl's birthday. And Arnold, you need to go through these contracts for the new production. Maggie Leonard's agent is kicking up a fuss about the fees—'

'Yes, Mrs Hackton,' Audrey snapped, slicing the secretary's tirade short. 'Carl is coming to get me in' – she checked the heavy clock on the sideboard – 'fifteen minutes, so if you wouldn't mind leaving us alone until then.' She turned back to the game, pretending to scrutinise the board even though she already knew exactly where she was moving next. Out of the corner of her eye, she saw Mrs Hackton appeal silently to Arnold, one hand outstretched in gesture toward Audrey, an expression of stern exasperation on her shaking head.

Arnold exhaled slowly through his lips and pulled his shoulders up into a shrug. He glanced back at Audrey and then spoke to Mrs Hackton. 'Just another fifteen minutes, Annabel,' he said. But his tone didn't have the reproach Audrey wanted to hear. Arnold never spoke to Mrs Hackton the way Audrey felt the old cow deserved. He was ever patient, ever tolerant and although he usually held himself back from ever quite siding with the woman, Audrey couldn't help but feel this was more out of pity for his daughter than because he actually thought Mrs Hackton out of line.

Mrs Hackton moved off to ready the papers in her hand, spreading them out across the shining oak dining table in the corner, making an audible fuss of organising them. Audrey stared at the chess pieces, willing all her patience into the game. She made her move and closed her eyes with a deep exhale. Somehow, she'd get out from under Mrs Hackton's ever-hovering thumb.

Carl arrived on time, as he always did, and Audrey reluctantly moved her knight for the win she'd been holding off on cementing. Arnold clapped the tops of his thighs with his palms and laughed deeply.

'I best be off then, Daddy,' Audrey said, getting to her feet and bending low to kiss her father on the top of his bald head.

'Have fun, my dear,' he replied, patting her thin arm with his chubby hand. 'Relax, enjoy yourself! And help yourself to some of Merv's whiskey – the old bastard still won't tell me who he's getting it through.' Arnold laughed again, but Audrey knew the rivalry over who had the best smuggler contacts for getting booze in since the temperance laws was more heated than just an easy laugh. If your supplier had better whiskey to offer you at a meeting, they had the upper hand. And if a supplier had the upper hand, negotiating them down on price was a job more difficult. *I know the right people – I have power in this town.* That's what having the right alcohol said at these meetings.

'I'll steal you a whole case, Daddy,' she replied with a smile.

'Smuggle it out under your dress!' He laughed, gesturing to her slim-fitting satin.

Audrey left and got in the car, for the twenty-minute journey over to the Gerritsens' large estate. Two gates with an elaborate G wound into the wrought-iron bars were pushed open at the base of a straight driveway, intersected by a fountain in the middle. The house stood among ten acres of perfectly manicured grounds. Audrey didn't like it. It looked pretty, but it didn't feel real. There was something more real, more homely about her own house, with its winding driveway taking you into the heavens away from everyone else. The untouched land around them was a buffer between the Lloyds and the world. She knew Daddy intended to develop it at some point, but she could be quite safe in the knowledge that it wouldn't be for a while yet. It always took Daddy time to ramp up to big plans like that, and he had enough productions on his roster to keep him busy for several years. She might even be gone by the time he got round to sorting out their land. That thought gave her a strange little jumble of emotions as she climbed out of the car and nodded her greeting to the penguin-suited doorman guiding her into the Gerritsens' extravagant hallway.

Audrey didn't really *want* to leave Daddy or her home, but she couldn't help but feel there might be somewhere better suited to *her*. She'd had a private tutor for her early years of education, but when it came to high school, Mrs Hackton had had her say, and told Arnold that Audrey wasn't enough like other children. She was secluded and strange, and school would be the best way to fix that.

Mrs Hackton had of course been wrong. School had been nothing but a year of sheer and utter boredom for Audrey. One that she could only inject life into by taking her sharpened pencil and pressing it into the backs of her hands or forearms until the pain burst with a satisfying sting and small bubbles of red bloomed beneath the lead. Eventually, the principal had suggested that Audrey might be beyond the remit of their usual high school curriculum and if she wanted to continue her education, perhaps another tutor or some classes at a local college might suit her better. All these suggestions were made with an air of disinterest, though, for it was fully expected that rather than worry about academics, Audrey would just get herself a husband to care for. Audrey had happily accepted another tutor, a retired math professor from Caltech, who had, of late, been putting ideas into Audrey's head about going away to study at college. And seeing as old Professor Ross was the only person she'd ever met with an intellect that impressed her, she'd begun to think college might not be the worst place for her.

She would have to work on Daddy, though. He would not want her to venture too far from home, and Professor Ross was adamant his old college's rival, MIT, was the best place for her – all the way across the country. His more local alma mater was not quite ready to accept women yet, unlike their East-Coast counterparts.

Daddy was protective, that was all. It was just the two of them now, had been for eight long years, but for someone so adept at spotting patterns it had surprised Audrey how long it had taken her to notice that her father had become increasingly reluctant to allow her to leave the house of her own volition. Aside from events like tonight, when Carl would be parked outside ready to whisk her off home at a moment's notice, Audrey had started to recognise that she didn't have quite as much freedom as some of the other girls her age. She had not paid much attention to it before – Audrey had no interest in shopping or horse-riding or sneaking into speakeasys with her peers. She'd never much missed not having a friend to while away the hours with, but now she had somewhere she would like to go, and she had become increasingly aware of quite how difficult that might be to manoeuvre under the iron-cladded guardianship of Arnold Lloyd.

She accepted a glass of honeyed champagne and brought the gold-rimmed glass to her lips, feeling the bubbles spit against her eyes as she tipped it up.

'Audrey Lloyd.' A smooth voice came to her through the crowd, parting to let through a young man with dark hair, swept back with a good amount of wax. It was Daniel Bowen, a few years older than her and recently cast in Lloyd Productions' latest film. Only a small role, but Daniel had performed an intricate tap solo, and Arnold was certain he had a new star on his hands.

Audrey watched Daniel approach and fixed herself with the easy smile she knew people liked. Audrey had spent her childhood in observation of and playing games with the people around her – she saw what made them tick, what opened their expressions to a gentle laugh, or caused them to duck their head to share a confidence. Audrey had seen it all, and she knew how to use it.

'Daniel,' she drawled with practised ease. 'How nice to see you.'

'We don't normally see you at these parties,' he said, moving closer.

'I don't normally attend them,' she replied with a laugh he reciprocated.

'You're a mysterious woman, Audrey Lloyd.' He raised his glass in cheers before draining it of its champagne.

'Isn't that the best way to be?'

He laughed again and looked around the room, pretending to take in the party atmosphere. But Audrey knew something was coming. In the same way she could see what her opponent would do next in chess, she could sense that in a moment he would lower his head conspiratorially. After another beat, Daniel obliged her prediction.

'Tell me, the mysterious Audrey Lloyd.' His voice was low, and he had to hold his head close to hers to make himself heard. She could feel his warm breath on her neck and shuddered inwardly. 'I hear your father is casting for *The Old Blue Ship*. Big male lead, so the rumour goes.'

And there it was. Just like everyone, all the time. The only reason humans bothered to interact with each other at all was to get something.

'Ah, now I'm afraid I wouldn't know anything about that,' Audrey said with a small shake of her head. 'Daddy doesn't talk to little old me about business.' That wasn't true, but who did Daniel Bowen think he was to expect a thing like honesty from her?

'Well,' he said, leaning back and raising his voice to a normal level. 'Perhaps *you* could talk to *him* about business.'

Audrey scrutinised him slowly as she took another sip of champagne, seeing the slight, desperate flit of his eyes as they darted across her face, waiting for her response. When she lowered her glass again and still said nothing, the muscles in his face dropped, his previous display of confidence falling with them. 'It really would mean the world to me,' he said, his voice softer, swallowing something thick in his throat. 'It's been a tough ride coming here.' He gestured around the party and Audrey understood he meant Hollywood. 'I grew up in Oregon; we had a farm. But then the war took both my brothers, and my poor dad couldn't afford any help and was too old to manage the workload on his own. He just keeled over one day feeding the cows.' Daniel shook his head, and Audrey noticed with surprise that his eyes were wet. 'Anyway, it's just my sisters, me and Mom now, trying to get by. Had to sell the farm of course and the three of them are holed up in a tiny house in Portland. Mom gave me the very last of the money from the sale of the farm for my ticket down here. My dream is their one last shot.'

Audrey nodded and placed her hand tenderly on his arm. 'I'll talk to Daddy.'

Carl picked her up a few hours later. Audrey bid farewell to Mrs Gerritsen, who had been talking for half an hour about the potential suitors for young girls of her and Melissa's set. 'It really is something you should be thinking about,' Mrs Gerritsen said with a stern expression, 'and with your mother no longer around you'll have to take action for yourself.'

Back at home, she climbed the terracotta steps and clicked her dancing heels through the marble corridor. The living room was empty, so she turned down toward her bedroom, seeing light escaping from underneath her father's study door.

Audrey pushed it open and leaned against the doorframe.

'Hello, darling,' Arnold said, looking up from his desk. 'How was the party?'

'Excellent, thank you,' she replied. 'I was speaking to someone about *The Old Blue Ship*.'

'Oh, yes?' Arnold put down his pen and looked up at her with interest.

'Yes, I think you should cast Rex Heatherington as the lead.'

'Rex?' Her father screwed up his face in thought. 'I was thinking of Daniel Bowen.'

Audrey waved her hand. 'Bowen? He's a bit-part actor. He couldn't handle a production as big as this. No, Daddy, trust me. Rex is leading man material. Bowen won't open a film for you.'

Arnold considered the notion and then nodded. 'Perhaps you're right,' he said. 'I think Rex will do the job well.'

'He will.' Audrey grinned. 'Good night.'

And as she walked back to her bedroom, she imagined Daniel Bowen returning home to Oregon having wasted the very last of his mother's money. No prospects. Forced to get a job in a factory. That handsome face covered in grime every day.

And then a laugh burst out of her, and she trotted the rest of the way down the corridor.

–

Audrey came back to the present, the black and white squares of the heavy old chessboard blurring back into focus. She tucked the lighter cardboard version under her arm, along with the box of pieces, and headed back out toward the terrace. On her way through, she checked the old clock in the kitchen. Eight thirty. Terri would be arriving soon. And Audrey was ready to play.

Eight

Don
Friday

In the parking lot of the hospital, Don settled into the comfortable leather of his driver's seat and picked up the handset of his newly installed car phone. It was time to tick a couple of basic things off his to-do list. He asked the operator for the offices of Thornton Kendal and then waited to be connected. No point carrying on much further if the base alibi was bullshit.

'Hello,' he told the secretary who answered. 'This is Detective Don Vernon, with the LAPD. I wanted to speak to someone about a colleague of yours – Theresa Nicholls?'

'Oh.' The secretary sounded alarmed at his formal introduction. 'Is Terri alright?'

'She's fine,' Don reassured her. 'She is in the hospital, but she'll be absolutely fine.'

'Oh dear, poor Terri. Let me connect you with Glenn Plummer; he heads her team.'

Don waited, and when he was on with a smarmy-sounding Glenn, he explained about Terri's predicament. The response was not what Don had been expecting.

Glenn burst out in a harsh laugh. 'The Lloyd Estate? She actually went?'

Don's attention pricked up. 'You didn't know she was going up there?'

'She was talking about it in the office. Stupid idea, everyone knows that mad old woman who owns it won't sell. I told her not to bother. This is why Thornton doesn't trust her with big acquisitions. She's an amateur,' Glenn finished, and Don felt like he could hear the eye-roll on the other end of the phone.

'Alright, Mr Plummer, thank you for your time.' Don found he had little patience for Glenn. 'Your colleague is in Sacred Heart being treated for a few minor injuries, so if you'd like to send your best wishes you know where to direct them.'

'Sacred Heart?' Glenn asked, finally picking up that his workmate was in hospital. 'What the hell is she doing there?'

Now it was Don's turn to roll his eyes. He briefly explained again about Terri's injuries before giving a professional goodbye and getting the asshole off the phone. It wasn't a firm alibi, but it was something. If she'd gone behind her boss's back to try and secure a deal herself, that might be a possible reason for the caginess he'd detected. But his instincts said her untruthfulness ran deeper than just office politics.

Before he set off, he made one more call to the station for a basic background check on Theresa Nicholls.

'I'm heading up to the house now – is there anyone still up there?'

'Two officers securing the scene, awaiting any further instructions from you.'

'Thanks. I'll call back for the background check when I park up.' Finally, he put his car into drive and pulled out of the hospital parking lot.

The entrance to the Lloyd Estate was a good forty-five minutes from the hospital. On his way he passed the Double Tree strip mall on the junction of Elm and Sycamore, noting the payphone where Terri had made her early morning call.

He reached the tall black gates he remembered, chain-link fences attached on either side. The gates had been left open, presumably for the stream of police, crime scene staff and ambulances that were required to deal with a potentially suspicious body. He curved his sedan around the long, winding driveway, certain that he must have missed the house after ten minutes of fruitless driving. But finally, he turned around one last bend, which levelled out to a gentle incline as it approached the house.

At the top of the driveway was a large, cracked turning circle, a squad car parked in the centre. Weeds had long broken through the weather-worn slabs of stone intricately arranged in concentric rings, spiky green sprouts dotted around the cracked grey.

Don pulled up and noticed a uniformed officer waiting for him, presumably alerted by the sound of his car up the driveway. He was at the head of a narrow, paved pathway that clung to the side of the building. Don raised a finger to signal that he'd be just a minute and dialled the station again from the phone console.

'OK, what have we got?' Don asked the officer on the other end when he was put through to her again.

'Clean as a whistle except for a couple of parking violations and' – her voice lowered, indicating something important – 'something that might interest you – an outstanding speeding ticket for three a.m. this morning.'

'A speeding ticket?'

'Yep, flashed a gun doing eighty down on Lexington.'

'Lexington? But that's the other side of town.'

'That's all I've got on her.'

'Alright, thanks, Debbie. Good to know.'

Don hung up and got out the car, thinking. Terri hadn't mentioned any car. In fact, *not* having a car was a crucial part of her alibi – limping away from this place in the early hours of the morning. Was that a lie to buy herself a few more hours? If so – for what? Or was this her supposedly out-of-town fiancé, still very much in town and racking up violations in his betrothed's name? It might not have anything at all to do with the body at the bottom of the stairs, but he made a note to look into it.

Horses, not zebras.

'Detective Vernon?' The officer approached him across the turning circle. 'Officer Chen.' He gestured to himself by way of introduction.

'Good to meet you,' Don said with a nod. 'What's the situation now?'

Officer Chen began walking back the way he'd come, leading Don along the narrow path around the side of the house while he spoke. 'Body's been taken, but the scene hasn't been cleaned yet. Thought you might want to take a look.'

'Good thinking.' Don followed Chen out onto a wide, curved patio and almost gasped at the view of the Holly-wood Hills that fell away from him, the white dome of the Griffith Observatory nestled into the greenery in the distance.

'Quite a place, isn't it?' Chen said with a brief flicker of his eyebrows.

'It's…' Don struggled for an appropriate adjective and blew out a sigh. 'Something, alright.'

'The deceased was found at the bottom of these steps here.' Chen stepped forward across the blonde stone patio toward a steep set of steps down the side of what looked like might have once been a hanging garden. Don could see a patch of blood at the very bottom of the stairs and winced at the thought of the fall. As they descended, he kept his eyes trained on the stone beneath his feet, his expertly honed instincts trying to imagine the details of such a fatal fall. There were a few reddish drops here and there, drying quickly orange in the Californian sun, but not as many as he would have assumed given the nature of the death. They reached the bottom and Don stared down at the large pool of drying blood, before turning back to gaze up the imposing steps, assessing.

Chen started to speak, describing the scene when they'd arrived and the placement of the body, which Don matched in his mind against the photograph he'd seen.

'How did you get called?' Don asked, wondering why it hadn't been in the file that Audrey Lloyd had apparently been alive when Terri had found her.

'Ambulance called it in when they got here.'

'Do you know what the woman who called 911 said?'

'Just said there'd been an accident. Didn't sound like they could get much sense out of her. Couple of the guys at the tail end of the night shift went to Double Tree to pick her up, took her to Sacred Heart when they saw the state of her. Ambulance came up here, found the vic dead, then called us in.'

Don took in the information and twisted his body to look out over the vast view of the ramshackle property. All these years later, here he was back at Lloyd House. In the photograph of her body, his first thought, stupidly, had been that Audrey looked far older than he remembered.

But of course she did. Three decades had passed by and, of course, it wasn't a photograph of her at all, was it? It was of her corpse. The twinkle in her eye he remembered, the small tug of her mouth into a straight-lipped smile, the feeling that you would never truly understand her. All gone, extinguished. It had been a bleak reminder of his own advancing years, his own impending death. He turned back toward the steps and hoped his own would be more natural, more peaceful.

'You and Officer—?' Don held out his hand, waiting for Chen to supply his partner's name.

'Sterne,' Chen answered. 'He's inside getting a head start on the paperwork.'

'I'll send him back out to you. Give the grounds a once-over – just the area surrounding the house. This garden' – he nodded to the patch of lawn through a small gate at the bottom of the stairs that played host to some kind of tribute to the Washington Memorial – 'and anywhere else easy to get to on foot.'

'What are we looking for?'

Don shook his head. 'I don't know. Probably nothing, but it never hurts to be thorough.' He shook away Ray's warning about zebras. He wasn't letting the past distract him; this was routine. 'I'm going to give the house a quick look.' He didn't have a warrant, but he wasn't performing an official search. He wasn't looking for evidence, just a few clues in plain sight that would wrap everything up nice and easy. It was nothing to do with finally having the authority and manpower to give this place a once-over. He was just doing his best to close the file on Audrey Lloyd and Theresa Nicholls.

'You might need more than one of you for that,' Chen said with a shake of his head. 'It's mammoth.'

Don remembered Theresa's words — *It's a maze.*

'Well, I best get started then.' He nodded back to the garden. 'As had you.'

Don embarked on the steps back to the house, feeling his adrenaline spike, like he was a young cop again, still excited by his job.

Finally, after all this time, he was getting his hands on Lloyd House.

Nine

Terri
Tuesday

Terri pulled up to the top of the driveway and turned off the ignition, silencing the Human League's pleas to a one-time cocktail waitress. She hadn't been sure what to wear that morning and had settled in the end on something smart-casual – high-waisted slacks and an off-the-shoulder tee. Not quite the power suits she donned for the office, believing them to be some kind of polyester armour in the battle she fought every day. Her hair she'd tied back at the nape of her neck, bangs fluffy and thick and freshly blown as she'd listened to a morning radio phone-in for Police tickets.

The front door was already propped open, but she still hovered on the doorstep for half a moment before stepping into the cool shade of the house and calling out a questioning 'Hello?' down the corridor. There was no answer forthcoming, so she carried on down the short hallway and into the curved glass living room. The door to the kitchen was ajar and Terri assumed Audrey was inside, perhaps making her pedantic breakfast tea. She pushed her way in, another 'Hello? Audrey?' accompanying her into the empty space.

Pausing on the threshold to the kitchen, Terri cricked her head over her shoulder, gazing down the corridor toward the office she'd found yesterday. Could she take this opportunity to root around? She felt a prickle of unease at the thought – Audrey's instructions to meet at nine a.m. had been clear and she would surely have heard Terri driving up, or would at least notice the parked car outside. And if Audrey found her snooping, then Terri would have blown any chance of success. Instead, she stepped determinedly forward into the kitchen, knowing she would have to play this slow and clever.

The kitchen was a bizarre room, large but divided by countertops and shelving into maze-like sections. She looked around at the extravagant facilities and knew they must be a hangover from the days when the Lloyd family had a whole roster of kitchen staff to cater their daily lives and glamorous events. Seeing it in the cold light of modern day was jarring. Through the back of the kitchen was a set of wooden-framed double doors, and even from her distance at the other end of the room, Terri could see they were barely hanging on their hinges from the splintered, rotting wood. But they were pushed wide open, unmoving in the breezeless morning with unkempt poplars and wild lemon trees framing their opening.

The sun was stronger on this side of the house. As Terri exited through the double doors, she was astounded by the beauty of the dilapidation she saw before her. She was standing on a wide wrap-around terrace of blonde stone, staggering down four levels of what she could only assume was once a magnificent hanging garden. There was no gardener now, though, and the terraced beds were mangled with burned weeds and dried-up soil. The view from this vantage point stretched out across the whole estate, and she couldn't help but think it really would be one hell of a place to live. She stood and stared a little longer, the reason she'd come all this way temporarily lost on her as she took in the jagged bushes and overgrown patches of trees among the dusty red clay.

'You let yourself in.' Audrey's voice jolted her wandering mind, as it rose up the stone steps from one of the terraces below. Terri could not tell if she was looking for an apology.

'I'm sorry,' she said, erring on the side of politeness. 'I did call out.'

Audrey gazed at her, eyes fluttering ever so briefly into the house behind Terri before they finally landed back on her face.

'I've set up iced tea down there,' Audrey said and moved to one side, gesturing down the steps she'd just climbed. 'I've some pastries too.' She pointed toward the kitchen doors.

Terri nodded with a bright smile. 'Can I help you with anything?'

'No, no. Go and make yourself comfortable. I'll be down in a moment.'

Audrey swished past her, today's satin robe pale peach, and paired with a dark purple turban squashing down her curls, a bewitching jewel at the centre of her head. Terri was starting to wonder if some of these outfits had come from the wardrobe department of her father's movies. She smiled to herself and took the steps Audrey had just climbed, heading down to the first stone terrace where an elegant white wire table and chairs was set up. One of those small sets that would not be out of place outside a Parisian cafe, intricate patterns twisted into the metal wire, white gloss picked and peeling off in huge chunks.

There was a small drinks trolley to one side with a large pitcher of iced tea, free from any garnish. It was in an ugly plastic jug, and seeing that totem of modernity among its decrepit surroundings brought Terri a reluctant twinge of affection toward the old woman.

On the table was a battered old chessboard – cardboard, with the rough board poking through the worn lining – and a polished wooden box on top. She waited, standing awkwardly, and glanced around the terrace. Audrey came down the steps, elegant and floating across the sandy stone tiles, a plate piled high with Danish pastries in one hand.

'Sit down,' Audrey said with her funny straight-lipped smile.

Terri found herself obeying and pulled out the chair on the far side of the table, taking only a brief moment to question why she had waited at all. Why was she falling so easily at the gauntlet of this woman's presence?

Audrey watched her with a smile before stepping forward to take her own seat, placing the plate of pastries next to the pitcher of iced tea on the drinks trolley.

'Help yourself,' Audrey said with a distracted nod as she busied herself opening the polished box of chess pieces. The pieces contrasted the shabby board as well as Audrey's own faded glamour contrasted the dereliction of her home. Each chess piece shone in the sunlight and was beautifully carved. They looked solid in Audrey's delicate hand and made a satisfying *thunk* as she placed them on the board. Terri watched her lay out the board and it occurred to her that Audrey hadn't even asked if she knew how to play. Perhaps in Audrey's circles every young lady was taught how to play chess. Terri had learned, albeit reluctantly, on her dad's cheap tin set, a few of the pawns replaced with thimbles or coins over the years, the cardboard board still bloomed with damp salt rings from where he'd kept it in his thin canvas bag on the various boats that had brought them to America.

Audrey finished setting up the board and looked at her, and then toward her empty glass.

'Well, pour out the tea, then,' she said, and Terri had a warm flashback to her *yaya* scolding her for not setting the table. She leaned over to the drinks trolley and decanted the iced tea into two cut-glass tumblers, passing one over to Audrey. Terri took a sip and the tart lemon shot down her jaw to the back of her throat. The punch of the unsweetened tea blew a welcome hole through the fuzziness caused by last night's bottle of wine, and she gulped down a few more mouthfuls, feeling herself come back. The shakes steadied, and the dull fug of a headache suddenly seemed surmountable. She put the glass down and leaned back into her chair, feeling the morning sun brush her face. The one thing she couldn't argue in her regrets about their move across the country – Californian mornings really couldn't be beaten. They could make you forget what you were meant to be doing – just for a moment.

'Right then.' Audrey put her own glass down. 'You're white. You go first.'

Terri surveyed the board and knew this woman probably had plays and tactics galore. Her dad barking at her to 'Control the centre – you control the centre, you control the game' came rushing back to her, and so she braved her first move. A small, insignificant pawn.

'Interesting,' Audrey said slowly, and Terri thought she might be mocking her.

'I haven't played in years,' Terri said, defending herself as Audrey made her own first move and the game progressed. 'My dad taught me when I was little – they used to play a lot back home, but you know' – she gave a shrug – 'these things fall by the wayside.'

'And where is home?'

Terri blinked. 'I grew up in Connecticut.'

'Oh.' Audrey leaned forward and made her move. 'You made it sound like this home where they played a lot of chess was further afield.'

'Oh, right,' Terri said. 'Greece. They came over in '54 – my mom was pregnant with me. I was the first Nicolaides born on American soil.' She shrugged. 'Although they changed the name to Nicholls pretty soon after.'

'Yes,' Audrey replied thoughtfully. 'We Americans do like to demand that of people, don't we? Many moons ago my father was apparently Arnold Lautman. But that got changed, too.' She sighed with a surprising air of sadness. 'And I found out too late.'

Terri raised her eyebrows in surprise – she hadn't known this little Hollywood factoid before. 'Why did he change it?'

Audrey didn't catch her eye as she answered, her focus instead on the brown liquid in the glass she brought to her thin lips. 'I believe Lloyd was considered more neutral.'

Terri took a punt and moved her knight to the centre, thankful to have something to do with her hands. Audrey moved her own knight, and from the look on her face Terri knew she was out of her depth – Audrey didn't seem to be fighting for control of the centre. Terri moved a bishop as a final bid for centre control, which Audrey considered carefully before swiping it quickly away. It only took another few short moves before Audrey placed Terri into checkmate. Terri didn't think this expert player could possibly have derived any satisfaction from the victory, but when she looked up, the old woman's eyes were glittering.

'Guess my dad's training wasn't up to scratch,' Terri said with a forced smile as Audrey began collecting the fallen white pieces and handing them back.

'It's easy to spot a Steinitz man,' Audrey said before she gave a single nod of apology, 'or woman in this case.'

'A Steinitz man?'

'You play within the scientific school of chess. Wilhelm Steinitz.'

Terri blinked in incomprehension.

Audrey continued. 'Well, whether you know that's what you are or not – you are indeed a Steinitz man.' Audrey waved a hand dismissively and leaned over to retrieve the few black pieces Terri had succeeded in taking.

'And you're not?'

Audrey shook her head. 'Controlling the centre is a fallacy. It might make sense on the surface, but you play against a hypermodernist like me and it's… well' – she gestured down to the board – 'deadly.'

She blinked innocently at her, but Terri was sure she heard an underlying tone, although she couldn't quite identify its meaning.

'So you *don't* control the centre?'

'Oh no, my dear girl.' Audrey's eyes flashed. 'You *weaponise* it.'

Terri swallowed thickly and started replacing her taken white pieces in their assigned starting positions across the small black and white squares. It was only as she tried to pick up her bishop from where it lay on its side that she noticed the tremor in her hand.

'It's been many years since I've had a competent chess partner,' Audrey said, and Terri recognised a shift in her voice. It was softer, as if the words were petals catching on a breeze, falling wistfully to the ground. 'It seems you really are just what I've been looking for.' Terri snapped her head up from where she'd been arranging her pieces on the board, the hairs on the back of her neck standing suddenly erect in high alert.

Audrey smiled, her bottom lip as straight and stiff as ever.

Ten

Audrey knew her instincts had been right.

Terri was not quite on the same level as Audrey. But so few people were that Audrey had learned not to expect such a thing.

But the young woman did at least have some tactics, some natural flair, which Audrey had sensed yesterday when she'd confessed her subterfuge. The way one navigated chess, Audrey had found, so often reflected the way one found their way around the real world. And Terri Nicholls was indeed a woman of strategy.

But Audrey was interested to notice the visible signs of − well, there was no other way to describe it − fear. The small tremor in her hand as she reset her pieces. The shift in her posture, a fraction more upright as if her instincts were readying her for flight. This woman did not know her own power. But that was alright, preferable in fact. Audrey could guide her, as she had done before. Although this time it would be better.

Audrey felt the air thicken as the silence of the remote nature fuzzed into her ears. She nodded down to the empty glass in front of Terri. 'You finished your iced tea quickly.'

Terri took a moment to gather herself and stretched her mouth into a tight, guilty expression. 'I'm afraid I drank a bit too much wine last night. And that iced tea has really helped my hangover.'

Audrey threw back her head and laughed. 'Don't look so worried!' she declared. 'I was young once, too.' She clapped her hands together. 'I've always found hair of the dog works wonders. I can go get you a little something to add to your iced tea.' Terri tried to refuse the offer of morning booze with a shake of her head and an awkward laugh, but Audrey ploughed on. 'Irina and I, gosh we'd get into such trouble pilfering all the booze Daddy was so careful to smuggle in from Mexico and Canada.' She puffed out her cheeks and put on a deep, gruff voice. '*I need that for my business associates!* He'd huff and puff, but he was never really too angry at us. I don't think Daddy knew *how* to be angry at me, actually.' She broke off and stared contemplatively at the wall behind Terri, strewn with dead vines, discoloured fuzzy moss creeping out between the uniform stone. When she spoke again her voice sounded as if it belonged to a stranger. 'Well, he figured it out once.'

Terri gave her a smile and raised her palm politely up. 'No, no thank you. I don't think I could have any alcohol today.' Audrey's brow gave a small twitch of a frown at the refusal. Audrey knew she was right – it would make her feel better. Why would Terri ignore that?

'Who is Irina?' Terri asked with the air of trying to make conversation out of Audrey's sudden, unexpected quiet.

'My friend.' Audrey swallowed away her frustration with Terri and felt the warmth of Irina instead. 'More than a friend in many ways.' She smiled. 'The missing piece of me.'

Audrey gazed down at the black and white board and fell back fifty-two years to another chess game sitting in that very spot.

A chess game that changed her life.

1930

She'd been sunbathing with mauve-lensed sunglasses shading most of her face, her bobbed hair covered with one of Mama's old Hermès scarves. Her body sank into the canvas of the deckchair, and she allowed the sun to press against her skin. Mama's memorial stood gleaming out in front of her, the newest addition to the landscape since Daddy had had the idea after visiting Washington for business last year.

'Audrey!' She heard her father call from the terrace above. 'Audrey my dear, are you out here?'

She pulled herself up from her relaxed spot on the deckchair and stood to wave at her father, who was now appearing over the top of the first hanging garden – fuchsias and daisies spilling out between lush greenery, pretty trails dangling down the blonde stone wall toward her. She waved one arm upwards.

'Down here, Daddy,' she called back.

'Oh good.' Arnold grinned down at her. 'Stay there, stay there! There's someone I want you to meet.'

Audrey frowned. She thought Daddy had given up on this by now. He'd brought by a couple of suitors over the years, as her peers had got married off in elaborate ceremonies, pressured no doubt by Mrs Hackton hissing in his ear. But as each suitor was turned away with her callous disinterest, he'd seemed to have given up on the project.

Arnold appeared at the top of the stairs, trailed by a tall man in a dark suit and a girl about Audrey's age. The trio filed down from the stairs and arced out in front of Audrey on the terrace.

'Audrey, this is Lev Popov – he's going to be my new lawyer.'

Audrey smiled in the way she knew she was meant to and stepped forward with her hand outstretched.

Mr Popov looked at her open palm for a brief moment, a small crinkle of surprise on his face. Then he smiled, looking positively delighted. 'What a charming young woman.' He beamed at her. His accent was foreign, but Audrey couldn't quite pinpoint from where.

'And this is his daughter, Irina.' Arnold gestured to the girl, who stood back a little from the two men, shoulders hunched, face anything but friendly. She had black, uncombed hair trailing around her shoulders and round features that still clung to teenage puppy fat.

'Hello, Irina.' Audrey smiled, sensing that to offer a hand to this girl would be a waste of her sociable efforts.

Irina did not reply.

'Irina is quite the chess player,' Lev addressed Audrey. 'As, your father tells me, you are too.'

'I enjoy the game,' Audrey replied blandly.

'You seem to do little else lately!' Arnold chortled. 'Badgering me every moment for a game, trying to teach the staff when they're meant to be on duty.'

Something like ice flickered through Audrey's veins. 'I have to keep occupied in some way,' she said tightly, trying to remember her usual rules for interactions in front of Daddy's colleagues. But she couldn't help herself. The disappointment and anger from her dashed hopes over the last few years wasn't so easy to pummel down. 'If you'd

73

have let me go to college like Professor Ross suggested, maybe you wouldn't find me such a burden on your time.'

She knew Daddy had heard her tone, but he waved it away like it was nothing more than a jovial jab. 'Oh, darling, what on earth would you do with a degree?' He laughed, sliding his eyes toward Lev, who nodded in sympathy with a tender roll of his own eyes. *Daughters*.

His reaction when she had attempted to persuade him to allow her to go to college had not been so jovial. But Audrey suspected Daddy's lawyer would never see that side of him – unless of course business demanded it. The side when a shadow fell across his face and his usually booming voice fell to a terrifying quiet.

She'd pushed him too far. She'd thought she under-stood Daddy, that she'd be able to push him the way his staff and business partners couldn't. But she'd been naive and foolish, and had woken one morning to find her bedroom door locked from the outside – only opened for Mrs Doyle or Mrs Hackton to bring her food.

'He's protective,' Mrs Hackton had told her sharply. 'You're all he has left with your mother gone.' But the way her eyes wouldn't quite meet Audrey's told her that perhaps this was one thing the loyal secretary didn't quite agree with her boss on. After three days of captivity, Audrey had told Arnold she'd come to her senses; she didn't want to go to college after all. But still, she couldn't help but push every now and again. Perhaps, just once, he would break.

'Anyway.' Arnold gestured once again to Irina, who seemed as reluctant as Audrey to participate in this play-date. 'I've found you a chess partner. They've just moved over from Berlin, and Irina's English is still coming along.'

'And what better way for her to learn than in conversation with a peer over a good game of chess!' Lev clapped his hands together with satisfaction.

'Of course.' Audrey smiled back, feeling the tendons in her throat flex. *Daddy's little pawn* – that was all she was good for in this house. She eyed Irina and wondered what kind of game she could play with *her*. This strange shy girl who could barely speak English.

'Meanwhile' – Arnold looked up to Lev, who had at least a foot in height on him – 'we have business to discuss. And you're in luck – I've found a whiskey smuggler to rival even Merv Gerritsen's!'

Lev laughed deeply and the two men climbed the stairs, abandoning Audrey with the uncomfortable Irina, dressed in black, no doubt sweating in the California heat. Audrey was in light linen shorts and a cotton blouse and could still feel damp patches spreading under her armpits.

'Will you come and sit down then?' she asked impatiently and the girl hesitated a moment before stepping forward. She took her seat opposite Audrey and stared quietly at her.

'So… Berlin,' Audrey said, sitting back in her seat and pulling apart the two edges of the mahogany chessboard on the table to reveal the pieces underneath. Often, Audrey enjoyed the power dynamic of someone else's discomfort, but this girl was making it too easy. In the world of Audrey's upbringing in Hollywood, Audrey had so rarely been faced with timidity she didn't quite know what to do with it. 'What was that like?'

Irina blinked, wide, round brown eyes. 'What… was… Berlin *like*?' she repeated slowly, her accent as thick as molasses. She seemed to mull the words over for a long time before giving a single nod. 'It was home.'

'What brings you all over here?'

A small frown creased beneath Irina's thick eyebrows, and she shook her head gently. 'It's not safe for us. Not anymore.'

Audrey raised her eyebrows. She didn't bother herself much with the news or foreign affairs. 'Well, it's safe here for everyone,' she declared happily, 'the land of the free and all that.'

Irina nodded but didn't say anything.

'Should we flip a coin for who goes first?' Audrey asked, holding up a white piece in gesture.

Irina shrugged noncommittally, irking Audrey.

'Well, how do you normally decide?' she asked, her lips pulled tight in frustration. Again, Irina shrugged and looked nonplussed at her chess partner. 'Alright,' Audrey said slowly and handed over the white piece. 'You're my guest. You can go first.'

All she heard in response was a gruff 'OK' in a heavy accent as a hand timidly reached out to accept the piece.

Audrey watched lazily as Irina commenced the game, assuming that this foreign girl would provide little more competition than Daddy. She moved a pawn and Audrey followed suit, and the first couple of opening turns progressed. But, just as Audrey was readying her bishop to swipe Irina's knight, Irina swept her rook neatly down the board and directly into Audrey's perfectly placed bishop. Audrey blinked in surprise as her piece was removed, Irina flashing a small hint of a smile as she did so. Audrey had underestimated her. She'd become lazy – too used to playing people beneath her.

Audrey readjusted her sit bones and rested her elbows on the table, concentrating on the board with more atten-tion than she'd ever needed to afford a chess partner before. Now she looked she could see exactly how Irina had trapped her – distracting her on one side by placing her knight temptingly in the path of Audrey's bishop. Audrey readied herself for battle and soon set a similar trap for Irina, before her new companion retaliated with a skill Audrey wasn't used to. As she watched her black pieces diminish from the board, Irina's white encroaching ever closer to Audrey's precious king, she found herself feeling something unfamiliar. For once she was not tied in anguish by boredom; her usual bursts of frustrated anger were sated, distracted. Her mind was being challenged. Her skill was being matched. She felt something she hadn't felt since Professor Ross had been let go from his duties when Audrey had turned nineteen and deemed too old for education – she felt respect.

When Irina finally completed her sophisticated attack and said in a gruff voice, 'Checkmate,' Audrey couldn't help but laugh.

'Good game,' Audrey said, impressed. '*Very* good game.' She looked up at her new partner with bright eyes, seeing the dowdy girl with a new reverence. People really could surprise you sometimes. 'Will we play again?'

Irina only nodded, but Audrey thought she saw another flicker of a smile beneath her dour expression. Audrey felt an unexpected warm glow that wasn't just from the hot sun tanning her olive skin. Irina opened the game again and Audrey followed suit – pawns stepping forward into battle. Irina played a tight and complicated game, similar to Audrey's, setting a guard around the centre, trying to lure her opponent's pieces to their death. But Audrey was just as skilful, and now she knew she'd met her match she wound her brain up to its full potential, allowing the patterns she loved so much to come to life inside her, every move predicted, every victory hard-won. As she manoeuvred her bishop directly in the path of Irina's king, who had nowhere else to escape to, Audrey felt a rare bubble of feeling at the triumph. Satisfaction. It was a win that she had earned.

'You play very well,' Irina said, gathering up Audrey's black pieces and handing them back.

'For once it seems like Daddy might have actually found a match for me.' Audrey grinned. Irina hesitated for a moment before nervously mirroring her. 'One more?' Audrey asked. 'The decider?' Irina nodded. While they set up this game Audrey found herself falling into a genuine conversation, with a real desire to get to know the person on the other side of the table. 'Your accent isn't just German,' she said, lining up her pawns one by one.

Irina shook her head. 'We go to Berlin in 1917. From St Petersburg.' She paused, considering. 'Petrograd.'

Audrey cocked her head, remembering a discussion on world events she'd overhead at some party or another. 'Leningrad now, though, isn't it?'

Irina's face scrunched up and Audrey saw two shades of pink tinge the tops of her cheeks. She pulled her lips together and then spat impressively over the table to land on the pale stone tile in an inelegant globule. Audrey watched, astonished.

And then she laughed.

'I think you'll like it here,' Audrey said confidently. 'The weather is much better than in Russia or Germany.'

'I don't mind cold,' Irina said thickly, gesturing with her open palm for Audrey to take her first move.

'How very odd,' Audrey mused quietly before focusing on the game.

Irina won again, but it was a tight fight for dominance, with several thwarted 'checks' on either side of the table, before finally Irina extracted Audrey's queen and set herself up for victory. Audrey was thrilled to have been trounced in such a manner and invited Irina to stay for afternoon tea so they could continue their tournament.

'I think we have to get back for this afternoon,' Irina replied slowly, her accent undulating over the carefully selected words.

Audrey felt a quick, sharp twisting in her chest. She didn't want Irina to go. She finally had someone to play with on her level. She gave a strained smile. 'But I hope you will come and play with me again?' She heard how tight the words sounded, something like desperation pinching at them.

But Irina didn't seem to notice and nodded shyly, averting her eyes from Audrey's in that nervous manner she had. Audrey felt the twist in her chest unwind a little but knew that a small knot would stay, until she was reunited with this girl again.

She led Irina up the steps of the terraced garden and back inside, through the kitchen where Mrs Doyle was boiling a ham for lunch. When they came into the living room, Audrey noticed a shift in the atmosphere – a thick coolness between the three men who were standing in the space between the dining table and couches, the gramophone spitting scratchy jazz from its trumpet.

'Audrey, my biggest fan!' a smooth voice said, turning away from where its speaker had been standing in the awkward triangle with Arnold and Lev. 'How nice to see you.'

'Rex,' Audrey replied with a steady nod, accepting an air kiss on her cheek from the man whose career she had accidentally bolstered four years previously, and who had not let her forget it since. Sometimes her games did go wrong – she was sure Daniel Bowen would never have been half as much trouble in the end. 'What are you doing here?'

'Come to talk to your father about a new script of his.'

'Oh, very good,' Audrey said, barely interested.

'Yes, well,' Lev interrupted, giving Arnold a look through heavy lids. 'We'd better get going. Did you girls have a good game?'

'We did,' Audrey answered brightly. 'Irina is a wonderful player.'

Arnold smiled enthusiastically. 'Really, my dear? Have I finally found you your match?'

'I think you might have, Daddy.'

They all laughed politely except for Rex, who had pushed his hands deep in his suit pockets, a cloudy expression falling again as his gaze darted between Lev and Irina. Lev had clearly not missed Rex's hostility, because he turned toward the door and gestured for Irina to follow him.

'Can we play again tomorrow?' Audrey called out after them.

Lev shot another look toward Rex before nodding with an edge of polite relief. 'Yes, yes,' he said, raising his hand in farewell, 'I'm sure I can get my driver to bring Irina over.'

'See you tomorrow,' Audrey said eagerly to Irina, her palm raised in farewell.

Irina gave a nervous smile and waved her own goodbye before following her father out of the door.

'You need to be careful mixing with the likes of them,' Rex said darkly when the front door had slammed closed.

'Not now, Rex,' Arnold said softly.

Rex turned to Audrey instead. 'You keep your eye on your new friend.' He shot another look back to Arnold. 'Your father should know better than to be introducing you to that kind.'

Arnold interrupted before Audrey had a chance to ask what on earth Rex was talking about.

'Rex, come on, no need to bore poor old Audrey with all of that. You wanted to talk about *Sunset Over the Desert*? I think you'd be perfect for General Porter, you know.'

Rex's expression cleared a little as he turned his attention instead to Arnold. 'That's exactly what I was thinking too.'

Arnold hustled Rex out toward his office, leaving Audrey to consider what he'd said. She took a moment's more contemplation before deciding that she didn't much care what *kind* Irina was, whatever that meant. The girl was what she'd been waiting for, in all of her twenty-two years of life. And now she was here, Audrey didn't plan on letting that go easily.

Eleven

Don
Friday

Don headed back up the stairway and followed the path around the house back to the turning circle. He ascended the four terracotta steps to the front door, and pushed it open, stopping still, forehead creasing upward in shock. The state of the place had degraded far more than he could have anticipated. Seeing how the years had scraped away at the once-grand home made him feel even older than contending with the demise of the once vivacious Audrey Lloyd. He picked his way through the entrance hall, feeling a terrible sadness for the old woman who had lived in such squalor.

Officer Sterne was perched against the back of a filthy couch, one leg propped up on an over-crowded occasional table as he filled out paperwork on a clipboard.

'Officer Sterne?' Don greeted him and the young man looked up, immediately straightening his posture as he did so. 'Detective Vernon,' he introduced himself. 'I've spoken to your partner, viewed the scene.' He nodded down to the clipboard. 'Don't worry about that now. Go help Officer Chen give the grounds a once-over. Not sure what we're looking for but stick mainly to the trails that can be easily accessed on foot for now.'

'Will do.' Officer Sterne nodded obediently before retracing the route out through the door Don had just entered. The door slammed shut behind him, and Don gave an audible exhale into the cluttered room, twisting his body in almost a three-sixty to take it all in. He felt a sudden strange sense of imposition standing in Lloyd House. He'd been in other people's homes countless times over the years, pawed through their possessions, found and discarded the most personal of items in the hunt for the truth. But that was something he hadn't had the chance to do last time he was there. And now he finally could, it felt different. Like a movie set, where he might be reprimanded for touching anything.

He picked his way over the debris and filth around the couches, finding it impossible that anyone could actually have lived in this place – it was like a haunted museum of mouldy glamour. He thought of Theresa Nicholls, coming here in the name of work, apparently staying late into the night for some reason. Surely the woman hadn't *chosen* to spend so much time up here unless it was absolutely necessary.

He walked around the edge of one of the couches, stopping himself from running his hand along the visibly soiled back of it. He peered into a rotting old cardboard box on the floor and couldn't help an awed smile as he saw a yellowing age-withered screenplay with Arnold Lloyd's name typewritten across the front. An original screenplay from the man himself. Don shook his head for something to do to stop him from reaching out and grabbing it. He turned on his heel toward the back of the living room, more boxes, an old lamp so strung with cobwebs it reminded Don of the silly string his grandkids had covered his car in last Halloween. A side chair, an old high-backed chesterfield, cradling more ancient Hollywood gems.

Last time Don had been present at Lloyd House – too many decades and too many pounds ago – Audrey Lloyd had pulled open the front door, just a touch, one heavily painted dark eyebrow raised in question at the young police officer standing on her doorstep.

'Can I help you?'

Don had had to steady his breath. Audrey Lloyd in the flesh. Opening the door of Lloyd House. He was just a rookie, a couple of years out of the academy he'd joined out of a misguided sense of patriotism, after being too young to sign up during the war. His brother had returned a hero, a chest full of glittering metal, and all Don had done in the same time was perfect his baseball swing. And so, Don had vowed, if there was no external threat, he would protect his country from within.

Up until that point the most action he'd seen was chasing down an opportunist who'd swiped the contents of a drugstore cash register. But Don loved the job. He loved the stories the older guys had told – tales of the mob and booze smugglers. The first days of Hollywood. He lapped it all up and didn't care that his days so far had consisted of paperwork and innocuous call-outs to quieten loud arguments or barking dogs. His time would come. And, standing there on Audrey Lloyd's doorstep, he felt it finally had.

'I'm here regarding a report we've received,' Don told her in reply with an awkward nod. He was suddenly too aware of his hands – didn't know where to put them, what to do with them. 'Could I—' He was focusing too hard on trying not to fidget under her unyielding gaze. 'Could I ask you some questions?'

He saw her eyes flicker over his shoulder toward his parents' Chevrolet parked on the turning circle. If she wondered why he hadn't arrived in a marked squad car, she had not said. But in the intervening years, as Don had revisited this interview in his memory, he knew that she had certainly noticed, and that, along with his evident ineptitude, had given her all the ammo she'd needed.

'Well of course.' Her demeanour changed suddenly, an unnerving straight-lipped smile pulling across her features as she stepped back from the door. 'You must come in and ask me whatever you wish.'

She had known, of course. Known that he was not there with the might of the LAPD behind him, but just the whims and excitement of an over-eager fan in the right place at the right time.

Audrey Lloyd had guided him through her crowded home and gestured to the same silk couches he was now standing at the head of, thirty-four years later. The couches had been crowded back then with throws and cushions, but he didn't remember them being so stained and threadbare, as he'd taken the seat she'd gestured to.

'Can I get you anything?' she'd asked. 'Tea?'

'Oh, no thank you, ma'am.'

'Now then, what is it you want to ask me about?'

And he'd stumbled. Don remembered it now with embarrassment, how easily and obviously this woman had seized control without him even realising. After a brief conversation, she'd gestured back toward the front door, guiding him out as he'd lingered, his gaze hungry for the inside of this infamous home, the glittering gold Oscars on proud display on a sideboard, a mannequin draped in a sparkling emerald gown just visible down a corridor off the living room.

'Unless,' she'd dared him, amber eyes bright, 'you'd feel more comfortable having a look around?'

She'd called his bluff, seen his innocence, seen his own personal interest in her home and she'd used it against him.

Knowing that he had no warrant and no permission to even be up there, Don had felt suddenly stripped bare in front of her, shame pricking pink into his fresh, clean-shaven cheeks.

'No,' he said hurriedly, ducking his head down and making at once for the front door. 'That won't be necessary. Thank you for your time, ma'am.'

Audrey followed him. 'Not at all, Officer...' Her hand had wafted elegantly in front of her, a silent demand for him to supply his name.

'Vernon.' He gave his choked reply. 'Donald Vernon.'

'I'd be happy to let your superiors know how well you've conducted this investigation if you'd like.' Those eyes glittered again, a snake about to strike.

'No.' The word had come out strained and desperate and he'd noticed her smile return. 'That's really not necessary, no need to waste their time. They're very important men.'

'Of course they are.'

'Well, I'll be getting off now.' He stumbled down the terracotta steps.

'And Officer Vernon?' He turned back to hear her parting wish. 'I hope that one day you too will be a very important man.'

He'd been certain she'd opened her mouth then and given a shrill, manic laugh as the door closed on him. A laugh that had woken him for weeks, ringing in his ears, a shudder rippling his muscles. As he'd matured, he'd convinced himself he was just spooking himself. A young cop, embarrassed to be caught out where he shouldn't have been. The legend of Audrey Lloyd, of the enigmatic house on the hill adding to the narrative.

But now, as Don stared out at that very same living room, the important man Audrey had once prophesised, he wondered how much that was true.

He jumped as the front door banged open, half-expecting to see the ghoul of Audrey Lloyd framed in the doorway, demanding of him what he was doing back here. But it was Officer Chen, red-faced and bending double over his thighs, drawing in great gasping breaths as if he'd just sprinted at full speed up those steep stone steps.

'Chen, what is it?' Don stepped toward him urgently.

'We've got something.'

Twelve

Terri
Tuesday

The midday sun was high and strong, and beads of sweat pricked around Terri's hairline. She noticed the edge of Audrey's turban was also edged darker with damp.

'Should we head inside?' she suggested, having been, yet again, magnanimous in another defeat. 'Get out of the sun for a little bit?' This seemed a reasonable excuse to get back in the house and maybe, once she was inside, make an excuse to peel away and search the office.

Audrey gave a single nod. 'Why not. I'll prepare lunch.'

'I'm happy to help,' Terri said, pushing back her chair as she stood and leaning over the table to start clearing the chess pieces away. Audrey eyed her for a moment from her seat, before deciding to allow her to continue clearing.

'I enjoy preparing food,' Audrey said. 'I used to sneak into the kitchen here as a child and Mrs Doyle would feed me cookies and pies. Later, when the staff were gone, I found her old cookbooks, annotated with all her secrets and tips.' She gave a smile that was both sad and tinged with a fond nostalgia. 'I get my ingredients sent up from the market once a week. They leave them on the doorstep, so I don't even have to bother to speak to anyone.' She gave a small titter and then her face turned surprisingly serious.

'I don't like just anyone coming into my house.' Terri felt an odd dart of warmth at the comment, before shaking herself free.

They carried the glasses and plates back up to the kitchen; one glistening Danish pastry still swirled at the centre of the plate.

'Go and sit down.' Audrey turned to her, gesturing to the door out to the living room. 'I'm sure there's an old book or magazine lying around you can read.'

Terri wasn't sure if Audrey was joking, or if her surroundings had just become so normal to her that they were now unnoticeable. Terri left Audrey in the kitchen but stopped just outside the door as she heard Audrey say something. Just as she was about to go back inside and ask what she wanted, Audrey spoke again. Terri frowned, trying to place the words. They sounded, bizarrely, Russian. The accent light and the words slow, sentences hardly fluent as Audrey talked to herself in long rambling sentences. Terri heard the word 'Irina', followed by a loud, deep laugh as if Audrey was sharing a joke with her old friend. Terri swallowed thickly and moved away from the kitchen, the sound of the one-sided conversation on the other side of the door unnerving her.

She walked deeper into the living room, the cool shade of being indoors a welcome relief. She glanced down the corridor that fed off toward the bathroom she'd used yesterday, and then cricked her neck back toward the kitchen. She had a few minutes at least. Picking up her pace, Terri trotted out of the living room and passed the bathroom, following the corridor around a bend. It brought her out onto a landing with a sweeping staircase circling around to at least three floors below.

'*Jesus*,' she breathed to herself in frustration. There could be God only knew how many rooms down there to explore. Making a plan, Terri turned back toward the office opposite the bathroom she'd found yesterday. Maybe the universe would smile on her for once and she'd find it neatly packed in the first box she tried. And if not, then tomorrow she would have to find a way to steal onto the floors below.

She pushed open the office door and made immediately for the boxes on the desk. The cardboard was old and dry, and as she moved a yellowed screenplay off the first one, the seams split and a flurry of dust billowed into the air, itching her eyes and causing her to splutter a cough from a scratched throat. A pile of paperwork slid out, revealing a stack of screenplays, comments and notes on the front in fading ink and a cursive hand. If Terri had more time she would marvel at the Hollywood history in this one box alone, but she didn't. She rifled through every sheet of paper, eyes scanning, looking for the words she needed, but to no avail.

She moved on and on, rummaging hurriedly through the boxes in easy reach, finding item after item of intense interest – just not of interest to her. The statue of a golden panther climbed out from one box, resting on a broken leather-wrapped pen pot underneath, a few more sheets of paper she read and dismissed – just a long-forgotten to-do list from decades ago. She could feel the time escaping second by second, could sense Audrey putting the finishing touches to their lunch as the minutes ticked by. When she'd finished the boxes on top of the desk, she turned to the drawers, yanking them violently open in turn, hearing the crack of old wood splinter under her force. She rifled only through more useless effects from a history she didn't care about.

There was nothing – it wasn't there.

Knowing that at least seven or eight minutes must have passed since she'd left Audrey in the kitchen, Terri gave the office one final, tense glance before racing back out the door, no time to replace anything she'd disturbed, just hope that Audrey didn't go in there enough to notice. She closed the office behind her and made it back to the living room in time to hear the kitchen door push open, Audrey backing out holding two plates. Terri stepped quickly toward a pile of books in a stack behind the sofa and picked up a heavy black hardback, its title inlaid in pale grey. She slid onto the sofa and pretended to have been engrossed in her reading material all along.

As Audrey made her way across the living room, Terri looked down at the front cover of the book. *Directions for Knowing All Dark Things – Ahmes and Modern Mathematical Analysis.* Terri gave a curious frown and flipped open the front cover, seeing that the publisher's page had been scrawled over with a handwritten message.

> *To Audrey, my most accomplished student. I hope you will continue to thrive and seek out the answers of the universe. Yours, Prof. Ross.*

Audrey came to a stop by the couch and handed a plate to Terri, who was surprised to see a cheese sandwich, some carrot sticks and a handful of chips. The food was so ordinary, so normal, it seemed completely out of place. But then again, what did she expect Audrey to be whipping up in there – pheasant pies and foie gras?

'Thank you,' Terri said, taking the plate and putting the book down on the cushion next to her.

'I see you've found my old math book,' Audrey said, taking a seat opposite her.

'Yeah,' Terri replied, absent-mindedly putting a chip in her mouth. 'Looks intense.'

Audrey smiled and Terri thought she detected a touch of tenderness in it.

'It's a very good book. My final tutor gave it to me. He was retired from Caltech. Very clever man. He gave me that on our final lesson.'

'He obviously had high hopes for you,' Terri said. 'Creepy title though.'

Audrey gave a little laugh. 'Do you know anything about the origins of mathematics?'

Terri raised an eyebrow in an expression she hoped Audrey understood to mean of course she didn't.

'The Rhind Papyrus, by the Egyptian philosopher Ahmes, is thought to be the first record of mathematics. The section that details the first ever calculations is titled' – she gestured down to the book – 'Directions for Knowing All Dark Things.'

Terri pulled a face she knew looked juvenile – her top lip scrunched up questioningly. 'Why?'

There was an unmistakable sheen across Audrey's eyes as she replied. 'Perhaps he understood what looking at those building blocks of the universe can do.' She held Terri's gaze. 'Knowledge is a very dangerous commodity to have. Especially for a woman.' She gave Terri a small nod. 'You must have learned that by now.'

Something fluttered inside Terri's chest, as she recognised, unexpectedly, flattery in Audrey's tone.

'Why do you say that?' Terri asked, finding herself craving the answer, craving this woman's compliments.

'I see a lot in you, Terri,' Audrey replied simply. Feeling a flash of embarrassment, Terri turned her attention to her food, picking up a chip between her thumb and forefinger. She could not remember the last time anyone had said they'd seen anything in her. Even Ethan had purposefully batted away her knowledge and skills, time and time again, his own ego taking top billing in his priorities. 'Oh, I haven't got you a drink yet to have with your lunch,' Audrey said, pulling Terri from her thoughts.

'I can get it,' Terri said, making to move and get up herself. 'I don't mind.'

'No.' Audrey's voice was surprisingly sharp, halting Terri on the sofa. Her face was unreadably stern for just a moment, but soon broke again with a bright smile. 'I like to take care of my guests. There's not much else for me to do with my days, after all.'

Terri gave a nervous laugh and picked up her sandwich. Audrey waited until she'd taken a bite before she swung around to go back into the kitchen. She returned with Terri's glass from earlier, freshly topped up with iced tea.

They ate in silence, the cheap plastic slices of cheese clinging to the roof of Terri's mouth, as she allowed herself to bask pathetically in the glow of Audrey's compliment.

Terri leaned forward and put her plate down; the salty chips had made her thirsty again, and she could feel her heavy night starting to catch back up with her. She reached for the glass of iced tea and took a large, desperate gulp – waiting for that tart lemon to work its wonders on her again. She managed to see off almost half of the short tumbler in one swallow, and stopped suddenly, an unexpected taste on her tongue. She held the glass out in front of her, frowning at it.

'Everything alright?' Audrey asked, biting into a carrot stick with a loud crack.

Terri brought the glass back toward her and peered into it, her frown furrowing deeper. 'This tastes…' She opened and closed her mouth a couple of times, tongue flicking out to lick her lips. 'Well, it tastes like gin.'

'I told you,' Audrey said with a smile that reached her amber eyes. 'Hair of the dog always works wonders. You'll feel right as rain in no time.'

Terri looked up at her. 'You put gin in my drink?'

Audrey just nodded, evidently pleased with herself.

'I – I – er…' Terri tried to cast about for the most polite way to refuse. 'I'm driving.' She gestured limply over her shoulder and in the rough direction of where the Maverick was parked outside on the turning circle. 'So I probably shouldn't…' She made to put the spiked iced tea back on the coffee table but stopped when she saw the smile fall from Audrey's eyes. It remained on her stretched lips though, unnerving and strained.

'You should drink it,' she said.

'No, really, I—'

'You should drink it. You'll feel much better.' The smile returned to her eyes and her next words were said with a brightness that did not befit the situation. 'Trust me!'

Terri felt Audrey's gaze bore into her, and those marionette strings tightened once again. She could think of no other way to get rid of the iced tea, aside from throwing the heavy cut-glass directly into Audrey's face. Watch as it cracked open the old woman's nose, iced tea flowing with blood down into her shocked, gaping mouth.

Terri shook herself free of the fantasy, knowing that violence did not come easily to her. She'd known that

94

since she was thirteen and a group of girls at school had wanted her to join in their campaign of bullying the new girl who was so temptingly quiet and awkward for them. But after seeing one fist pound into the side of the new girl's face, Terri had felt a rush of sickness rise up her throat and fled home. She had not bullied the new girl, who had transferred to yet another school just one week later. But she'd not helped her either, and in that incident Terri had learned something about herself – she was a coward.

She drank the gin and iced tea, swallowing the burning liquor down in one, knowing that Audrey had given her far more than just a single measure.

'See,' Audrey said with a satisfied gaze, 'you'll feel as good as new in no time.'

Thirteen

Audrey
Tuesday

It disappointed Audrey that, when the afternoon started to pull to a close, Terri began looking hopefully at her watch. Surely she couldn't expect to drive home? Not after four fingers of gin?

'Terri, if you want to be getting home...' Audrey tested her, feeling a sharp spike of black as Terri's face immediately cleared in relief.

'Yes, I will,' she replied, practically running for the handbag she'd left on the side earlier that morning. She fished her car key from inside and then paused, turning back to her host. 'Thank you for such a lovely day. I'm looking forward to tomorrow.'

'Are you feeling alright to drive?' Audrey pushed some more. She could, of course, *make* Terri stay, but that was not the point of any of this. Not yet, at least.

'Oh yes,' Terri said, already walking toward the door. 'You were right after all. That gin did wonders for me! I'll see you tomorrow, Audrey.'

Audrey frowned. She knew Terri was being disingenuous – Audrey had had a long life of learning to read people, learning their patterns, their quirks. She heard the door slam shut and, moments later, the sound of the sports car engine revving loudly before taking off down the hill.

It was a shame Terri didn't want Audrey's care, and Audrey felt an overwhelming sense of sadness as she sat back down on the sofa. Her hand stretched out and found the black hardcover volume that Terri had discovered earlier that day. She flipped it open and ran her finger under Professor Ross's inscription, surprised when heavy thick droplets fell onto the page, crinkling the paper in small circles.

'Don't cry,' Irina said from behind the far sofa, hovering at the edge of the corridor that led into the rest of the house. She was wearing Audrey's favourite silk kimono, swirled in silver dragons against royal blue. Audrey wiped away the tears from beneath her eyes with her fingers, cheering a little.

'*No llores,*' Irina repeated, this time in Spanish, and Audrey smiled at the language shift. Irina had learned English very quickly after they'd first met, and then they'd passed the time with Audrey teaching her Mama's Spanish and, in return, Irina teaching her Russian and – German. Audrey's throat grew thick at the memory. Irina came over to the sofa. She moved slowly and Audrey watched her every step of the way.

'Sometimes memories get the best of me,' Audrey admitted sadly when she was joined by her companion.

'*Vamos,*' Irina said gently, *come on*, the Spanish, reminding Audrey of Mama telling her bedtime stories. She placed her hands on the book in Audrey's lap and closed it firmly. '*No point dwelling on memories that make us cry now is there?*' And she smiled up at Audrey with a smile only the young could produce.

It was raining heavily outside the tall glass windows of Lloyd House's living room, on the day that spawned Audrey's greatest regret. Thick droplets sauntered down the panes, glistening in the gun-metal grey of the sky outside.

'I imagine this feels more like home, does it?' Audrey said.

'Turn the temperature down several degrees and you might have an idea,' Irina replied with the easy-flowing English she'd learned over the last three years of their friendship. It was still weighed down by her distinctive Russian-Germanic accent, which it would be all her life.

'Sounds dreadful,' Audrey said, swiping the last of Irina's pawns in a ploy for checkmate.

'You would hate it,' Irina agreed with a nod and reached for a bite of the Danish pastry on the gold-rimmed plate just to the right of where they'd set up the chessboard on the dining table. There was a cafetière of thick black coffee next to it, the aroma of the roasted beans making Audrey feel quite ill as she drank her tea. But Irina was insistent – coffee was all she would accept.

The door to Arnold's study clicked open and Mrs Hackton strode out, heels clacking the short way down the corridor and into the living room. Audrey felt the usual small knot of tightness twist in her chest, knowing that this meant Lev and Daddy had finished their meeting and Irina would soon be taken away from her. Audrey did not like when Irina was taken away from her – she needed her. They needed each other. Audrey had seen that for herself over the summer.

Mrs Hackton eyed them warily now, her scrutiny zeroing in on Audrey as it always did. Audrey knew that, when she watched her closely like this, Mrs Hackton was thinking about Palm Springs, and what she had heard Daddy's secretary refer to as the *incident*. Audrey had tried to laugh with Irina about Mrs Hackton using such a turn of phrase, so grandiose and over-dramatic to describe two best friends, two *soulmates*, being reunited during a summer vacation. But Irina had looked strangely uncomfortable for a moment before muttering that 'Sascha was quite frightened you know,' and solemnly continuing the game they'd been playing.

Audrey had waved Irina's discomfort away; it wasn't her fault. She was wonderful but weak in so many ways – she often bowed to agree with her father or what other people around them said. That was why it was so important Audrey was there for her. To guide her. To care for her.

Mrs Hackton eyed the young women for another moment before snapping, 'Irina, your father is ready to leave now. Wrap up your game.'

Mrs Hackton was soon trailed by Lev Popov, Arnold and one of Lev's colleagues in law who had joined whatever complicated project Arnold seemed to be working on. He'd been there at least once a week for most of the year. The three men looked grave, but Arnold soon covered his expression with a bright smile when he saw his daughter, as he always did.

Over the last year or so Arnold had stopped bringing Audrey in on his creative decisions, stopped chatting with her about his work, stopped asking her advice on who to cast or where to shoot. In fact, the last idea he'd listened to was to film *Sunset Over the Desert* on their own land. Audrey shot Mrs Hackton a dark look, confident she knew who to blame for this new dynamic with her father's business. Somehow, the woman was still getting in her way.

'Good game, girls?' Lev asked, not quite as adept as Arnold at hiding the strain from the meeting they'd just had.

'Yes,' Audrey said smoothly, finishing her tactic with a successful flourish, putting her queen directly in front of Irina's king. 'Checkmate,' she told her friend with a smile.

'Come on, Irina,' Lev said, 'we best get going. Leon, do you need a ride?'

The other man, Leon Lewis, nodded. 'If you don't mind, Lev. I need to get back to the office downtown. It was nice to see you again, Miss Lloyd.' He waved a polite farewell to Audrey.

Irina got to her feet and followed her father and Mr Lewis toward the door. Before they reached the entrance hall, Lewis turned back to Arnold.

'Be careful, Arnold,' he said in a low voice. 'You're on dangerous ground, so please – be careful.'

Arnold nodded and clapped him on the back. 'It's the right thing to take the risk,' he said with a tense smile.

'You're a good man,' Lewis said with a nod. 'A good man.'

Audrey watched them leave and heard the door close behind them.

'What was all that about, Daddy?' she asked, standing up from the dining table and walking toward her father, stopping to lean on the back of the sofa.

'None of your business,' Mrs Hackton cut in sharply, with a stern look to Arnold. 'Best you stay out of it all, do you hear?'

'I don't know who you think you are' – Audrey straightened up, riling for a fight – 'but what Daddy and I discuss—'

'She's *right*,' Arnold snapped suddenly, and Audrey felt smugly vindicated. She flashed a look to Mrs Hackton, and then to her father, and felt a horrible dread descend as she realised Daddy was talking to *her*. 'Annabel is right. It's best you stay out of any of this business. Best for everyone.' Arnold visibly steadied himself, taking several deep breaths before looking back to his daughter. 'We have company coming in an hour,' he said. 'We'll be entertaining for drinks before I have' – he inhaled shakily – 'business to discuss. Please make yourself presentable for cocktails.'

Audrey watched in horror as Mrs Hackton led her father away with no more conversation. No offer of a quick game of chess before their guests arrived, no consolatory recognition that Audrey might not *want* to entertain guests. Just an order and then abandonment. She blew out an angry exhale and stormed off to her room.

Despite her fury at her father, she knew she would not let him down. She was clever enough to understand that messing up a business occasion like this would only give Mrs Hackton even more weaponry in her arsenal against Audrey. And so Audrey tamed her hair with wax, revitalised her face with blush and thick mascara and dressed in a neat black dress that fell to her shins, with structured puffed sleeves and heavy white buttons.

'You look marvellous, *bebita*.' Audrey saw Mama in the mirror behind her, ruby red lips pulled into a proud smile.

'*Gracias, Mama*,' Audrey whispered to the empty room. 'I'm doing my best for Daddy.'

'I know you are, *mi amor*.'

Palm Springs had been entirely Mama's idea. It had been a blisteringly hot July, and Irina had been wrenched away by Lev for a two-week stay in some ludicrous holiday home owned by one of his clients, an actress whose career Audrey had vowed to destroy for facilitating their separation. With Irina gone, Audrey had never felt more alone – thick black walls pressed closer and closer each day, and only Mama was there to help hold them back and save her from true suffocation. Daddy was busy with the *Sunset Over the Desert* production, wide tracks cut into the wilderness of their land so trucks holding the necessary equipment could traverse the property. Audrey's forearms were a wilderness of their own with scabs and scratches. At first the boredom and loneliness had only been relieved by the press of a sharp pencil, as it had in high school. And then it had progressed, and she found relief only in digging her nails deep into her skin and feeling the satisfying sting as her inner flesh was exposed to the air.

'If you feel like this, imagine how Irina must feel too,' Mama had said one day, watching Audrey pick at a deep scab, releasing the warm blood beneath it. 'You should go to her.'

'You're right, Mama,' Audrey replied, amazed she hadn't had the idea herself. She'd left immediately, fetching the keys to the Phantom Carl had taught her to drive for her eighteenth birthday, and setting off for Palm Springs.

Dusk had fallen by the time she arrived, having found the address on correspondence in Arnold's office. And it had been Irina's youngest brother, Sascha, who'd spotted her through the large French windows at the back of the home, illuminated only by moonlight, arms still streaked with dried blood, her sand-coloured slacks equally stained with rusty pools. His screams had had a touch of melodrama to them, Audrey had thought, but the rest of the family had swarmed to his aid at once. When things had settled, and Sascha had been safely taken back to his room, Lev had allowed Audrey to stay for the remaining three days of their vacation, calling Daddy to let him know where she was. And what a good thing Audrey had gone when she had. Even for just three days she had had a full-time job batting away Irina's brothers, who kept trying to engage their sister in table tennis games, the culmination of an apparent tournament Audrey knew Irina had no interest in competing in.

Audrey climbed the staircase back up to the living room, toward the cocktail party, such as it was, that had already started.

Rex Heatherington turned around with a martini glass in his hand, a saccharine smile pulled beneath his moustache. 'Audrey, my biggest fan!' He greeted her as he always did. 'I'm delighted you're joining us.'

At the sound of her name, Arnold turned away from another gentleman, who Audrey did not recognise. He wore a grey suit and had sheer blonde hair and pale grey eyes – he was devoid of colour in every way.

'Audrey, my dear,' Arnold said delightedly. But as Audrey stepped forward, she was surprised to see the tell-tale sign of strain in her father's eyes. 'I'd like you to meet Herr Scholtz. He's from the German consulate. Herr Scholtz – my daughter, Audrey.'

Herr Scholtz seemed to hesitate before stretching out his hand, and Audrey felt his eyes drop all the way down her body to her feet, and then back up to her face. Audrey took his hand and forced a smile.

'How nice to meet you,' she said. 'A friend of mine is from Berlin. She's been teaching me some German. *Willkommen in unserem Zuhause.*'

Herr Scholtz smiled then, evidently warming to hearing his native language. '*Danke.*' He nodded. 'And it is a magnificent home you have.'

'Daddy designed it himself.'

'Oh, I had help from an artist.' Arnold waved a hand dismissively.

Herr Scholtz turned to survey the rain-dabbled windows. 'And so much land to go with it.'

'I have it in mind to develop one day,' Arnold said jovially. 'Just haven't quite got round to it yet.'

'Of course.' Herr Scholtz smiled in the way Audrey recognised – it didn't quite reach his eyes. He turned back to the dining table he was standing near, bringing one hand down to rest on the screenplay Audrey now could see had been placed there. The chessboard she and Irina had been sitting at earlier had been tidied away. 'I appreciated the opportunity to read your latest script, Arnold.' He lightly lifted all his fingers one by one, until only his middle finger was left resting on the bound papers. It was a slow, hypnotic process and Audrey noticed that she, Arnold, Rex and Mrs Hackton had all watched it intently. 'The German market is of great importance to you, is it not?'

Arnold nodded hurriedly. 'Of course.'

'Which is why I am so appreciative of this insight into your creative process.' Scholtz smiled at Audrey. Then he pounded the script decisively with a full fist, in a sudden, loud movement that sent a shock through the room. 'I have made some notes.'

It took a moment for Arnold to reply. 'I…' He paused and blinked. 'I look forward to reading them.'

Herr Scholtz took another swig of the cocktail in his other hand, before unclenching the fist that had smacked the script and holding it out in gesture toward Arnold.

'Now, will we discuss our business?'

'Yes, yes of course.' Arnold stepped back and held his arms out, guiding the way to his office. 'My office is just down here. I'm sure we can come to some sort of arrangement.'

Mrs Hackton bustled forward and grabbed the now empty martini glass with both hands. 'Let me get you a fresh drink, Herr Scholtz. I'll bring it through with some nibbles Mrs Doyle has been preparing.'

'*Danke*, that is most kind,' Scholtz said with a smarmy grin Audrey knew Mrs Hackton would fall for. Sure enough, the woman giggled infuriatingly and hurried off into the kitchen.

Scholtz and Arnold disappeared off into the office, leaving Audrey alone with Rex.

'Well, I'm glad I got all dressed up for such a short party,' she said flippantly.

Rex laughed. 'You look beautiful as always, Audrey, just like your mother.' He took a final swig from his own glass and set it down on the sideboard. 'Although, alas, I have learned my advances will always be rebuffed by you.'

'It doesn't stop you trying, though,' Audrey replied, making her way to the bar cart to pour herself a drink. She held out a hand as she passed by, and he handed her his empty glass. She set them down on the cart and began selecting her gin and vermouth, taking the small knife to peel a few curls of rind off a lemon in the overflowing bowl picked from their own trees.

Just then Mrs Hackton came back through from the kitchen, holding a tray of canapés. She paused just long enough to pick Audrey's completed cocktail directly off the trolley, place it on her tray and carry it off toward Arnold's office. Audrey gave an irritated exhale and turned to hand Rex his refilled drink, before getting another glass and starting again on her own.

'She has quite a way, doesn't she, that Mrs Hackton?' Rex said with a laugh.

'Something like that.'

'Now.' Rex's tone became business-like as Audrey finished off her drink and turned toward him. 'Won't you join me on the couch?'

'This is my house,' Audrey replied, taking a sip. 'How very presumptuous of you to invite me to sit in my own home.'

Rex gave a nod with an amused smile. 'Very well. Would *you* care to invite *me* to sit?'

Audrey gave a small roll of her eyes before walking past him toward the couches. She put her drink down on the side table and reclined comfortably, while Rex joined her opposite.

'I've been meaning to ask you about something,' he said as he relaxed. 'The last few times I've been here.'

'Oh yes?' Audrey said lazily. 'And what would that be?'

'That book.' Rex nodded and Audrey was taken by surprise at his answer. She followed the direction of his nod to see it was the copy of *Directions for Knowing All Dark Things* she'd rested her drink on.

'My math book?' she asked drily, picking her glass up for another swig.

'Yes,' Rex said slowly. 'It's quite impressive. I had a flip through the last time I was here. Your father says you read it a lot.'

Audrey gave a shrug with one shoulder. 'I don't have much chance to keep in with math since my tutor was let go. This is the one little tendril of exercise my brain gets.'

Rex beamed.

'What if I said there might be a way for you to exercise those math skills after all?'

Fourteen

Terri
Tuesday

'You're back.' Ethan rushed her as soon as she stepped through the door. He was agitated, eyes wide and bloodshot, hair overgrown and ungroomed, so different from the neat, professional crop he'd first got done when they'd moved to California. He was wearing his work suit, but it hung limply from his ever-reducing frame, the tie pulled away from his neck so the knot hung somewhere around his chest. 'Did you get it?' He gripped her shoulders, pushing her roughly back against the door. She could smell the bourbon on his breath.

'Ow,' she said, trying to manoeuvre herself out of his grasp. 'You're hurting me.'

'Did you get it?' He ignored her, and only pressed her harder against the door.

'No,' she said, feeling pathetic as the word slid out her mouth. 'I tried, but there's so much stuff. I told you, it's a big house – I'll keep looking tomorrow. And all week, I'll even go back next week if I have to!' A whimpering plea had crept into her tone now, one she found she was glad Audrey wasn't there to hear. As Ethan slammed away from her with a groan, Terri didn't allow herself to wonder why Audrey had jumped to her mind at that moment.

'We don't have until next week!' Ethan shouted, hands coming to his hairline to tug on the blonde strands with white-hot knuckles. He fell against the back of the sofa, his breath rising. 'We don't even have until fucking tomorrow, Terri!'

'Wh—' Terri stepped forward. 'What do you mean?'

'Jason is coming.' Ethan looked up at her, drained and pallid. 'Tonight.'

Terri's mind jumped into overdrive, trying to process what Ethan was telling her. 'So, you'll talk to him — explain everything, it'll be OK. You're old friends, right?' The words fell out of her, hurried and desperate as she moved closer to him, her hands yearning to grab him and hold him, but wary how he might react to her touch.

'We're not at fucking Pacific High tossing the pigskin to each other anymore, Terri!' He seemed to explode from his perch, his fury aimed directly at her.

'But you said he took one of the trucks from the business!' she screamed back, his desperation catching now. 'You said that would tide you over!'

Ethan sagged a little, but his stance was still combative, fight or flight clearly raging within him. 'Well, it wasn't! His boss said it's not enough, he needs more. It's been too long, the interest has got too high, I—'

'So what does he want from us tonight?' Terri interrupted, trying to make a plan — one of them had to keep a clear head if they had any hope of sorting out Ethan's mistake. His stupid, stupid mistake six months ago, accepting a loan from an old high school friend. Terri would never have gone along with it, but by then she was already cut out — the long nights in the bar had started, the terse way he snapped at almost everything she said. She'd never warmed to Jason, not since the first night she'd met him at a pool party a few months after they'd first arrived. He'd slipped Ethan a little bag of white powder and taken him to a nearby strip club, leaving Terri to wander a house of strangers wondering where her fiancé had gone. Back then Ethan still bothered to apologise, and he'd grovelled for days until she'd finally forgiven him. But the deal with Jason had been agreed late night at some dive bar, a shaken hand with a guy who worked for questionable people, enforcing questionable 'business deals'. Illegal loans with illegal interest rates were no doubt just the start of it.

'He wants his money,' Ethan said slowly, panting over the words.

'We don't have it, though.'

'Or he wants me.'

'What do you mean he wants you?'

'He's going to hurt me, Terri. Maybe even kill me.'

An eerie calmness settled over Terri then, some evolutionary instinct to be still and focus. 'Then he'll never get his money.' She attempted reason.

Ethan shook his head. 'He doesn't think he ever will. And he can't let it get round that he's going soft on old friends.'

'But we're so close.' Terri braved another step closer to the man she'd loved for over a decade. 'I'll find it. I will.'

'It might be too late.'

'There must be something we can do!' Frustration suddenly burst out of her, frustration not just at Ethan, but the assholes at work who laughed at her ideas and never trusted her with anything important. The only person who seemed to think she had any type of worth was a mad old woman sitting high on a hill in a rotting old house.

Ethan blinked into her rage, shock stopping him from responding immediately.

'I have to go,' he said suddenly, his body animating again in quick, agitated movements as he swung from one side to the other as if trying to decide which direction to flee.

'Go? Go where?'

Ethan had paced into the bedroom, where he grabbed an old gym bag from under the bed and yanked open his underwear drawer.

'I'll just go – it's me he wants. He—' He paused and jerked momentarily toward Terri, who had trailed him to their bedroom door, before turning back to his packing. 'He won't hurt you.' He did not sound completely convinced by his own words.

'No, no, no, no, no.' Terri's words were staccato and panicked. Surely he wouldn't leave her here all alone to deal with this – this gangster? She tried to grab at his arms, to stop him from packing, but he shoved her off, hard, so she staggered awkwardly back.

'Yes, yes.' He seemed to be settling into his plan of abandonment now. 'This is it. This is the best way. Give him whatever he wants to tide him over, show him we're serious – give him the TV or something, I don't know. Tell him you don't know where I am but—' He paused to pull the zip around the flap of the royal blue nylon canvas, before straightening up to look her in the eye. 'Tell him we've nearly got all of it – the whole repayment. Tell him we're close.'

'Wh... what if he doesn't believe me?'

'*Make* him believe you.'

Ethan picked up the bag and pushed past her out of the room.

'Where are you going to go?' She chased after him, pleading as he got to the front door.

'I don't know — it's best that you don't know either, be believable for Jason.' Horrible thoughts of his location being tortured out of her flashed unwittingly through her mind. 'But I'll take the bus somewhere. You need the car. You need to get back up to that house.' He pulled the door toward him and looked back one last time. 'You have to get it, Terri — we've run out of options.'

And he was gone. He hadn't even kissed her goodbye.

A thousand questions were on her tongue. How long would he be gone? How would she tell him if she succeeded? Did he not want her to go with him? Escape into the night together — head down to Mexico and live a simple life on the beach? Tears crept out of the corners of her eyes, a thick swallow straining down her throat.

She slumped heavily on the sofa. With no other ideas, she simply did was she was told. She hadn't even taken her vows yet, but here she was — ready to honour and obey.

In the end Jason didn't just take the TV.

He and his goons stripped their home of everything. The black leather couch she'd bought so proudly with her first commission check. The TV, her jewellery, even the plain old radio that stood in the kitchen. Only the rickety wooden dining set was left, deemed too worthless to clog up the van with. They'd been saving up for a new one. Some glass and chrome model Terri now winced at the price of.

When he was done, the last of his men carrying their brand new VHS player out the door, Jason stopped in the entrance way and turned toward where she was silently sobbing against the wall.

'It's a shame it's had to come to this, Terri,' he said, fluffy, shoulder-length chestnut hair framing tanned and unnervingly handsome features. 'You need to keep better track of that husband of yours.' He waggled his finger like a teacher reprimanding a student.

She turned to him and swallowed away a rising sob. 'He's not my husband yet.'

'No.' Jason's eyes fell to the solitary ring on Terri's left hand, a round-cut diamond on a golden band. 'But you've got his ring.'

'Please,' she whimpered and pulled the hand up to her chest. He stepped closer to her, holding his hand expectantly out. 'No,' she said, attempting firmness and stepping away from him again.

'Please,' Jason said, sounding bored, 'let's not play this game.'

'No,' she said again, and cradled her left hand protectively against her chest.

But Jason did not accept the word 'no'. The knuckles of his fist slammed into her cheekbone before she'd even registered that he'd closed the gap between them. He pushed her to her knees and gripped her wrist with an iron-like grasp, bending her ring finger so far back on itself she was sure she could feel the bones crumble under the pressure.

She let out a soft yelp of pain and he smiled in satisfaction as he slid the ring off. He twisted her finger even harder in the wrong direction for another moment, before releasing it so suddenly she was disorientated about where the agony had gone. Jason slipped the ring into the pocket of his Levi's and stopped at the small side table by the door on his way out.

'And I'll be taking this, too,' he said, hooking her car key onto his finger and spinning it elegantly around.

'No!' Her voice was more urgent this time, and she clambered to her feet. 'No, you can't. I need it – I need it for work. I told you, I *told* you I'm working on something to get you the money. But I can't do that without my car! Please, please. I'm begging you – I need it.'

Jason watched her beg and then he laughed.

'You seem like a resourceful kinda gal. I'm sure you'll think of another way to get to work.'

'You don't understand, I—'

But he was in her face before she could finish the sentence, before she could even realise what had happened. His nose was so close to hers she was sure their hairs were touching. The laughter had gone.

'No, *you* don't understand,' he spat. 'You tell that no-good loser of a man of yours that running out on a debt to *my* people is not the smartest plan. All of this' – he swung one arm around the newly empty house – 'is only a tiny fraction of what you owe. And this...' He brought the arm back toward her, so she flinched, expecting another pound in the face. But he slowed at the last moment and brushed the back of his index finger against the tender spot on her cheek. 'This is a warning. And he's out of warnings.' Jason stepped away. 'You have one week. Or I'm coming back to burn this place to the ground, whether you're in it or not.'

And then he was gone.

Terri fell to the floor in the moments after the door slammed shut behind him, the breath ripped from her lungs.

Fifteen

Don followed Chen back down the steps, feeling his age and bulk as he struggled to keep up with the younger officer's nimble footwork. They jogged through the gate and past the lawn with the white obelisk, Don noticing how Chen purposefully held back his pace to keep the older detective alongside.

Off from the lawn, a narrow dirt track ran through high, dried-out bushes that scratched at Don's jacket and face where they had overgrown the path. The path veered sharply uphill, and Don felt an unfortunate sharpness in his chest, which he pushed aside as he continued to plough on in Chen's wake. At the crest of the hill, they came out onto a wide plateau of dusty soil, a few other tracks falling away, off into the rest of the grounds.

Don bent over and coughed up a large, painful globule of phlegm from somewhere deeper than he wanted to imagine. Black spots drifted across his vision as he waited for the oxygen to return to his body. He drew in several deep breaths and then stood up, a little embarrassed as the two younger officers waited awkwardly for him to recover from the unexpected sprint. He remembered being like them, silently vowing to themselves that they'd never become that spluttering old man.

But Don's attention did not remain on them long, as his sightline was interrupted by a dark red Chevrolet from what looked like the Forties.

'What the—' he said to himself, stepping forward between Chen and Sterne, toward the bonnet of the car and bending down to run his hand across the silver grille along the front. He stood upright and looked over to the officers. 'Looks like a 1947,' he said knowledgeably. 'My parents had one around the time I joined the force.'

'It's not the car we called you for,' Chen said, and Don noticed he was purposefully keeping his head turned at a forty-five-degree angle away from the vehicle.

'Well, what is it, then?'

The two officers looked at each other. 'It's what's inside the car,' Sterne answered. He nodded toward it. 'Back seat.'

Don walked around the long hood of the car and bent down to peer in through the back windows. They were grimy with years of dust and muck, but his eyes soon focused through the film of dirt, although it took another moment for him to realise what he was looking at.

'Jesus Christ,' he hissed, stepping back from the car in alarm. He shook himself off and returned to the window, this time focusing keenly on the yellowing skeleton draped across the bench-style back seat. He stood up and looked at Chen and Sterne over the top of the car. 'Have you had a closer look?'

Sterne shook his head. 'We found the car, thought it was odd' – he gestured around the abandoned landscape that didn't naturally lend itself to a parking lot – 'then we saw the skeleton and came to get you immediately.'

Don nodded. 'Right. One of you, get the licence plate number and call it in. We're going to need another team from the coroner's, forensics, crime scene photographer – everyone down here. While you're there, call in a check on the licence plate; I want to know who this car belonged to and when.' Don already thought he had a good idea but going in answer-first with only a recollection from thirty-four years ago was no way to do police work. 'And tell Captain Glover I'm calling in one of the many favours he owes me, and get us a warrant for the house and grounds.'

Chen nodded, looking a little apprehensive at having to demand a favour from the captain. 'Will do.' Then he turned on his heel and headed back the way he'd just led Don, up to their squad car and the radio within.

'Sterne.' Don gestured to the remaining officer to join him on his side of the car. 'Let's see what we're dealing with.' While Sterne moved around the back of the car to stand beside him, Don placed both hands on the silver handle and tugged it hard. Nothing moved.

'Locked,' Sterne said.

'No. I think it's just stuck. God knows how long it's been here for. Rusted. But the handle has some give, so I don't think it's locked. Just needs brute force.'

Don gave it another few tugs before stepping aside and gesturing in a gentlemanly manner for the younger, and stronger, man to take a turn. Sterne gave the handle a few sharp tugs, and Don could see the young muscles ripple under his uniform shirt, lamenting the days when his own shoulders had wielded so much power. After three strong pulls, Sterne leveraged his right foot against the driver side door, and gave one strong yank that unstuck the door and caused him to fall back and land on his butt in the dirt.

Don approached the open door slowly, and peered into the back seat, the yellowing skeleton as real and grinning as it had been through the window. Dark stains tainted the passenger footwells, where Don guessed the organic matter had pooled as it rotted off its host's bones. Scraps of material clung to what had once been living, working legs – the last remnants of not-yet-decomposed nylon stockings. Don took in the rest of the scene before stepping back from the car toward Officer Sterne.

'What do you think?' he asked, turning to Don.

Don shook his head. 'I'm not sure. But I'm starting to think that whatever we're hearing, it might not be horses after all.' Sterne frowned in confusion, but Don didn't give him time to question. 'Stay here with the car until the teams come. I'm going to continue the search of the house. See if I can't find anything that might tell us who that might be.'

'Surely it's not connected to this, though?' Sterne asked. 'I mean…' He raised a hand toward the car. 'Whoever that was, it must have been years ago.'

Don nodded and followed the direction of his gesture. 'If I've learned one thing in thirty-five years on the force…' He turned back to the young officer. 'You never know what might come back to haunt you.'

Like your own incompetence.

Like a case you gave up on too easily.

Like Lloyd House.

Sixteen

Terri
Tuesday

It took a monumental effort to haul herself upright, her cheek throbbing and feeling tight enough to burst. The air felt suddenly hotter and more humid than it had before, and she could feel it cloying down her throat, as if it had its own sweaty little hands and was trying to rob her of her innards. But eventually she got her breath back, filled her lungs and pushed herself onto her feet as a gentle knock came from the front door.

Panic seized her where she stood, terrified it was Jason coming back for more. But he'd not knocked so politely when he'd arrived – a hard thud and catcall through the window. The knock came again, and she approached timidly, pulling the door open a fraction so only a sliver of her face would be visible from the other side.

It was Mrs Washington, standing awkwardly on the top step, holding a small television. Terri frowned and pulled the door further open, trying to ignore her neighbour's gasp of shock when her quickly bruising cheek was revealed.

'Mrs Washington,' Terri said with a sigh. 'Now is really not a good—'

'I saw those men leave with your TV,' she inter-rupted. 'And we had this old black and white one just lying around. Never knew what to do with it when we got our new one, felt wrong to throw it away.' Terri stared in surprise at the television. 'Is—' Mrs Washington stalled herself before ploughing on with her question. 'Is everything alright?'

No, Terri thought was the obvious answer, but that's not what she told her neighbour. 'Bailiffs,' she said. 'From the bank. We've had some troubles and fallen behind on a couple of mortgage payments.' She could see that Mrs Washington did not believe her. The bank did not send goons wearing leather jackets and acid-wash jeans, driving blacked-out vans. 'But we'll get back on track.' She forced a smile. 'We always do.'

Mrs Washington nodded jerkily and then held out the television with an awkward motion. 'Do,' she said in a low voice as Terri leaned in to accept the gift, 'you need me to call the police?'

'No.' Terri answered abruptly, not wanting to know what Jason's sprawling network would do to her if she did. She forced lightness into her tone. 'Really, that's not necessary. We'll be fine.'

It took another minute or so for Terri to get rid of Mrs Washington, making promises of lucrative new deals for both her work and Ethan's business.

'Alright,' she said eventually, still not sounding entirely convinced, 'but if you need anything – anything at all – you let me know.'

Fifty grand would be nice, Terri did not say in reply.

She let the door slam on her retreating neighbour and closed her eyes as a tension headache pricked at her temples. The last thing she needed was a nosy neighbour calling the cops. Terri knew it would make no difference; the likes of Jason, and whoever he worked for, were not so easily put to justice. And Terri had no problem believing that Jason's parting promise was more than just an idle threat.

Dropping the TV on the floor, she padded her way into the kitchen and stared fruitlessly into the open refrigerator. She'd drained the last of the wine the day before and so, having already had an unexpected cocktail at lunch, Terri poured herself a gin, mixing it with a little orange juice she had left, pretty sure it was several days past its use-by date. Her finger was throbbing now, sapping all her energy, so she could not dwell too long on what Audrey spiking her drink had meant. Perhaps the old woman had genuinely thought she was trying to help.

She carried her drink into the living room and set it down on the floor, plugging the TV in and flickering it to life. She fetched the first aid kit from the bathroom, and watched re-runs of *Mork & Mindy* as she sat on the floor and manufactured a splint from the stick of a popsicle she'd found in the freezer.

The strawberry ice was sickly sweet, and she felt the sugar start to rejuvenate her, along with the gin and more-than-recommended dose of aspirin helping to dull the pain to manageable levels. Her mouth was sticky and covered in red, like a child playing dress-up in her mother's make-up. Terri barked a half-drunken laugh at a joke on the show while she wrapped the medical tape one final time around her fingers. She held out her hand in front of her and felt the laugh churn up her throat into a sob as she stared at her sad, broken finger. Bereft of engagement ring and now swollen and bruised.

Oh, Ethan, what have you done? When did it all go so wrong?

He'd proposed on Coney Island, where they'd gone for a day out from their Manhattan apartment about six months after Ethan's dad had died. Terri had taken him to the amusement park for a break, and as the Ferris wheel had reached the peak of its ascent, the glittering multicoloured lights sprawled beneath them, Ethan had cleared his throat.

'I think I'm going to have to move back to California,' he'd said. She felt a rock plummet in her stomach. He was leaving her. 'I need to take over my dad's business.'

She blinked in an effort to work out what to say. 'But you've just got published,' she settled on, as if one short story in a science fiction magazine meant his writing dreams were taking off.

'I can write around the business,' he said, with what she now knew was a fool's confidence.

'Oh.' She couldn't keep the disappointment out of her voice. 'Well, I guess you gotta do what you gotta do.'

His eyes had sparkled in that moment, just before. His long blonde hair, which would soon be cut in favour of a more business-like look, framed tanned, freckled features and blue eyes, which danced with Coney Island's illuminations. He'd dug his hand into the inside pocket of his jacket, and pulled out a square, velvet box.

'I'd love for you to come with me,' he'd said softly, and popped it open to reveal a small, glittering diamond. Terri had never expected she would be that girl, but she'd burst at once into tears, and they immediately began planning their future together. Now she felt like she was still on that Ferris wheel, feeling it swoop through the air and watching the dancing lights glow in her new engagement ring – but her mind was fuzzy, and tension pinched at her lungs.

She woke with a start on the floor, her glass empty, the TV displaying a late-night card imploring her to come back in the morning. The contents of the first aid kit were strewn around her and she leaned forward, her brain only just adjusting to the sound that had dragged her from that dreamed memory of the Ferris wheel.

The loud trilling of the phone travelled piercingly through the house from the kitchen. Groggily, with no idea of what time it was, Terri clambered to her feet and held her cheek against the newly awakened pain. Without thinking, or wondering who it could be, she pulled the receiver off the base and pressed it against her ear.

'Hello?'

'Did he come? What happened?' Ethan came down the line, urgent and breathy.

'Ethan?' She ignored his questions and fired her own back. 'Where are you? Are you coming home?'

'I'm at a motel. Got a bus out of town. It's alright, he won't find me here. What happened? Did he come?'

'He came,' she confirmed, leaning one shoulder against the wall and gazing out of the kitchen window into the moonlit garden.

'Are you alright?' Ethan sounded reluctant to ask the question.

'Yeah,' she lied, gazing down at her taped-up fingers. There was nothing to be gained by telling him of her injuries. 'But he took everything.'

'Everything?'

'Everything,' she confirmed. 'TV, sofa, my jewellery, my' – her eyes creased out fresh tears – 'engagement ring. The car.'

'The car?'

'It's over, Ethan.' She said it so weakly, she didn't know what she was saying until the words were out of her mouth. 'I can't get back up to Lloyd House without it. Jason said he's going to come and burn down the house if he doesn't have his money in one week. We're out of time.'

'No.' Ethan sounded so determined, and Terri thought bitterly that it was easy to be determined when you were well hidden at the end of a bus line somewhere. 'You can get back up there – there'll be a way. You *have* to go back, Terri.'

'I'm tired, Ethan.' And in that moment she was. Exhaustion was all she could think about. 'I'm tired of fighting for survival. I think' – the idea formulated as she said the words, knowing at once they sounded right – 'I'm gonna go back east.'

'No! No, Terri, please, please don't. I need you – I can't do this without you. You know that, right?' His voice sounded so urgent, so desperate for her. She yearned for him to want her again, to need her like he used to. 'Just you and me, baby, right? As it's always been – we're a team.'

And with her memories still soaring on that Coney Island Ferris wheel, Terri relented. As she always did. She retreated from her own life, her own wants, to do what Ethan needed of her. As she had when she'd struggled to pay the rent solo on their New York apartment while he chased his dreams, unable to hold down another job because it 'interfered with his creativity'. As she had when she'd turned down her dream job as an assistant for a producer when they'd first moved to LA. A wild idea she'd applied for on a whim and regretted immediately when Ethan had screwed up his handsome, perfect face in a facsimile of confusion. 'But that's like a fifteen grand pay cut?' he'd said, slipping his arms around her waist and holding her close. 'I thought we had our eye on that red Maverick.'

And now the Maverick was gone. Her dreams were gone.

All that was left was Ethan.

'Just you and me,' she said quietly. 'I'll get it for you, don't worry, baby.'

Seventeen

Audrey
Wednesday

Terri arrived late, looking more than a little dishevelled. The fingers on her right hand were bandaged together and she had deep crevices gouged into the skin underneath her eyes, a fresh purpling bruise across her left cheekbone.

'Sorry,' Terri said, voice weary as if she had no energy for a real apology. 'Car trouble this morning. I had to get a couple of buses.'

Audrey's eyes fell to her injured hand. 'Can I help you with that?'

'No.' Terri gave a weak smile, but Audrey thought there was no humour behind it. 'It's fine.'

Audrey narrowed her eyes. 'If you insist,' she said, feeling the refusal as a rebuke. 'You can carry the tray of drinks down to the terrace, then. I'll bring the chessboard.'

Audrey collected the flimsy chessboard and tucked it under her arm, along with the wooden box of pieces. She led Terri through into the kitchen and nodded down at the tray, set up with the jug of iced tea, two glasses, and the Danish pastries. Terri struggled with the tray with her injured hand, trying to balance it partly on the kitchen counter so she could place her forearm underneath it to take the weight of the tray, steadied by her good hand.

'Very impressive,' Audrey said, not without a hint of truth. 'You do like to get along by yourself, don't you?'

Terri gave an embarrassed sort of smile. 'Stubborn, I guess.'

Audrey headed out of the kitchen, across the top terrace and then down the steep steps to the small white table. It took Terri a little while to navigate the steps with the awkward tray, but eventually they were all set up in front of the chessboard again, two glasses of iced tea poured and ready to be drunk. The landscape today was dull and grey, the thick smog having pooled across the city below, wisps infiltrating Audrey's haven up on the hill. Audrey did not like the reminder of how intrinsically linked to other people she was – no matter how hard she tried to control her own world up here, the actions of the people down there could ruin her view and her air. It made her shudder to think about.

'Stubborn is not a good trait,' Audrey told Terri, watching as she tenderly inspected her obviously sore fingers. 'What happened?'

'Oh, just an accident,' Terri said dismissively.

'More stubbornness,' Audrey said, recognising the lie but pulling half her mouth into a knowing smile all the same.

Terri gave a small laugh and brought her eyes to Audrey's. 'I'm going to guess you were stubborn, too, in your day?'

'Ah yes,' Audrey said sadly. 'Stubborn, rebellious, all the things a clever girl in my position could be to get through the day without boredom. But these things never end well.'

Terri frowned. 'How do you mean?'

Audrey sighed and turned her head out toward the muggy, overcast view of her land.

'A girl like me – I had everything, of course, no need to strive for anything. But equally nothing was expected of me, nothing was *wanted* from me. No one wanted to hear my thoughts or ideas. No one wanted me to make a change to anything. Sit and look pretty and make polite conversation – that was all I ever needed to do.'

'I can imagine that must have been difficult,' Terri said diplomatically.

Audrey watched her for a moment, mind flitting between past and present, as it so often did these days. It was as if her life was looping back on itself. Another challenging young woman, sitting across the chessboard from her. Not challenging in quite the same way of course, but Terri was getting better, and she had a spark, an intelligence the girl herself didn't even seem to appreciate she had. Another chance, Audrey thought. Another companion, finally.

'It's a burden in life,' Audrey said eventually. 'One that only a few will ever understand.'

Terri gave a small, awkward nod and then gestured to the game. 'Do you want to play?' But there was something in the way she said it that told Audrey chess was not at the forefront of Terri's mind today. It seemed almost as if Terri was trying to distract her. Audrey frowned and nodded, vowing to keep a close eye on her visitor today.

Audrey waited for Terri to open the game with a white pawn, deciding on how long she'd drag this game out for. She could usually finish it within just a few turns, but Audrey had learned that wasn't too much fun. Sometimes it was best to dull your own shine to fit in with those around you.

In her youth Audrey had not done as well at reconciling her genius with the rest of the world. Keeping her brain active and occupied was her foremost priority in life. And that, she had learned, came with terrible consequences.

1934

She had been sitting in the small office on the second floor down, working furiously at her roll-top desk. It had once been the study room that she and Professor Ross crowded into, working on equations and calculations long past his allotted hours, when Mrs Hackton would interrupt and demand Audrey join her father for dinner. But now Audrey had her own little project to work on, her pen scribbling into the notebook Rex had given her – the one that was apparently a gift from Herr Scholtz – quickly checking back at the grid of numbers in the front every now and again.

It had been a few months ago when Rex had first asked her to help him and Herr Scholtz in furthering their cause for LA, and Audrey had not thought much about it. 'Just some math problems we need help with,' was how Rex had put it. The first one she'd done had resulted in just a stream of letters, which she'd passed back with a nonplussed expression.

'That was impressive,' Rex had breathed slowly, eyes flicking up to her. Arnold was holed up in his office with Scholtz again, while she and Rex sat at the dining table. And then he had explained. He was helping Scholtz with a very important mission for their country. There was a threat within their borders, fermenting right in the heart of Los Angeles. Did Audrey know what the threat was? Audrey had told him she didn't much care for politics.

Rex had watched her a moment and then laughed, throwing his head back and chortling as dramatically as if he were on set. 'No,' he said, collecting himself, 'no, I don't suppose you do need to worry about that.' His eyes had turned serious again. 'But just know, you are doing important work for our country. Now then, what do you know of the Vigenère square?'

'Not a thing,' Audrey admitted.

'You can be taught — it's simple when you know how. We have a contact down in San Diego who we're talking to, but it's imperative that our communication remains private. And our contact is not happy with just the usual cipher. He wants an extra level of encryption. He's developed a rather complicated code, one based on an understanding of mathematics I cannot claim to have. He's begun sending our transmissions using this code, not caring whether we can read the blasted things at the other end. And in return' — Rex gave a deep nod — 'he wants our messages to be coded in the same way.' Rex gave a small flick of his hand. 'He's a math graduate himself, can see numbers the way you do.'

'Ah,' Audrey said, looking down to the paper she had just handed back to Rex.

'Are you willing to join our important cause? Your father is working with us to defeat the enemy.' Rex nodded to the tall windows, which looked out over the Lloyds' vast land, dappled in the California winter sun. Dotted across that land were twenty men dressed in a uniform of tall black boots, white shirts, black neck ties and flashes of red armbands. They were on their second day of practising military-style drills. Audrey had asked her father what they were doing, but he'd not answered, turning instead away from the window and walking with melancholy back to his office.

'I don't care much for causes,' Audrey had replied. 'But I'm happy to help with the math.' She'd grinned, and when Rex had handed her a dark green notebook with an inlaid gold emblem on the front, opened the first page and shown her a twenty-six by twenty-six grid of letters, she'd felt a spark of life she only got these days from her chess games with Irina. That had been two months ago now, and 1933 had come to an end, New Year celebrations spent in a strange, quiet party at the Popovs', which Arnold had forbidden her from telling anyone about.

Audrey translated the end of the final transmission and placed the ribbon of the notebook down the page to hold her place. When Rex had first given her the notebook and tasks for her mission, she'd thought perhaps this would renew the bond with her father. They had a shared work now after all; he could be proud of what she was doing to help his cause. But when she'd knocked on his office door and pushed it open, she'd found her father with his head in his hands, leaning on his desk.

'Daddy, I've agreed to—' she began, ready to show him her new notebook.

'Not now, Audrey,' Arnold had snapped. 'I don't have time for this now.' And then Mrs Hackton had risen from a chair hidden in the shadows in one corner and shut the door in Audrey's face. Fine. If he wanted them to have secrets — she could have her own secrets.

The only person she felt wrong about keeping in the dark was Irina, who today Audrey had a date with for a chess game upstairs. But every time she opened her mouth to tell her of her work a bubble of suffocation rose up her throat and stopped her from sharing. She closed her notebook on top of the ribbon, slid it into the pocket of her slacks and closed the cover of the roll-top desk.

'Hello, dear,' Audrey called into the living room, where she could see Irina already set up at the dining table with a cup of coffee from Mrs Doyle and unpacking the chess pieces from inside the board.

'I didn't sleep well last night,' Irina said gruffly as Audrey sat down opposite her. 'I can be white?'

Audrey nodded and smiled a thanks to Mrs Doyle, who placed the tray holding a teapot and cup and saucer down next to her.

'Why didn't you sleep?'

'Sascha,' Irina said, flicking her eyes awkwardly up to Audrey's face for a moment. 'His nightmares.'

'Ah,' Audrey replied, pouring herself a hot cup of tea.

'He still misses his friends,' Irina said sadly, and Audrey noticed her soften as she spoke. 'He never got a chance to say goodbye. One day he was pulled out of school, and we were all on a plane over here.'

'Why *did* you leave Berlin so abruptly?' Audrey had never quite got to the bottom of what prompted the Popovs' move to America.

Irina gave a shrug and made her opening move. 'I think they didn't want to sit around just to wait to be run out of our home again.'

'Surely that wouldn't have happened again,' Audrey said reassuringly. 'Not that I'm not happy you're here.' She paused to think. 'I think I'd have gone completely mad by now without you.' Suddenly the thought of life without Irina gripped her in a panic so tight she thought she would never draw breath again.

But then Irina gave her a small smile of acceptance, and Audrey felt the air come again, as her friend reached for her coffee cup. Irina raised her cup in a silent cheers and Audrey nodded, raising her own in return. She kept her eyes trained steadily on Irina, as if this act alone could ensure she would never be without her.

There was a party that afternoon at the Chateau Marmont – a relatively new hotel that in its five years of operation had done well to court the Hollywood elite Audrey had spent her life mingling with. Mrs Hackton interrupted their conversation to tell Audrey she was expected to be ready to attend the celebratory luncheon for her father in just twenty minutes.

'You could have given me more warning,' Audrey snapped, getting to her feet at once.

Mrs Hackton looked genuinely befuddled for a moment. 'I usually get in trouble for interrupting your game.' She glanced down at the board. 'At least I let you finish it.'

Audrey narrowed her eyes at her.

'Irina,' she said, looking down at her friend, 'will you accompany me to the luncheon? I think I might need your presence.' The thought of an afternoon of air kisses and inane chatter brought a gnawing sensation to Audrey's stomach.

Irina looked alarmed. As did Mrs Hackton.

'I don't think I should,' Irina stuttered.

Audrey stiffened at Irina's refusal, but then gave a small sigh of understanding. 'I know you hate these things, but please, Reeny – for me. We can have a few cocktails, show our faces and then make our escape.'

Irina looked reluctant.

'Audrey, can't you see the girl doesn't want to,' Mrs Hackton snapped. 'Stop pushing her. Now go and get ready, your father needs you.'

'I won't go without Irina,' Audrey said stubbornly, even more irritated by Mrs Hackton trying to dissuade her friend.

'Audrey, I really don't know,' Irina protested.

'You don't have to get dressed up,' Audrey barked. 'Come on, I can do your hair and lend you a jacket.'

Irina looked ready to argue again, but she caught Audrey's eye directly, and after a beat, nodded solemnly. 'OK.'

Audrey loaned Irina a dogtooth blazer and braided her hair with a long plum-coloured ribbon wound through it. She dressed in her favourite matte silver skirt suit, and, seeing the flyaway baby hairs at her roots and knowing she wouldn't have time to reset her waves, she pulled a blue cloche hat down over her head.

When they made it back up to the hallway by the door, where Arnold was already waiting, chatting amenably to Carl, Audrey was surprised to see his face flicker a little when he saw Irina accompanying his daughter.

'Joining us this afternoon, Irina?' he asked with an odd tone.

'Yes,' Audrey said with a determined nod. 'I invited her.'

'Excellent!' Arnold clapped his hands together, but Audrey couldn't help but think his tone failed to match the enthusiasm of the word.

They pulled up outside the turreted hotel and Irina gazed up at it with awe-filled eyes.

'It looks like a *Schloss*,' she said quietly, and Audrey felt confident she had done the right thing in making her come.

Inside the party, the first person Audrey saw after claiming two glasses of champagne spun around on his

polished brogues and declared, 'Audrey, my biggest fan!'
She gave an inward grunt of annoyance and handed Irina
a glass, waiting for Rex to approach.

'Hello, Rex,' she said. 'How have you been?' But Rex's
expression had fallen, his eyes grazing up and down Irina.
'Oh – do you know Irina?' Audrey added. 'Irina Popov.
Her father's Daddy's lawyer.' She paused in recollection.
'In fact, I think you met a few years ago at our house.'

Irina nodded awkwardly at Rex and raised her free
hand in a small wave. 'Nice to see you again,' she
muttered.

'Hmm, yes,' Rex said, scraping his eyes back to Audrey.
'Your father still using Lev Popov then, is he?'

Audrey blinked. 'Yes, as far as I know.'

'Interesting,' Rex said, and returned his eyes to Irina.
'I'll have to warn him about that.' He looked quickly back
to Audrey. 'I'll see you later, Audrey.' And like that he was
off to the other side of the reception.

'What on earth was that about?' Audrey frowned.

'Rex doesn't like my father,' Irina said.

'I've never understood why not, though.'

Irina gave a matter-of-fact shrug. 'The same reason as
a lot of people.'

'Audrey,' her father interrupted, waving at her from
near the buffet table.

'Come on,' she said to Irina, 'let's go meet whoever
Daddy wants us to meet.'

Irina gave a small laugh and followed Audrey over to
where Arnold was standing on his tiptoes waving at her.

'Got her mother's height,' he was saying to his
companion as they approached. 'Luckily for me, so I can
always find her in a crowded room.'

Audrey laughed and turned to greet her father's companion, feeling a small tremble of unease as Herr Scholtz leaned forward to kiss her on the cheek.

'*Fraulein*,' he said silkily. 'How lovely to see you again.'

Even though Audrey knew the work she and Daddy were doing was to support Scholtz's cause to help America, she still didn't like him. This wasn't unusual for Audrey – she didn't like most people.

'Herr Scholtz,' she said. 'This is my friend, Irina. She used to live in Berlin; I think I've mentioned her to you before.'

She twisted one shoulder to reveal Irina from where she was hiding behind her, and was surprised to see her friend look even more timid than usual.

'*Guten Tag*,' Scholtz said with a less than enthusiastic air himself.

Irina merely nodded in response. 'I think I should go home,' she said in a low voice, leaning in close to Audrey's ear and tugging on her forearm. 'This was a mistake. I'll see you tomorrow.'

'Oh,' Audrey said as disappointment flared into something else inside her. Something that burned hot in her stomach. 'OK,' she said, swallowing what felt like thick lava, 'I'll see you tomorrow.' It was not an invitation or question. It was a command, and both she and Irina seemed equally surprised by it for just a moment, before Irina gave a small nod and bid her a quiet farewell.

Audrey watched Irina's retreating back until she was out of the front door, before turning back to her father and Scholtz. She was surprised to see Scholtz too watching Irina's hasty exit with stony eyes.

Audrey and her father travelled home from the Chateau Marmont in an impenetrable silence, each lost in deep thought. As Carl pulled the car up their winding driveway, Audrey watched the pinks and oranges of sunset glow against the black silhouettes of the dogwoods lining the path. They both bid Carl good night as Mrs Doyle opened the front door, before walking down the entrance corridor and into the living room.

'I'm going to bed,' Audrey said, bending to kiss the top of her father's head. 'Good night, Daddy.'

'Good night, dear,' Arnold said wearily, and patted her arm before setting off in the direction of the drinks trolley.

Audrey walked toward the corridor off the living room and paused, turning to watch her once-sparkling father pour himself a neat vodka with a shaking hand. This afternoon he'd been his usual vivacious self, but she'd noticed the extra strain that energy seemed to take these days. His skin hung tired and waxy from his cheeks, dragging the bags under his eyes deeper and longer. The grey hair that still clung to the base of his head was thinner and greyer than ever before.

'Daddy,' Audrey said softly as her father looked up from his glass. 'Why do Rex and Scholtz not like the Popovs?'

Arnold took a deep breath and answered into his glass. 'Because they believe they are a threat.'

'And are they?'

He looked at Audrey then, dead in the eyes, half his face in the shadow of the dusk falling through the unlit room. 'No more so than I am.'

–

Audrey blinked her father's drab, sombre face away and turned her attention back to the chessboard and her new companion. The recollections had been coming back more and more lately. Perhaps it was because she was using her mind again, after forcing it to lie dormant for so many years. She'd learned that was safer, in the end. But a sharp mind finds its own entertainment when not fulfilled, and hers liked to play tricks on her. She knew what they were, but she enjoyed them all the same. After all, what else was she supposed to do all alone in this big house?

Her gaze settled on Terri. It would be different this time, better. *She* was better. She took in Terri's wayward hair, her beaten face, her swaddled hand. And Audrey knew she could make *her* better too.

Audrey was finding her purpose again.

Eighteen

Don
Friday

Don trudged back up to the house, taking the steps more slowly than he'd come on his way down. As he walked across the turning circle, he saw Officer Chen sitting in the front seat of the car, door open, on the radio to dispatch. Don gestured inside to indicate he was going to keep looking around and Chen nodded in understanding before saying something else into the radio receiver in his hand. He placed it back in its holder and climbed out of the car to face Don.

'Circus should be back in a half hour.' Don nodded. 'And I have a message from Captain Glover, too. He said he's called in his own favour with a judge and got you the warrant, will send it up with the cavalry.'

'Thanks, Chen,' Don said. Chen shifted his weight from one foot to another, scratching awkwardly at his neck. 'Anything else?'

'He – er – he also wanted me to remind you not to make him look like a damned old fool.'

Don barked a laugh, which seemed to relax Chen a little. 'Alright, thank you, son. You go and hold the fort with Sterne for now, liaise with the team when they

139

arrive.' Chen nodded in understanding and Don climbed the terracotta steps, heading inside.

Coming to the end of the entrance hall, he gazed around the over-crowded living room feeling suddenly overwhelmed at the prospect of looking for something of use in this house. Maybe asking for the warrant was just a step toward his own personal zebra hunt. He passed through the living room, thinking over what he thought he knew. A body killed by a fall. A banged-up witness apparently knocked over during the fall, but still with several unexplained injuries. A decades-old skeleton inside a car in the grounds. If they linked together, he did not know how, or even trust that he would ever find out. It felt like too many dangling threads in the wind. There was a history in this house, secrets he hadn't even got close to scratching the surface of last time – he'd been too young, given up too easily. But now he was back, this time *with* the might of the police force behind him, and a thirty-odd-year career to back up his instincts. He couldn't just leave it. That's not what he'd become a cop for.

He walked down a hallway and passed a mannequin draped in a dark emerald ball gown. Don smiled to himself, remembering how his young self had itched to walk down this corridor, drawn in by the tease of this dress. But he was older now, and did not stop to admire the finery. He came to a door on his right-hand side and pushed it open, extending his arm and patting the wall by the door until he found a light switch to illuminate the dull room. It had only one window covered by unruly foliage pressed up against the glass from the outside. In the new light, provided by an intricate golden chandelier, Don saw a large oak desk pushed against the window.

The carpet felt thick beneath his shoes, but from the tickling cough that scraped at the back of his throat was clearly covered in layers of dust. He made his way over to the desk and surveyed the boxes on top, noting that they appeared jumbled and out of place, a few tears down the old cardboard seams, as if someone had been looking through them hurriedly. One was pulled over onto its side, spilling a pile of notebooks and pens onto the desk, the drawers all yanked open.

Don frowned as he took this in.

Someone had been looking for something. It was hard to tell when exactly, but it seemed recent — the displaced dust had not had time to settle again in the patches where the boxes had been moved. Audrey? But this was her house. Granted it was crowded beyond belief and perhaps her memory could have been failing her into her later years, but Don struggled to believe the formidable woman he'd met all those years ago would scrabble so inelegantly around her own home. Even if she had lost something. Which left Terri. Don pulled out his book and added a quick note to the pages underneath the ones detailing his unsuccessful interview with her that morning. Was she just being nosy? Perhaps she'd offered to help the old woman find the deeds for the purchase she was apparently seeking? But something about the displacement of the drawers and boxes felt more frantic, more desperate.

He began picking through the debris from the knocked and torn boxes, finding some fifty-year-old account ledgers, a copy of *The Age of Innocence*, another priceless screenplay, and, underneath, a few thin sheets of paper that looked like a form of some sort. The text was a mixture of smudged type and scrawling handwriting Don struggled to read. He pulled the pages free, and carried them to the centre of the room, directly underneath the light. The top right-hand corner had a logo for the 'Desert Palm Sanatorium' underneath a medical-looking icon of two wings above a twisted base.

The heading read 'Temporary Discharge Form', and the date filled in by the scrawling hand seemed to be for some time in 1937, although the day and month were illegible. Don read down the form, squinting where he needed to try and decipher the doctor's spiky hand-writing.

> Name of patient: Audrey Lloyd
>
> Discharged into the custody of: Annabel Hackton

Don paused here, his gaze lingering on the name.

> Reasons for granting of temporary discharge: On the occasion of her father's death it has been deemed helpful for the patient to be able to attend his funeral, only under the care of Mrs Annabel Hackton, who is well familiar with the patient's delusions, outbursts, tendencies for falsehoods and violent aggression. Conditions for discharge are centred around the continued regimen of care and medication as prescribed by myself, Dr Schofield, and as managed by the team here at Desert Palm Sanatorium. Three-day furlough granted.

Don frowned as he twisted his mouth to one side, thinking. What did this mean? That the woman who had fallen down a flight of stairs in the middle of the night had spent time in what seemed to be some kind of mental institution almost fifty years previously. According to this, she'd been released for only three days after her father's death. To Annabel Hackton. He moved back to the box, and pawed through some more loose sheets of paper, not finding any other information on Audrey Lloyd's apparent commitment. How long had she spent there? When had she finally come home for good? He turned back to the paper in his hand and read the details again.

He thought of Annabel Hackton. Of Audrey's maniacal laugh. Of the skeleton in the car. Of Theresa Nicholls's injuries, and felt a tumble of bile warm his stomach. A theory was forming in his mind, and it was daubed with black and white stripes.

Clutching the discharge form in his hand, he headed back out to his car, where he slid it into an evidence bag and placed it on the passenger seat. Then he picked up the phone and asked for Information.

'Desert Palm Sanatorium,' he said, without confidence. He didn't think a fifty-year-old mental asylum would still be standing, but it was only a quick check to see. He heard the operator tapping before coming back on the line.

'I'm sorry, I can't find that. Do you have any other details?'

Don leaned over and read the address off the form through the plastic bag, where it was printed underneath the logo.

'OK,' the operator said, tapping again. 'We do have a listing at that address – oh, here is why I couldn't find it earlier, the name we have listed is Desert Palm Rehabilitation Centre. Is that what you would be looking for?'

'Yes!' Don alarmed himself with the outburst of surprise that they were still open all these years later. 'Yes,' he corrected himself. 'Please connect me.'

Nineteen

Terri
Wednesday

Audrey seemed distracted as they played their game, taking longer to mull over her moves than usual. But by now Terri was getting used to not knowing what was happening underneath that head of silver-streaked dark curls. Today they were wrapped in an Hermès scarf, gold chains imprinted on satin shackling her head. It clashed surprisingly stylishly with the multi-tonal blues of her paisley caftan, and it occurred to Terri that this woman had more drive to get up and get dressed in the morning than she did. They both had nowhere to go except that dusty old house, and yet Audrey's resolution was stronger than hers. The thought made her uncomfortable.

They made it to lunchtime in a silence Terri thought was awkward, even if Audrey herself showed no signs of discomfort.

'I have some tins of soup for lunch,' Audrey said after finally swiping Terri's king from the board, and getting to her feet. Terri nodded politely, too distracted by her own plan for the day to worry about how long those cans might have been sitting in that mouldy old kitchen.

'Thank you,' she said, clambering to her feet. 'Should I clear up?' She nodded down to the chessboard.

'I'm sure we'll come back to it,' Audrey said mildly, already heading for the stone steps. Terri followed her up and into the kitchen, where Audrey opened a door to a surprisingly well-stocked pantry full of tins, spices and glass bottles of olive oil.

'Do you need any help?' Terri asked, hoping she'd be turned away like she had every other time she'd offered to help. She was not disappointed.

'No,' Audrey replied simply.

'I'll go find something to read in the living room,' Terri said, and Audrey blinked in distracted agreement.

When she got back to the living room though, the kitchen door slamming behind her, she did not go anywhere near the stacks of books and magazines behind the sofa, and instead headed immediately for the corridor off the living room that led into the maze of the house below.

Terri came to a stop at the top of the stairs she'd found yesterday, gazing down at the architectural oddity of this side of the house. There was another clear glass wall in front of her, reaching from the very top floor all the way down to the bottom of the three floors that fell away below her. Terri knew she must be facing the approach road, but the view was ambushed by bracken and broken trees, parasitic vines wrapping tightly around their trunks and leaping between their host and the brick of the house. With the overcast, smoggy day, the grey sky reached down with long spindly fingers and Terri was faced with a haunted wood from a child's fairy tale. There was none of the barren beauty of the land rolling out into the open views of the Hollywood Hills from the garden side – this was wild abandonment to the point of strangulation.

It took a minute for her to brave taking the first step on the stairs, the imposing windows making her feel as if she was walking directly into the wood. Unable to take one eye off the nature pressing in at her, she descended the stairs to the landing below, leaning a little over the bannister to count the floors beneath her. God only knew what possible use Arnold Lloyd envisaged for this many rooms. The landing she was on was carpeted in thick scarlet and was less crowded with junk than the floor above. There was a marble plinth in the centre with a beautiful carved statue of a woman draped in a veil that was cut so intricately Terri swore she could see the material moving. She was dulled by dust. As Terri breathed in, she could taste the years layered together in the granules that coated the entire landing.

Something creaked overhead, and Terri froze, squinting her eyes to concentrate on whether it sounded like footsteps. She exhaled after a few beats, confident the noise was just an old house shifting through its day. There were corridors on either side of the landing and a crowded floor-to-ceiling bookshelf along the back wall. She moved closer and browsed it idly, seeing mainly expensive-looking leatherbound dictionaries and encyclopaedias.

Terri decided to take the right-hand corridor, which led to a warren of rooms and doors. She pushed one open and found an actual movie theatre, with about twenty old velvet-covered chairs, their bases flipped upright, no doubt unused for decades. The grin spread unconsciously across her face as she stepped into the room, forgetting her purpose for just a moment. It had four rows of seats and a screen at one end, curtained in thick red velvet gathered into golden ties. She turned her neck and saw an ancient projectionist's booth, the old-fashioned camera pointed like a gun at the screen.

Leaving the movie theatre, she headed for another door a little way down, and found another office, smaller than the one upstairs. A roll-top desk was pushed into one corner with climbing shelves along one wall and a small window looking out to yet another part of the grounds Terri hadn't seen. There were some weathered math books on top of the desk, and she twisted the old iron key in the lock of the roll-top and heard it click open. It rolled stiffly as the slats of wood got caught in their runners, but she managed to shimmy it up. There was a pad of mathematical graph paper with a couple of graphite scribbles on top, as well as a solid-looking fountain pen sitting on top of a dark green leather notebook. The pen obscured the symbol on the front, but Terri frowned as she recognised the outline of a blocky bird's wing – something from her high school history class reigniting in her brain. She knocked the pen off the notebook and picked it up, swallowing thickly as she ran her thumb across the gold inlaid symbol of an eagle – a spiked wreath holding a swastika clutched in its talons.

Fucking *hell*.

Were the Lloyds *Nazis?*

This was the very last thing Terri had expected to discover about Audrey Lloyd and her family. She flipped open the cover of the book and saw a grid of letters on the first page, a stream of numbers underneath it. There were pencil markings all over the page, underlining sections of the grid, circling streams of the numbers, the odd equation scattered down the side. She flipped over the page again and saw a block capital sentence at the top of one page.

THOMPSONFIFTEEN. She flicked another page. TWOHUNDREDSTJUDE. There were pages and pages, these capitalised words circled triumphantly, littered among incomprehensible mathematics.

Terri dropped the book back down onto the roll-top desk with the burn of bile rising in her throat. Could Arnold Lloyd have been a Nazi spy? But, she remembered, he had died in 1937, before the war had even started.

Confused, Terri scanned the desk again, looking for something – anything else that might be a clue. There was a pile of papers to one side, which Terri reached hungrily for. But they were of no interest – some more old pages of Lloyd Productions accounts, a couple of transactions angrily circled in red ink. She threw them down and picked up the newspaper page underneath, seemingly torn from the *LA Recorder* from February 1934.

Eminent Lawyer to Warn of Anti-Semitism Risk

Prominent lawyer Lev Popov is due to speak at the Laurel Bryce Country Club next week, founded in 1920 for the Jewish members of our community. The membership of the club, including the upper echelons of our Hollywood elite, are gathering to discuss the apparent rise in fascism and anti-Semitism in our city, concerns sparked by the election of German Chancellor Adolf Hitler last March. As a recent émigré from Berlin, Popov is expected to lead the discussion with troubling news for his community about their treatment overseas.

'We have reason to believe the Los Angeles branch of the German National Socialist movement is attempting to mobilise on our own shores,' Leon Lewis, a legal colleague of Popov and Laurel Bryce member, told our reporter. 'They have targeted Hollywood as a focal point for communicating with the whole country.'

LAPD Chief of Police James E. Davies responded with confirmation that there is no concrete evidence to believe in a threat within American borders.

The event is set to take place on 15 February.

A Nazi plot right there in Hollywood? It didn't seem real, but then Terri had the gold-embossed notebook in front of her to prove it.

Terri folded the paper back up and returned it to its spot on the roll-top desk, hidden again by the old accounting ledgers, before closing the lid and locking it back into place.

This changed nothing.

Whatever secrets Audrey's tragic past contained, Terri could not concern herself with them. She had her own tragic present to worry about. A new determination surged through her, and she abandoned the office, pocketing the weighty fountain pen as she did so. Even if she couldn't find what she was looking for, maybe she could find enough to pawn and raise some cash to get Jason and his men off their back. Or at least enough to start a new life again somewhere else. But she'd have to be careful — it couldn't be anything that could be traced back to the Lloyds.

Knowing that she needed to get back to Audrey – she'd been gone far longer than she intended – Terri stormed into the next room along and found more jumbled storage: leather suitcases stacked on old satin sofas, a small balcony visible outside the smeared French windows. She flipped open the first suitcase and found towels and sheets, moving quickly on to three others. Finally, in one, there was a leather vanity case buried among the floaty material of summer dresses. It was embossed in gold with *EL* but Terri felt no burden of reverence to stop her pawing through Estella's travel case. Inside she found a solid silver mirror with matching brush, and then, underneath, a pair of large diamond earrings. Terri gave a sigh of disbelief, that a pair of earrings so valuable could have been simply misplaced in an old vanity case. She gazed around the rest of the room, wondering what else she could find if she only had the time to look. But no – now she needed to focus. She hadn't got what she'd come for, but she had something. And maybe that something would be enough to bring Ethan back to her. Her stomach churned, heavy and volatile, her mind unconsciously ticking off the days she had left. Would it be enough to keep Jason's burning torch away?

Slipping the earrings into her pocket alongside the fountain pen, Terri headed back out, returning to Audrey, pockets jingling with her treasure.

Twenty

Audrey was cooking the soup, methodically stirring as the thick orange started to bubble and catch, spitting onto the stove, tendrils of black smoke curling from the side of the pot. A heavy droplet spat out of the pan and landed on her forearm, smarting the skin in a sharp, circular red burn. It felt good. Physical pain was sometimes what she needed to centre herself, to focus her mind. She couldn't go wandering off into the past anymore; she was needed here in the present. And it felt good. She'd forgotten what it was like to feel useful, to feel purposeful – as if her entire existence might actually have a point after all.

But before she could stop it, past and present merged in a confusing kaleidoscope of memory and reason and the pain from the fresh burn on her arm anchored her back to another, similar agony from years ago.

1934

It had been three days since the party at the Chateau Marmont, and the conversation with her father had churned Audrey's insides ever since. She'd spent the time running over everything from the last few months as she flicked an old silver lighter to life before extinguishing it and plunging the hot metal against her naked forearms. The delicious sting of the pain helped her to concentrate. To reason that she was just solving some math problems, that was all, there was nothing to think that it could hurt Irina or her family in any way. But still, she'd found herself going back through her notebook, running her finger across the messages she'd decoded and handed back to Rex, or the encrypted equations she'd received from him in return. They were generally nonsensical – harmless, surely.

TWOHUNDREDSTJUDE

THOMPSONFIFTEEN

THREEHUNDREDSTCHAD

THOMPSONTWENTY-FIVE

TWOHUNDREDSTJUDE

COLTTWENTY

She shut the book and slid it into her pocket, before swinging her legs off the couch and heading into the kitchen, and out into the sun on the terrace. She'd avoided coming out here lately; she didn't care for the sight of the young men in white shirts and red armbands parading around their land. Their numbers seemed to have grown in the last few weeks and now Audrey could count at least thirty-five. She sat down at the table and leaned back in the wooden chair, letting herself feel the sun for just a moment. Then she tipped her head forward, retrieved her notebook and began examining it once again.

For the first time, she forced herself to examine the question she'd been avoiding – why hadn't she told Irina? They told each other everything. Irina was the only person in this world that Audrey felt understood her and her raw core. If anyone had a brain to help Audrey with some of the more difficult solves, then surely it would be Irina. And yet, each time she'd opened her mouth to bring it up, she'd remembered Rex's warning the first time they'd met the Popovs. She'd always known Rex disliked them, and she hadn't wanted to delve too deeply into it. But now, as she ruminated on the Chateau Marmont party, she knew that the avoidance was merely selfish preservation. What if she lost Irina?

The thought didn't bear considering. What if she lost the work? Another eventuality she couldn't conceive of. Sometimes it felt like it was the only thing that took the edge off her over-active, brilliant mind. Irina couldn't be there all day, as much as that pained Audrey, and without her equations to pore over and the knowledge that she was doing something *concrete*, something real with her talent, Audrey didn't like to think where she would spiral.

'Working overtime, my biggest fan?' Rex said over her shoulder, pulling out the chair next to her and sitting down, taking in the sight of the military drills on the Lloyd land. She hadn't heard the front door, but she assumed Rex's appearance meant that Herr Scholtz had arrived and was in yet another meeting with Daddy.

Audrey followed his gaze. 'What are they training for?'

Rex smiled. 'War, of course.'

She raised her eyebrows. 'Surely you don't think *war* is coming to California?'

'An uprising is,' Rex said. 'A much-needed uprising that only our German allies are interested in helping us with.'

'Who are these men?' Audrey asked. She'd seen a few of them up close as she'd come home one afternoon. They had been marching down the driveway toward the bus that parked on the side of the road to take them back to God knew where. There had been some as old as forty, pockmarked faces and weary expressions, and some as young and fresh-faced as the grocery delivery boy.

'Veterans.' Rex nodded. 'Or sons of veterans. But they will all be soldiers. The first soldiers of the new America.' Audrey turned to him with a questioning frown. 'My father fought for this country in the war,' Rex continued with a glazed expression. 'I was just a bit too young to join up, but boy did I want to. I wanted to be a hero like my old man.' He puckered his bottom lip and scrunched his face. 'But they didn't treat him like a hero.' A shake of his head. 'He came home hearing shellfire, and seeing his dead friends in his nightmares. His hands trembled constantly, couldn't keep them steady. The factory he'd worked at for years, assembling radios, wouldn't take him back. Said he just couldn't do the job anymore. And this country did *nothing*. We got nothing for my father putting his life on the line for our freedom. And do you know who that factory owner was, who got away with firing my hero father without even a severance check?' He looked back to Audrey, then and spat the name, 'Mr Levenstein. A fucking Jew. Not a real American – not like my father. All he'd done over the years of the war was sit in his office counting the gold that came rolling in from military contracts.' He held up a finger to highlight his point. 'And that's what they do. They think we can't

155

see it – they manufacture these wars so our countries will buy their damned radios and keep paying and paying and paying them until we're destitute on the street and they can lord their wealth over us.' Rex swallowed thickly and turned back out to face the ramshackle group of troops in training. 'But not this time. This time we'll strike first. Their underhand ways haven't gone as unnoticed as they might think.'

'Rex,' Audrey said slowly, mulling over the tale he'd just told. 'You can't really think the Jews are planning to take over *America*.' She held a hand out. 'You can't think this is *really* necessary.'

Rex snapped his head back to her, his face darker than she'd ever seen. Long gone was the handsome, charismatic movie star. In its place was bitter, putrid fury.

'Of course it's necessary!' He gestured violently at her notebook. 'What do you think all this has been about! You're either with our cause or you're against it!' Audrey didn't know what to say and Rex narrowed his eyes. 'You've been taken in by the Popovs, haven't you? I can see it in your face. Your loyalties are torn because of the Popov girl's forked tongue in your ear, her father's in Arnold's. I told Arnold to fire Popov, told him not to let you and the girl play chess. And now look – both of you, once allies to our great cause, now confused and weak. *That's* the power of the Jews, Audrey.' He shook his head violently. 'But not for much longer. Tonight, it will all change. Laurel Bryce is our chance.' He stared out to the troops once again. 'The start of our future.'

Twenty-One

Don
Friday

'Desert Palm Rehabilitation Centre, this is Jenny.'

Responding to the gentle female voice on the other end of the line, Don introduced himself and briefly explained the circumstances and what he was calling for.

'She would have been a resident in 1937,' he finished. 'So forty-five years ago now.'

The woman on the other end made a *yeeesh*-type sound that Don recognised with a fond smile as one his daughter often made when she'd heard something improbable.

'I'm not sure we have records from that far back,' Jenny said, clearly thinking hard, and Don appreciated her willingness to help. 'Although,' she corrected herself and Don felt a little glimmer of hope. 'The name changed in the fifties when it was bought by the current management company, and I know they did some construction work with the takeover. I work in the new building, but the old one is still in use, storage mainly and some shared therapy rooms.'

'Would they have kept the old files when they were taken over?' Don asked.

'I wouldn't know.' She sounded apologetic. 'I've only worked here a few years. But' – her voice turned suddenly determined – 'let me ask Blanche. She's been here longest out of everyone, not sure if it's quite forty-five years but she might remember the takeover.'

'Thanks,' Don said, as he was placed on hold. He watched the hands of his watch tick painfully by, but eventually she returned.

'Alright, thanks for waiting. Blanche joined just after the takeover, but said they moved all the old files into storage in the old building. If you give me ten minutes I can go and see if the details on your Audrey Lloyd are still there?'

'Thank you,' Don said with a genuine rush of gratitude. 'Thank you. Yes, please do that. I'll wait.'

While he waited with the fuzzy hold music pulsing into his ear, he fished out his notebook and added, *Deceased escaped mental institution? Unmedicated?* underneath his notes to ask Theresa about her mysterious speeding ticket, and if she'd been rooting through the Lloyds' office. He read the words again to himself and shook his head. This was starting to look like a hunt for unicorns, never mind zebras.

Eventually Jenny came back on the line.

'I have her file,' she declared triumphantly. 'She came in September of 1934. The records don't make for very pleasant reading I'm afraid. Fortunately, our treatments no longer follow the same theories as they did back then. But I can see here that she was granted a temporary discharge on 15 October 1937, into the care of a Mrs Annabel Hackton.'

'That's what the form I've found says, too. Is there any way to find out if she returned after that three-day furlough?'

'There's nothing else in the file I'm afraid. But that discharge form was at the back; nothing was ever added after it – no more details on accommodation or medication, final discharge or even her death, which is usually what you'd expect for a closed patient file.'

'If she didn't return what would have happened?'

Jenny made that *yeesh* sound again. 'Hard to say. Things were different back then. I can't imagine they'd have had the authority to force her back here – it doesn't look like she was here under a court order. Seems she was in the care of this Annabel Hackton – she might be your best bet if you want to know what happened to her after she left here?'

Don's heart sank at the suggestion. 'OK, thanks, Jenny,' he said, making a note of everything she'd told him. 'I really appreciate your help.'

'No worries, Detective.' Jenny said the word with an air of pride. 'You wait till I tell the aerobics girls tonight that *I* helped out a police investigation. I'll be looking out for my name in the paper.' She laughed, and Don bid her another farewell.

He hung the boxy phone back up on its console and got out of the car, slamming the door behind him. He headed back down toward where the car and body had been found, thinking that the crew they were waiting on must have started to arrive by now. Sure enough, as he heaved himself over that last steep bit of dirt track, he saw the clearing now had three other cars parked haphazardly around.

'We found another track off the driveway that comes straight here,' Sterne explained, gesturing down a dirt track that was as overgrown with brambles as the others, but did at least seem wide enough for a car to make it through.

Don nodded and turned back toward the car, which the crime scene photographer was now snapping from different angles. 'Well, that'll make it easier for moving everything.' He turned back to Sterne. 'I want you and Chen to spread out further into the grounds. We should have a warrant coming.' Sterne raised his eyebrows and Don knew he was thinking about how long it would take to thoroughly search this mammoth estate. 'You don't need to cover every inch. Just stick to the trails again like you did before.' He nodded back at the car as if to remind him what they'd already uncovered. 'Anywhere you can easily get on foot.' He suddenly remembered the rumours of coyotes. 'But for the love of God, don't venture too far, or off the paths. And if you're still out here by sundown – don't be.'

Sterne nodded and Chen approached from where he'd been talking to another uniformed officer who had just parked up. In his hand were two pieces of paper.

'These are for you, Detective,' he said, handing them over. 'Warrant to search the property signed by Judge Hoffman. And details on the licence plate check we ran.' He nodded toward the old Chevrolet.

'What did it turn up?'

'Not much. Just when it was last registered and to who.'

Don slid the warrant behind the slip of pink memo paper from the station and stared down at it. There in neat black type was the name of the person charged with caring for Audrey on her temporary discharge from the sanatorium. The car, with a rotting skeleton inside, belonged to Annabel Hackton.

He looked back up at the dark red Chevrolet and then up to the house and felt a pang of frustration for his younger self, who'd been so damned close after all.

'Does that name mean anything to you?' Chen asked, interrupting Don's thought-filled silence.

Don twisted his lips to one side before speaking. 'I found that name on some paperwork in the house,' he answered vaguely, trying to organise his memories from decades ago. 'Someone close to the Lloyds.'

Chen nodded and his gaze drifted back to the car, and the skeleton still inside. 'Do you think it's connected to…' He raised a hand to gesture in the direction of the steep stone steps.

Don shook his head. 'I don't know. This is what, thirty-odd years old?' He raised his eyebrows and gave a shrug. 'I can't see the connection just yet, but that doesn't mean there isn't one.'

'Revenge?' Chen asked and then clarified. 'If the skeleton in the car was murdered.'

'She's waited an awfully long time to do it,' Don said, distractedly. 'But I'll do some digging. See if Theresa Nicholls could be connected to Annabel Hackton.' He fished out his notebook and made a mark to remind him to check this perhaps tenuous link out.

'Alright.' He nodded to Chen. 'Let's get back to work.'

Twenty-Two

Terri
Wednesday

Just as Terri reached the top of the wide, curved staircase, the fountain pen poking awkwardly through her pocket and into her thigh, she froze. She thought she heard movement from the floor below. But Audrey was meant to be in the kitchen, unless – had she come looking for Terri while she'd been pawing through old family heirlooms to rob? Wondered where her guest had gone?

She held her breath as several loud creaks carried up the elliptical staircase, squinting in concentration as she tried to determine if they were simply the sounds of an old house settling, as she'd thought before, or if she was now conjuring the spectre of Audrey Lloyd up wherever she went. She remained still for another few moments before turning into the corridor with the bathroom. She walked back down into the empty living room, stopping to listen for another moment. It still didn't sound like anyone was behind her, but now she knew the rabbit warren of corridors and rooms in the belly of this house, it was not inconceivable that Audrey had another way back outside.

Feeling disconcerted at the thought that Audrey might have seen her sneaking off, Terri prepared herself with a cover story if confronted. She pushed open the kitchen door and moved through it, seeing a pan ringed with a light scum of congealed orange around the sides on the counter next to a jaggedly opened can of Campbell's soup. The rotting doors were still hanging at an angle on their hinges, and Terri wondered if Audrey ever actually closed them. Considering the odd mound of animal faeces, she suspected not.

As she stepped back out onto the blonde stone, Terri saw that Audrey was back at the table on the first terrace, two bowls of bright orange untouched in front of her. She continued across the patio, trying to think. Her mind was still on the floors below, trying to imagine how many other rooms there would be for her to search in just two days. Maybe she should just take her treasure from today and call it time. Get the hell out of town before Jason returned. Her mind flitted briefly to the idea of calling the police, but the swollen tenderness of her cheek and uncomfortable bind of her fingers reminded her of just the warnings Jason was capable of. She did not want to find out the real threat.

'Sorry!' she called out distractedly as she embarked down the stone steps, her brain still whirring with her fate outside of these rolling, abandoned grounds. 'Bit of stomach trouble.'

Audrey twisted in her seat to face her and gave a nonplussed smile. 'Soup's ready,' was all she said.

Terri started walking down the stairs but, just as she was nearly at the first terrace, her foot slid out from underneath her. She hadn't been concentrating. One foot, still in the air, flailed upwards, as the one she was relying on for support shot off the edge. Terri crashed backwards, falling awkwardly as instinct tried to twist her body so she could

163

use her hands to catch her fall. She failed on all accounts and succeeded only in trapping her ankle at an awkward angle beneath her and the sharp edge of the step, stone cracking into the back of her head as she landed on her back.

She blinked dazedly into the dark clouds overhead, feeling pain ricochet around her body, new receptors buzzing to life as the realisation of what had just happened settled in on her.

She heard Audrey jump to her feet, a soft gasp of shock floating toward her.

Terri started to feel dizzy, blotches clouding her vision, distorting the face that looked down at her, creased with concern.

'Are you conscious?' Audrey asked in her girlish voice, now even higher with what Terri thought sounded like panic. 'Terri, Terri?' Audrey clicked her fingers in front of her. 'Hello? Can you hear me?'

'I-I can hear you,' Terri stammered weakly, feeling faintness rush welcomingly at her in waves.

'Come on, we need to get you inside,' Audrey said, pulling at her arms. 'But you have to help me. I'm not strong enough to move you by myself.'

It took every effort of Terri's very being to allow herself to be pulled upright, to fight the concussion for long enough to manoeuvre her good leg up the steps. She hopped weakly and leaned heavily, too heavily from the way Audrey bowed below her weight. Her mind swam, lurching between wakefulness and blackness, so she had no idea how long it took to make the journey, but at some point she felt the welcome relief of support from the couch beneath her. She smelled the fetid stench of the cushions she lay on but couldn't muster the energy to care – the blackness could come now; the pain in her ankle was the only thing she noticed.

'Try not to fall asleep.' She heard a voice from somewhere overhead, but didn't heed its warning. She let herself slip away, the agony from her battered body dissolving into the air as she did.

Twenty-Three

Audrey
Wednesday

Audrey flipped shut the cap on the olive oil and placed it back in the pantry alongside the last remaining few bottles from the haul they'd had that one summer Daddy had decided to collect and press the olives from the grove on the back half of the land. Mrs Doyle had used it for over a year, until she'd started to complain it had gone bad and made her dressings taste rancid. By that time Audrey was gone and Daddy was too distracted to be pressing more olives, and so the bottles had stayed in their spot on the bottom pantry shelf, just waiting for a use.

When Irina had taken her into the pantry and pointed at them, Audrey had said, 'Absolutely not. The poor girl could kill herself.'

'There's something not quite right about her,' Irina said before putting the bottle in Audrey's hands. 'About why she's here. You can see that.'

'She's right, my darling,' Daddy said from next to Irina. 'Do what you do best and take care of her. She clearly needs you.'

Audrey had considered this, as she'd poured the silky golden oil down the steps and returned to the table to wait for her new companion. Terri had taken herself off down to the fourth floor, for what Audrey couldn't think. Irina and Daddy were right, there was something not quite right about this girl. Best for everyone if she stayed here for the time being.

Audrey had learned long ago that things did not go well when she prioritised her own mind. But she'd been on her own for so long she'd forgotten that perhaps she did need somebody. Irina, Daddy and Mama kept her company of course. But sometimes she'd watch them fade away, the backdrop of her old, empty house emerging into focus in their absence. Her brilliant mind was not always willing to be tricked for too long, even by itself.

Much better to have someone there who would stay. Someone, as Daddy pointed out, that needed her. Somebody she could make better.

1934

It was taking a moment for Audrey to comprehend what Rex had just said, when she heard the front door slam loudly from around the side of the terrace. Rex got to his feet and followed the sound, Audrey hot on his heels, moving around the house toward the turning circle outside the front door.

'Get in, Rex,' Scholtz snapped gruffly, gesturing to the black car he was half standing out of. 'We have no use for traitors.'

Rex nodded and obeyed at once, not giving Audrey another look. The car set off down the driveway and Audrey raced inside.

'Daddy!' she called, and ran to his office, where he was slamming the phone down onto the receiver. 'Daddy, I demand to know what's going on! What has happened with Herr Scholtz?'

But Arnold wasn't listening; he was frantic, pacing up and down his office before pushing past his daughter and heading straight to the bar cart. Audrey followed him, watching with wide eyes as his shaking hands emptied out the vodka bottle.

'Daddy,' she said, her tone dropping, 'please.'

Arnold looked up at her and then went to sit on the sofa, resting his elbows on his knees, taking a big slug of the clear liquid. Audrey sat down opposite him.

'Rex said the Popovs are a threat to America,' she said softly. 'Because they're Jews.'

Arnold laughed with a bitter sigh. 'Did I ever tell you that I changed my name when I was twenty?'

Audrey was surprised. 'No.'

Arnold nodded. 'My family still goes by the name of Lautman. Back in Ohio' – he creased his forehead – 'as far as I know. It's been a long time since I spoke to them. I was going to make something of myself, moved out to New York to work in the theatre. But people didn't like the name Lautman. I'd get turned down for jobs on productions without even a word.' He took another deep gulp. 'I changed it to Lloyd' – he raised his hands out to his side – 'and suddenly the world was my oyster, New York my pearl.' Audrey stared at her father. 'If the Popovs are a threat to America' – he held his glass out in front of him – 'then so are we, my sweetheart.'

'Why have you been helping them, then?' Audrey asked, feeling a burning itch soar through her. She saw Mama standing behind Daddy, shaking her head with disappointment.

'Because Leon asked me to,' Arnold said. 'Leon has been watching these cells, these Nazi cells the Germans are trying to plant all over our city. All over our country, I think. But they're focused on Los Angeles – keen on Hollywood. Hollywood is' – he stopped and thought of his words carefully before continuing – 'the epicentre of communication to our country. We speak directly to the normal people who go to the theatres and watch our movies. The German consulate knows the power of that, and they want it for their own ends.' He stopped and shook his head, taking another mouthful of vodka. 'Leon asked me to give my land over to them. He knew they were trying to mobilise, in whatever small way they could. There have been murmurings of training camps, and Leon wanted them somewhere we could keep an eye on them. It was the perfect way to keep Scholtz in my pocket, to gather information.' Arnold shook his head. 'But I've messed up. My stupid, *stupid* loyalty has messed it all up.'

'What do you mean, Daddy?'

'Rex warned me to stop using Lev as my lawyer. I thought I could get away with it, that he wouldn't need to find out.' He paused and shook his head again. 'But I guess there are no secrets in this town.' Audrey felt another sear of guilt across her skin. *She* had told Rex that Daddy was still using Lev. In fact, *she* was the reason Rex was in their lives at all.

There was a knock on the front door then, loud and echoing into the hall. Mrs Doyle scurried out of the kitchen to go and answer it, retreating back to her sanc-tuary of domesticity as soon as Leon Lewis had followed her into the living room.

'Leon, I'm out,' Arnold said, getting to his feet and heading back to the bar to refill his empty glass.

'Mr Lewis,' Audrey said with a polite nod. 'Nice to see you again.' But Lewis was not looking at her.

'What happened, Arnold?'

'He found out I was still using Lev as my lawyer.' Arnold turned from the bar briefly to gesture with a bottle to Lewis, who nodded gratefully. 'And from there it unravelled.'

Lewis sighed deeply and accepted the drink Arnold handed him. 'Are you in danger?' he asked with concern. 'Does he have anything on you?'

Arnold shook his head. 'No, no. I don't think so. But I won't be able to get you any more information.'

Lewis put his large hand on Arnold's shoulder. 'Don't worry about that for now. We have other spies we can turn to. All that matters is that you' – he turned to Audrey for the first time – 'and your family are safe.'

'Thank you, Leon,' Arnold said, and Audrey thought she saw, for the first time in a while, a shade of darkness lift from her father's expression. 'And I will continue to donate whatever you need to keep the operation going.'

'It's much appreciated.'

'Well, seeing as I'm exposed,' Arnold said with an exhausted smile, 'I suppose I can now come and hear Lev speak tonight at the Laurel Bryce Club.'

'We'd be happy to have you.' Lewis forced a smile and took a deep gulp of vodka.

The burning itch inside of Audrey had intensified while she watched the conversation. But she didn't know how to get to it, didn't know how to scratch it, to cleanse it from her body. She saw Mama in the corner, still shaking her head – so disappointed, and she felt the burn reach her forearms, a deep, agonising sting, a warm trickle spill onto her thighs. She looked down in dazed surprise to see a pool of blood spreading across her slacks, her fingers buried into the flesh on her arms, nails unconsciously trying to excavate the burning itch from within.

'Audrey!' Her father's shrill voice pierced her dazed panic. He rushed to her, fell to his knees while Lewis moved closer to the sofa, peering at her with concern.

'Did you say Laurel Bryce?' she croaked, feeling the burn flare again as her fingers dug even deeper.

Mrs Doyle had wrapped warm damp towels around Audrey's arms and sat her at the dining table with them outstretched in front of her, with strict instructions not to touch them. Audrey could still see Mama in the corner, and so turned her head away, hunching her neck so she stared down at a spot on the polished floor.

Opposite her Lewis was poring over Audrey's notebook, Arnold desperately trying to get through to Lev on the phone on the sideboard. Audrey had told them everything, including Rex's cryptic mention of the very club Lev was due to speak at tonight. Neither man had spoken to Audrey directly since she'd finished speaking, and she did not know what that meant.

'Arnold.' Lewis looked up from the notebook, his fingers placeholding several pages. 'Have you got a map of San Diego?'

Arnold had just hung up the phone with a grunt. 'Housekeeper says they've already gone over to the club for an early dinner before the speech tonight,' he said tensely before seemingly hearing Lewis's request. He thought for a moment, 'Yes,' he said with a frown, 'I've a collection of driving maps for the whole of California.' He disappeared into the entrance hallway and returned with two large books of San Diego, handed them to Lewis and took the seat at the head of the table between where Audrey sat opposite him. Lewis read the front of the books, selected the one he needed and flipped through the pages, scouring the intricately drawn maps.

'Aha,' he said under his breath, tapping a point with his fingertip. He looked again and nodded with satisfaction, 'and St Jude.' He tapped another point nearby, and then he looked up to Audrey and sighed deeply. 'I won't say it's not a blow to discover you've been helping out our enemies – whether accidentally or not. But I'm glad you've brought this to us when you did.' He looked to Arnold. 'But... it's not good news.'

'What have you found?'

Lewis slid the book over to Arnold as he spoke. 'We'd heard rumours from one of our men at the Aryan bookstore on Alvarado Street – he'd overheard some conversations, just snippets really, not much to go on. But piecing it together we think they're buying weapons from a rogue group selling illegally from the naval base down in San Diego.' He nodded to the book and flipped a couple of pages. 'These here are the orders they're placing' – he gave a glance to Audrey – 'that your daughter handily encoded for them.' She swallowed thickly. 'Thompson machine guns, Colt revolvers.' He flipped another page. 'And here – St Jude and St Chad – they're churches near the naval base. I assume they were meeting for the handover in the early hours of the morning, two hundred, three hundred military time.' He gave another sigh and a shrug. 'Obviously it's too late to do anything about it now; this arsenal is no doubt already in Los Angeles and – based on Rex's little comment earlier – the event tonight is the target.'

'But you have to do something!' Audrey wailed suddenly, feeling only the physical desire to claw out even more of her flesh.

Lewis eyed her calmly. He was not flustered. 'Of course we're going to do something.' He looked back to Arnold. 'When we've spoken to Chief Davies before, he's said we haven't had enough evidence for him to do anything. More worried about chasing communists than Nazis.' He gave a slight roll of his eyes before jabbing a finger back down onto Audrey's book. 'But this – this is concrete, this is enough.' He checked his watch. 'We have two hours until the event starts; we best get going.'

'Sh-should I come?' Audrey asked, her eyes following Lewis as he got to his feet.

'I don't think that's a good idea.'

'Please,' she said. 'Let me help.'

Lewis looked to Arnold, who turned his attention to his daughter. Then he nodded. 'Yes. She should come.'

'Right, I'll go to Davies. He needs to search the Alvarado Street HQ. I've been telling him for a year they've been smuggling weapons and propaganda in, but he wouldn't listen,' he added in frustration under his breath. 'Arnold, you and Audrey go to the club. Warn Lev, and warn the staff that they're all targets.'

Arnold nodded and they all headed for the door, Audrey scraping the now cold wet towels off her florid forearms and dropping them to the floor. She climbed into the passenger seat of the Rolls-Royce Phantom, thinking she would have laughed at the sight of her diminutive father behind the wheel of such a huge car in other circumstances.

Audrey had never been to the Laurel Bryce Club, a beautiful brick building with an elaborate porchway held up by thick trunk-like pillars. Arnold abandoned the car and leaped out, leaving Audrey to follow awkwardly and nod her thanks to the valet who stepped questioningly forward. Audrey frowned – she thought she recognised him. He must work at other venues in town as well. She followed her father into a terracotta-tiled hallway with a large, a curved reception desk at one end.

'Good evening,' the woman behind it greeted cheerily. She had short dark hair and bright lipsticked smile. 'Are you here for the event?'

'Where is Lev?' Arnold interrupted. 'There's an attack planned on this club, *tonight*.' He took a deep breath. 'I'm working with Leon.' At the mention of Mr Lewis's name, the receptionist seemed to nod in recognition. 'He's gone to get the police, but you need to call whoever is on the guest list and warn them not to come.'

Audrey turned at the sound of a waiter, who was carrying a tray of dirty glasses, stumbling on his feet. He caught her eye before picking up his pace and heading toward a door at the back of the entrance hall. From the steam that billowed out as he slammed through it, Audrey thought it must be the kitchen. But that old, pockmarked face looked as familiar as the young man who'd driven the Phantom off to the parking lot.

The receptionist looked alarmed but oddly prepared and nodded at once. 'Of course, I'll get right on it. But many of those on the guest list are already here enjoying dinner – in the restaurant upstairs.'

'Shit,' Arnold hissed and ran toward the stairs to the left of the reception desk. 'Audrey, hurry!' he called over his shoulder.

Audrey said nothing but followed her father, staring up at the six-pointed star carved into the large stone wall that gazed down at the staircase. They burst into the dining room just as the recognition of the faces she'd seen at the club swam into place.

'Daddy!' She grabbed his arm, spinning him frantically toward her. 'Those men, the men, downstairs – the valet,' she gabbled; she couldn't catch her breath. The words refused to come even as she tried to choke them out.

Arnold ignored her, turning back to the dining room and rushing forward to a table by the window, which Lev Popov sat at the head of, slurping tomato soup from a deep spoon. Next to him was his wife, their four sons zig-zagging down the table, ending in the youngest – poor Sascha, whose nightmares would not be soothed by the events tonight.

But Audrey's breath steadied a little as she realised Irina wasn't there.

'Lev, you have to cancel your talk tonight,' Arnold said hurriedly, reaching his friend's chair and resting his hands on the table.

'I can't cancel it!' Lev said. 'People need to hear, they need to take this threat seriously, I have to—'

'It *is* serious,' Arnold interrupted him. 'Tonight – the target is tonight!' Lev's eyes widened as he stared down the table at his sons and wife. 'Lewis is getting the police, but you all must leave now.'

It took a minute for Lev to take action, and Audrey watched as if it was one of her father's films as he got to his feet, throwing his napkin down and ushering his family up too.

'Daddy,' she said weakly, grabbing at his arm, 'the waiter… he's been training on our land.' She finally found the words. 'I recognise him.'

Her father moved as if in slow motion, the information settling on him in milliseconds she felt she could see individually. 'They're already here,' he said with horror.

Many things happened at once then.

First was the screech of cars stopping abruptly in the driveway downstairs, the sound of boots thundering into the building. Next was an indecipherable cry. The pock-marked waiter had entered the dining room from a back set of stairs reserved for staff, a Colt revolver brandished in his flailing hand. Finally, Irina exited a nearby door labelled *Restroom* in neat gold letters, stopping in shock at the chaos of the scene before her. She found Audrey's face as the police pounded in from the dining room's front entrance, and Audrey watched as her best friend's expression crumpled under the barrage of three bullets discharged into her back.

Audrey stilled and the world shrieked.

Twenty-Four

Don
Friday

Don watched as the circus performed around him, unloading boxes and zipping up white coveralls, and unwound his recollections from the years gone by. His memory had never failed him yet, and this case had been the first that had held any real interest – details scribbled down in his journal at home, suspicions raised over beers in the basement cop bar with Ray over the years. They all had those cases. The ones they couldn't let go. And Ray knew that the Lloyd Estate was one of Don's. Even though, as he'd often enjoyed pointing out whenever Don brought it up, it wasn't even really a case. Not officially anyway.

Thirty-four years ago, Don had been told to find Annabel Hackton. Told that she could give him some answers about Audrey Lloyd. But his superiors had no time for mysterious treasure hunts and instructed him to leave it. And Don had, for a while, until it was too late. For, a few weeks after he'd driven his parents' Chevrolet away from the laughing Audrey, that same name – Annabel Hackton – had appeared on the form for a missing person's report.

'I'll look into this one, Sarge,' Don had volunteered, standing eagerly in front of his sergeant's desk.

'Sounds like a time-waster to me,' the sergeant had said, leaning back in his chair, picking up the report with one hand to remind himself of the details. 'Nothing suspicious on here.'

'But it's a missing person,' Don had pressed.

'Just file the paperwork, Vernon.' The sergeant had dismissed him with a quick wave of his hand. Don had done what he was told for the rest of his shift, but, on his way home to his mom's meatloaf dinner, he'd taken a detour out to Glendale and the address on the form of the woman who'd made the report.

He pulled up outside the neat-looking family home and headed up the garden path to the front door, round grey slabs arranged like stepping-stones across the over-grown grass.

'Officer?' An older woman with tight grey curls and a plaid skirt over too-baggy stockings answered the door. 'Is this about Annabel?'

'Yes,' Don confirmed. 'Yes, it is.'

'Come inside. I've got some home-made raspberry lemonade just looking for a taker.'

Don got into the house and settled on the printed chintz couch. The woman who'd introduced herself as Mrs Miller bustled back from the kitchen with a tray of lemonade and shortbread. She was halfway through describing her secret family recipe for the shortbread and how her late husband, God rest his soul, had never tasted shortbread so good when Don understood why the sarge had been so keen to label her a time-waster. Mrs Miller was one of those witnesses he'd heard about from guys who'd been on the job longer than him. Nothing much to say, but in need of company and attention, and so would happily take hours of your time to say it.

Don thought of his mother fuming over her drying meatloaf as he was held hostage by this busybody neighbour.

'Delicious,' he said politely, taking a bite of the shortbread. It did taste nice. 'Now then, your neighbour—'

'Annabel, yes.' Mrs Miller nodded seriously.

'Why did you report her missing?'

'I haven't seen her in two weeks. And that isn't like Annabel at all.'

'When was the last time you saw her?'

'Like I said, two weeks ago.' Mrs Miller nodded importantly. 'When they came over to say goodbye. You know, I didn't think you were interested. Your colleagues were very dismissive on the phone. Just because I told them she'd driven away in her own car and had said she was going to visit her cousin – no one took me seriously!'

Don felt a sinking in his chest. 'Sorry,' he said, holding up one hand to slow her down. 'When did she say she was going to see her cousin?'

'The day they left, of course. Annabel told me they were going to see her cousin, but she would be back in a few days.'

'So why did you report her missing?' Don couldn't avoid the exhale of exasperation this time.

'Because she hasn't been back for two weeks!' One arm flew out toward the house. 'And she still hasn't been back! The house is just sitting there.'

'And you don't have a contact for this cousin?'

Mrs Miller shook her head. Don closed his eyes and exhaled through his nose. He forced a polite smile. 'But it *really* isn't like her to just disappear. We've been neighbours for ten years, and she's very kind to me. She gave me this jug, you know.' She gestured proudly to the plastic jug containing the raspberry lemonade. 'And she was in the paper. *Very* impressive woman.' She shook her head seriously.

'The paper?' Don asked mildly.

'Oh yes, I've a cutting here somewhere.' She got to her feet and bustled over to a neatly kept sideboard, where she rifled through a few things before returning with a neatly clipped advertorial.

Tupperware gives local woman new chance to live her American Dream!

Annabel Hackton has discovered an exciting new career all thanks to the innovations of Tupperware!

'Tupperware keeps your food fresh and secure – for all those leftovers we just don't know what to do with,' Annabel says. 'It's the nicest thing to happen to your kitchen.'

And now Tupperware is giving entrepreneurial women like Annabel the chance to run their very own business!

'My friends love hosting Tupperware parties and hearing all my tips for how best to use the exciting range of products. I'm making my own money and providing local women an excellent service at the same time.'

Annabel offers the host of each party a free gift or discount on their purchase, so it really is a win–win for everyone involved. Get in

touch with Annabel for your chance to host
one of these prestigious events!

There was a picture of the woman too, smiling above a table with a plaid tablecloth stacked with a full range of Tupperware. Her hands were spread proudly above her stock, and she was dressed in a full-skirted dress with a white frilled apron.

'She's doing very well for herself,' Mrs Miller was saying. 'Always brings me her latest products – never charged me for them either! She used to work for Arnold Lloyd, you know. As his secretary, from the day he moved to Los Angeles to the day he died.'

Finally, they'd come to something Don was interested in hearing.

'She worked for him, then?' he said. 'And was she close to the family at all? I believe Arnold Lloyd had a daughter?'

At this Mrs Miller threw back her head and cackled. 'A horrible girl, apparently! Gosh, Annabel would tell me some stories about her. Quite strange it sounded like. They didn't get on at all.'

'Really?' Don said, setting the newspaper clipping aside. 'Now that is interesting.'

Mrs Miller seemed buoyed by this encouragement from Don. 'Yes. She was planning to go over there, too.'

'Over where?' Don said, sitting up a little straighter.

'To Lloyd House. Told me she was looking for an investment.' Mrs Miller nodded importantly back down at the advertorial clipping. 'For her business.'

'And she went to ask Audrey Lloyd for this? When?'

Mrs Miller's expression grew serious as she shook her head. 'She *didn't* go in the end. She was just planning to. I think she must have changed her mind because she was talking about selling her car after that.'

'And then, two weeks ago, she told you she was going to visit her cousin, and she hasn't been back since?'

'That's exactly it, Detective.'

Don didn't correct his title, but he did now understand why his sarge had told him to just file the paperwork and be done with it.

A woman with, it sounded like, money troubles, driving off of her own volition to stay with family did not a suspicious case make. There was no way his superiors would listen to the gut instincts of a young rookie and divert precious resources to a case that would go nowhere. Especially when that young rookie had used his uniform to conduct not one, but two interviews to investigate reports he'd had direct instructions to drop. Don had bidden Mrs Miller farewell and gone home to fill up the pages of his journal with scratchy handwriting, trying to connect two unsubstantiated reports to a Hollywood heiress.

Eventually, he had closed his journal over his pen and laid back on the single bed in his childhood room, an LA Angels poster peeling down by its corners on the wall opposite. A couple of wrestling trophies from his high school glory days twinkled in the illumination of the streetlamp outside. A dusty carriage from his favourite train set hid in the shadows next to them. Don had a sudden jerk of embarrassment for the juvenility of his room. He was a cop for God's sake, not a child. Yet there he was, wilfully ignoring the expertise and instructions of better men to chase a mystery that didn't exist. A folly like the mysteries he used to solve as a child, excitedly telling his parents how he'd deduced that Mr Jackson from down the road was stealing the newspaper of his neighbour Mrs

Whitehead. It was time for him to grow out of his childish hunt for cases that didn't exist and take this job seriously.

And that was the vow he'd made that had seen him abandon the Lloyd Estate. A vow that had only wavered on sticky bar stools next to Ray. Or whenever he'd been instructed to drop another case or ignore another lead over the next decades of his career. One instruction of this kind had seen Don not pursue the complaint of a woman claiming her ex-boyfriend was stalking her. 'Hysterical,' his sarge had dismissed with a roll of his eyes. But when they'd found her, purple fingerprints around her neck, she had not looked hysterical in death. She'd looked terrified. And so Don had always kept one ear out to any suggestions that he'd made a similar mistake with the first case he ever followed instructions to drop. And thirty-four long years had passed without any hint he'd made a mistake.

But now, here he was, in the grounds of the place where Annabel Hackton used to work, staring at the car she'd driven away in, now abandoned to time – with human remains inside.

One question came back to him from his recollection. Something his young, rookie self had not probed. Something Don had paid no attention to himself over the years. But now, decades late, a whirring red alarm flashed at him from the past.

Had Mrs Miller said the day *they* left?

Twenty-Five

Terri
Thursday

Terri woke, disorientated and drowsy, and gazed around the unfamiliar room. She had no doubt she was somewhere in the bowels of the house. She could practically feel the weight of the floors above her, pushing down through the ceiling, each one another layer of the labyrinth.

Pain radiated from the back of her skull, but her ankle was well tended to – it felt soft and secure. She tentatively brushed her good foot against it, feeling layers of tightly wrapped bandages underneath her toes. But there was still a swollen balloon of agony just below the gauze, and it blossomed with pain as her toes gently explored the dressing. She was cocooned in a comfortable four-poster bed complete with dramatic green drapes and musty-smelling pistachio sheets.

At some point she thought she remembered waking to the feel of breath on her face and the sight of thick black curls bent low over her. She'd jerked instinctively at the shock and then groaned from the pain in her ankle. The face, shrouded in shadow and unidentifiable in Terri's blurred and confused vision, seemed to smile at her pain. The soft silk of a kimono brushed against her hand.

'Shh,' the voice had said as she'd groaned into wakefulness. 'Go back to sleep.' And then one hand cradled her head, carefully avoiding the pain from the base of her skull, and brought a glass to her lips. Terri felt cold water flood her mouth and slide welcomingly down her sandpapered throat.

She'd listened to the voice and let herself wash away again.

Now she was properly awake, she realised the sharp pain in both ankle and head had subsided to a barely perceptible ache. She tilted her head to one side, feeling the silky-smooth material of the sheets against her cheek, and twisted herself a little more upright on the thick pillow, seeing four thin mahogany poles at each corner of the bed, an elaborate art-deco style carved board at her feet.

The room itself was large, with a golden chaise longue in one corner by a large vanity table with a cracked mirror. The grand window looked out into an imposing mass of unkempt woodland. There was a glass of water on the mahogany bedside table and she quenched her thirst again, gulping down heavy mouthfuls that settled uncomfortably in her empty stomach.

She pushed herself fully upright, grabbing at the unused pillow on the other side of the king-sized bed, and propping it up behind her head. It smelled stale but did at least seem relatively clean. She remembered the stench of the sofa with a gag and felt grateful she was moved from there, even if she didn't understand what magic trick had done it. There was a beautiful painting of cherry blossoms on the far wall from where she was lying, the pinks picked out against the pale green wallpaper with satiny swirls shining in the glancing blows of sunlight. Sunlight. It was sunny again – the smoggy clouds must have finally cleared.

She needed to collect herself, and she needed to organise. She knew that somewhere out there, in the world beyond the reaches of the Lloyd Estate, she and Ethan were running out of time. A busted ankle was nothing compared to what Jason had promised. Something clutched tightly in her abdomen as she saw flickering orange flames consuming their condo, perhaps even licking across the small divide to devour kind Mrs Washington too. She forced herself to shake that thought away and concentrate on her own predicament.

She was still fully dressed under the bedclothes and moved her hand down to feel for her pockets. The fountain pen and earrings were still safe inside. If she could just get out of this, then perhaps she still had something to show for her week there. She no longer cared about getting anything else. Terri just wanted to get out, with Ethan. With the Ethan she used to know – before he had the pressures of his dad's business. She knew she could get him back. Sometimes she could still see that old twinkle in his green eyes beneath the veil of stress, the odd twitch of a smile that briefly shone with the radiance she'd fallen in love with. All she needed was to get them away, but where could they go to start again? Her family flashed to mind at once, the welcoming smiles, the endless offers of places to stay.

But terror stopped her from languishing too long on that thought – she didn't know how far Jason would follow them if they skipped town without clearing Ethan's debts. She couldn't risk him turning up on her family's doorstep holding the flaming torch promised for their own house. Before she could bring together something that might well resemble a plan of survival, there was a heavy click in the lock and the handle turned slowly as the door pushed softly inwards.

'Audrey?' Terri asked, hearing her voice sound strange and strangled. 'Is that you?'

'You're awake,' Audrey said, coming into the room, closing the door firmly behind her. Her hair was uncovered — it was the first time Terri had seen her like this, and she was surprised by the serenely dense silver of Audrey's roots. Audrey must have noticed her eyes focus on it, because one hand went instinctively to her crown.

'Mama always taught me to show the best of myself to the world,' she said, 'and I fear these greys are not the best of me.' Terri didn't respond and Audrey stepped closer. 'How are you feeling?'

'Fine, thank you,' Terri answered out of instinct.

'Your ankle?'

'Feels OK,' she said. 'The pain's gone down a lot.'

Audrey's eyes slid over to the empty glass on the side-board and she pulled one edge of her mouth down.

'You finished all the water?' One knobbly finger pointed to the glass.

Terri nodded.

'Good,' Audrey said. 'That will be why you feel so well, then. There was some old laudanum in there to help you with the pain. Do you feel disorientated in any way?' Terri widened her eyes and felt a shard of terror dart through her. Had she just been spiked with decades-old opium? Audrey narrowed her eyes seriously when Terri didn't respond. 'It's important you tell me how you feel, Terri. Or else I won't know if I've given you the right amount.'

'I... I feel OK; I don't need any more medicine.' The words came out rushed and garbled, tumbling over themselves as she tried desperately to persuade this woman to stop putting things in her drink.

Audrey gave a single nod. 'I'll be keeping an eye on you.' She smoothed her hands across the sheets covering Terri's chest. 'It looks like you might be with me for a little while.' Her eyes lit up as if with a sudden idea. 'You can teach me Greek!' she said excitedly. 'I do like to keep my mind active, and new languages are such a challenge. And I can teach you Russian. And Spanish, if you'd like.'

'That's really not necessary,' Terri said hurriedly, thinking only of the days ticking away. The more of a head start they could get on Jason the better. 'It's no trouble, I can call a taxi,' she garbled, and Audrey's face seemed to darken at Terri's reasoned attempt at escape.

'You're in much better hands with me, here,' she said. 'You must trust me.' Audrey's hand had now drifted down the smoothed sheet to Terri's upper arm, where she felt the pressure increase slowly on her bicep until it was pinched and burning. Terri was reminded of Jason's strong hands bending back her finger. Audrey had more physical strength than Terri had given her credit for.

'How did I get down here?' Terri asked distractedly, willing Audrey to release the pressure on her arm.

Audrey gripped her for a beat longer before relinquishing her grasp to gesture over at the far side of the room. 'In Mama's old chair.' Tucked against the back wall of the room was an old-fashioned wooden wheelchair. 'I brought you down in the elevator. Daddy had it put in for Mama. She was already weak by the time we moved here.'

'What did your mother die of?' Terri didn't know where the question had come from. Perhaps it was some tiny form of protest, one small part of her will trying to dislodge Audrey's footing.

Audrey gave a dazed sort of sigh. 'Spanish influenza in the end. It was quite bad that year.' She looked Terri straight in the eye. 'It's no fun to watch someone go slowly lame,' she said with one of her unnerving, straight-lipped smiles. 'And so we must do for them what we can.' Her voice was quieter when she spoke next, just above a whisper. 'That's what Daddy told me.'

Terri felt unease paw at her extremities, crawling up her skin with sharp pinpricks. Audrey leaned closer over her, dark curls dangling once again over Terri's prone body.

'Now you stay here until you feel better. You're safe here.' There was something about Audrey specifying this that made Terri acutely aware of the opposite. 'We'll take care of you.'

Terri swallowed thickly and when she spoke her voice sounded like a child's. 'We?'

Audrey twisted her head slowly over one shoulder, a creaking, jerky movement laboured by age. She gazed into the empty space by the door and breathed deeply before turning back with a blank smile. 'Oh yes,' she said softly. 'We'll take care of you.'

When the door closed behind her, Terri heard the loud, distinct sound of a lock clicking into place.

Twenty-Six

Audrey

Thursday

Audrey had put Terri where she knew she would be safe, in her parents' bedroom. That was where you put precious things that needed to be guarded, things that could implode your life. But Audrey cheered herself a little; she didn't think Terri would be quite so volatile as the last thing she'd hidden in that room.

Audrey thought that at least she'd be able to take care of her now. That was what you did for the people in your custody.

Daddy smiled at her with a knowing nod. That was what he had done for her all those years ago when she'd needed it most.

1934

Audrey woke every day with Irina's face still imprinted behind her lids. The sound of gunshots. The blackness that had followed. She awakened in her parents' old room, smiling into the familiar scent of Mama that still somehow clung to the walls, the whole room the colour of the pistachios that grew from the trees in the grove just beyond the window. When she was a child, Mrs Doyle would take Audrey out into that grove and teach her how to pick the fragrant green nuts and fill their baskets with olives and lemons too.

She blinked into the green hanging above her on the four-poster bed as her dreamed memories swirled lucidly through her still half-slumbering mind. The remembrance hit her as it always did, with a solid thump to her guts. She rolled over on her side to face the dark green spine of the leather notebook on the bedside table next to her. Mrs Hackton had returned it to her that first week after Irina's death, placing it silently next to her pillow with nothing more than a pinch-mouthed look. If Audrey had had the energy, she would have hated Hackton harder than she ever had before just for that one act. Now she saw Mrs Hackton only on Mrs Doyle's days off, when she would silently dump the trays of Audrey's three meals on the dresser before disappearing off again down the long corridor lined with the mannequins dressed in Mama's favourite gowns, toward the elevator which took her back up to the rest of the house.

Every day, Arnold would visit her down there, in the room she could not leave. It was separate from the rest of the house – an extra excavation down into the hillside so that Arnold and Estella could have their own wing. But Estella had died before the rest of the wing could be developed and now there was just one basement corridor leading to a pistachio-coloured room that had not been touched in twenty years.

No words had escaped Audrey's lips since she'd watched her best friend crumble under a shower of bullets.

That was, until recently.

Audrey pushed herself upright and turned to the golden chaise longue at an angle against the floor-to-ceiling window, next to the large, mirrored dresser.

'Good morning, Reeny,' she said in a croaky voice.

Irina smiled from her seat on the gold satin fabric. 'Good morning, Audrey. Who wants to be white today?'

Audrey smiled and sat back against her pillows, muttering the positions of chess pieces on a board that existed only in her mind, with a companion that also existed only in her mind.

Sometimes Mama would come to visit her, too. But Mama would lament with disappointed anguish that Audrey was letting herself go. 'You even told Mrs Hackton, *mi amor*—'

'Beautiful things can still be beautiful even without the eyes of the world on them,' Audrey finished.

Mama was right. And when Audrey had finished her game with Irina, a muttered crescendo of a finale which Irina eventually won, Audrey pushed herself out of bed and walked on wasted muscles toward her mother's dresser. Inside the stiff drawer she found old brushes and compacts, a gold-backed hairbrush that she dragged through her matted nest – her cleanliness maintained only by bed baths conducted by a determined Mrs Doyle, who washed Audrey's lacklustre body. She swept blusher across her cheekbones, shadow across her eyes, kohl around her lashline and then sat back and smiled into her reflection. It was a grin she shared with Irina and Mama, who stood behind her in the mirror, nodding their encouragement.

The magic was shattered by Mrs Hackton opening the door to the room, a tray containing a bowl of oatmeal and glass of orange juice in her hands.

'Oatmeal with brown sugar,' she said, without looking up. When she did, she dropped the tray in alarm, thick oatmeal sludging onto the green carpet in a congealed mound.

'Audrey!' She gasped, stepping back. 'You're out of bed! And wh— *what have you done to your face*?!' She screamed the last sentence, horror snaking down the bloodshot veins of the whites of her eyes. 'Arnold!' she shrieked, and Audrey could hear the torment, confused but satisfied. 'Arnold!' Mrs Hackton turned and raced from the room, her feet pounding down the isolated corridor, disturbing the peace of Mama's dresses.

Audrey frowned into the mirror.

She cocked her head and saw the stripes of pink, the thick rings of lipstick that stretched far beyond the boundaries of her mouth, the deep circles of black encasing each eye. And she laughed. And she laughed and laughed and looked to Mama and Irina in the mirror behind her. But they were fading.

Mrs Hackton had scared them away.

'Come back,' Audrey croaked, reaching one hand out toward the mirror, resting on the glass where her friend was disappearing. 'Come back!' she screeched, louder this time, reaching for Mama's heavy gold compact and flinging it into the deceitful mirror. A crack reverberated through her reflection. Her face now as fractured as the brilliant mind inside.

'Audrey, Audrey my dear.' Arnold came running into the room and stopped when he saw the broken mirror, his daughter's splintered multi-coloured reflection staring back at him. 'You're out of bed,' he breathed.

Audrey's shoulders hunched up and she fell forward onto the dresser, a sob wracking its way through her body.

'Irina's gone,' she wailed. 'She's gone!'

'Oh, my darling girl,' Arnold rushed to her, his hands on her shuddering shoulders, and kneeled down beside her stool, gripping her tightly.

Later, Audrey awoke again, back in bed, her memory fuzzy. Her father sat by her bedside, the dark green leather notebook now removed.

'Dr Schofield came,' he said, answering her unasked question. 'He gave you something to help you sleep.'

'Oh,' Audrey said softly.

'Are — are you feeling better now?' Arnold said, and Audrey thought she sensed him holding his breath. Waiting to see if she would reply.

'I — I,' she stumbled, but she could not answer. Without Reeny there was no reason to speak.

He leaned forward in his chair and grasped her hand where it lay on the old silk sheets. 'Please,' he choked, 'my daughter, please. Talk to me.'

Audrey felt her eyes grow wet and turned her head away from her father. Her throat was swollen and aching. It could not give him the words he wanted it to.

'Please,' Arnold begged, 'let us move on. It's been six months.' *Six months*. Audrey looked around her self-imposed prison. Half a year had passed by without her notice. 'Dr Schofield...' Arnold spoke the name carefully and Audrey furrowed her brow. 'He's recommended a place. A place for you to get better.' Arnold patted her hand, his eyes unconsciously sliding to the smashed mirror at the far side of the room. 'They'll help you. They know what they're doing.'

Audrey nodded. She knew she had no choice. She knew she was destined to be sent wherever her father, or anyone else, deemed fit. And why shouldn't she listen?

Why shouldn't she do whatever he wanted her to do? When she tried to take control of her own life – tried to take agency over just one thing... she couldn't let herself complete the thought. She summoned all of her energy, grasping at the tiniest of fragments from where it lay decimated and abandoned. She saw herself on her knees, reaching desperately for the smallest grains she could muster—

'I-I-Irina.' She choked out the name.

Arnold stared at her a moment before understanding what his daughter needed.

'The family have moved,' he confirmed. 'To San Francisco I believe. To start again.'

Audrey nodded sadly. The family cursed to start again over and over. She thought, in that moment, oddly, of young Sascha. Never able to settle. Guilt squeezed hot wet tears from her eyes and her father patted her hand, before pushing himself upright.

'I'll call Dr Schofield. Tell him we'll be accepting his placement.'

Twenty-Seven

Terri
Thursday

Not long had passed since Audrey had left Terri to rest. Now, Terri found herself smiling idly toward the locked door, some corner of her brain trying to prod something awake in her. But she found she couldn't quite let herself succumb to it. She was starting to feel perfectly calm, happy in fact. There was nothing wrong with just staying right here in this bed. She turned her head to gaze around the room and caught sight of the glass of water she'd gulped so greedily down.

Laudanum.

That was why she felt so good. Somewhere inside Terri wanted to wonder what else Audrey had been putting in her food and drink all week. But then she turned her head away and stared instead at the pretty cherry blossoms dancing on the opposite wall. She felt her eyes grow heavy as the pinks and greens blurred together.

She was woken as the agony in her ankle returned with a vengeance. She'd rolled over, and must have flexed her foot, because pain shot right up her leg and kicked her in the stomach. Dusk had fallen while Terri had slept; she could no longer see bright sparks of sun breaking through the overgrown trees that crowded the window. The light in the room had taken on a pale grey hue, almost ethereal. It must be late evening, nightfall not too far away.

A gaping black smog filled her from within as she regained consciousness, feeling the agony in her ankle and head; even the previously dulled pain from her finger seemed to pulse brighter than before. The laudanum had worn off. And with it any feeling of calm or happiness that had settled Terri into a cosy slumber.

Now she felt only panic tighten her chest. Sadness bloomed melancholy in her stomach.

She rolled over again, and it took another few moments for the shock of the pain that had woken her to seep out of her clenched stomach muscles and settle into a puddling ache inside the bandages. She stared straight up at the green drapes framing the four-poster bed and knew that she needed to get out. The woman was mad, and dangerous in a way Terri still didn't quite understand. She was so old and frail, it seemed ridiculous to fear her. If it came to a feat of physicality the younger and stronger Terri would surely be the victor. And yet there Terri was, banged up and on an opioid come-down – all of her energy seeping away at the thought of doing anything other than remaining cocooned in the silky sheets.

No, it was definitely time to go. She had her treasure to help them start something of a new life, and maybe she could even grab something else on her way out too.

Fuck.

Thinking about her way out had darted a memory of yesterday morning – of having to leave her home at five a.m. to get two buses, and the seventy-minute walk that had finally brought her to Audrey's front door. How would she manage all of that in reverse with her ankle?

Terri forced herself to concentrate. She needed a plan – she couldn't let herself be defeated at the first hurdle. She had to survive – she would get out of there. She was already weak, had already been at Audrey's mercy for too long. God only knew what other drugs she would try and pump Terri full of. Audrey could keep her there in that basement room for as long as she wanted her entertainment, and no one would ever know to look for her. She would get away with it all, because no one ever thinks about the lonely hermit heiress, living with ghosts and vermin, driven to insanity.

First things first: Terri needed to get out of this room. She pulled the covers off and pushed herself upright, noticing the headache gathering even more strength at the base of her skull where she had cracked it on the step. She glanced over at the door and remembered that it would be locked. She let out a frustrated scream into the room, hearing the echoing screech bounce back into her ears as she felt self-hatred bubble around her until she was consumed. This was all because of her own stupidity. She'd played Audrey's games. She'd let herself be sucked in, been easily flattered and let herself drop her guard, so exhausted from having it up all the damn time. The comedown from her laudanum high wanted her to curl into a ball and weep. To give up and stay in bed and just let herself succumb to the mad old bitch's whims. At least she'd be out of Jason's grasp.

It was the thought of Ethan that snapped her out of it. The Ethan from before. The Ethan with his long golden hair, tapping away on the electric typewriter she'd bought him as a surprise with her first bonus check. His ideas, his stories of far-away planets and the adventures of his heroes. He'd hold her at night and describe the latest worlds he'd been building in that wonderful, magnificent head of his and she would glow with pride. They could get back to that. There was a hope – it was small, but she had to try.

Carefully, she manoeuvred herself out of bed and hobbled, slow and wincing, toward the door. She bent low, kneeling onto her good leg, and looked through the old keyhole, trying to gauge whether Audrey was keeping watch outside her room. It was blocked by the black end of a key. Audrey had left the key in the lock. As long as her captor wasn't keeping vigil outside the room, Terri had a way out.

Hoisting herself back up, she scanned around the room looking for any tools that might help her. She limped back to the right side of the bed and yanked at the drawer at the top of the nightstand. It stuck after years of neglect, but with a forceful shimmy, Terri pulled it open. Inside was a time capsule from over sixty years ago. Brown glass bottles of pills rolled toward her inside the drawer, their labels handwritten with the name *Estella Lloyd* and peeling off. A mother-of-pearl compact mirror, a small comb. Terri reached for the mirror and clicked it open, the glass clear and bright, protected inside from years of dust. She added it to the collection in her pocket, and silently gave thanks to the ghost of Estella Lloyd for her donations to Terri and Ethan's new life.

Terri climbed across the bed to the other nightstand, already distracted by the vanity table, thinking that perhaps she'd be more likely to find tools to help her break out there, and wrenched open the drawer of what had been presumably Arnold Lloyd's bedside table. Terri was not thinking properly as she gave the mainly empty drawer a once-over, eyes only searching for something that would help her with the job at hand. But as she was abandoning the nightstand, dismissing its contents as useless, a talon extended from somewhere inside her and pulled her back toward the still-open drawer.

She stared down into it. A yellowed sheet of paper, unfolded but creased. A couple of cufflinks had rolled onto it as she'd jerked the drawer open. The life raft she never thought would come. She picked it up, the cufflinks dropping with thuds as they slid off, and stared down at the page in her hands. She read and re-read the words, adrenaline filling her veins with the potency of gas in her beloved Maverick. They were saved. She let out a loud laugh of relief, the sound misplaced and alien in this abandoned room.

Now all she needed to do was get the hell out of there. She folded the paper up along its creases and shoved it deep into her pocket. She limped to the vanity table and swiped a handful of hairpins from the dusty drawer before casting desperately about for the other bit she needed to execute her escape plan, catching her reflection in the broken mirror.

She stared back at herself, dishevelled and pallid, her hair matted and knotted, throwing rogue wisps up above her crown. She looked like one of those stray dogs she'd seen on bus posters for the local shelter, ungroomed and unwanted, ready to be put down. There was a concentric crack radiating from the reflection of her right shoulder, fracturing across her in jerked segments. The central wound to the mirror sent one large break up to the top, so the two halves of her face didn't quite line up, and there were smaller, perpendicular breaks cutting up the segments like a spider's web.

Terri took a deep, preparative breath. And then she plunged her hands into the mirror, tearing at the small fractures in the centre, feeling the edges of the glass scratch and tear and her fingertips. She ignored the pain and continued digging, clumsy and uncoordinated with her bound fingers. Scarlet trickled down the reflective glass and dropped a slow puddle onto the table's surface. She picked and peeled the fractures of mirror out of her way, dropping the bloody shards to join the small pool, until finally she wrenched out a piece that looked about the right size.

Holding the pins in one hand and the shard of mirror in the other, she focused all her energy on not tipping over as she perfected her half-limp, half-hop back to the door. With her weapons at the ready she kneeled and pressed her head to the wood of the door, trying to hear if Audrey was on the other side. Keeping watch.

Hearing nothing, Terri slid the piece of mirror under the door, shoving it roughly as it caught on the thick carpet. She waited a beat, holding her breath, expecting Audrey to barge in at any moment. But all remained still, and so Terri lined up the shard of mirror as best she could underneath the lock, before taking out the thick setting hairpins. The key sat snugly in its home and did not respond to her initial prods with the pin through the keyhole. But Terri persisted, pounding the pin harder and harder into the lock until finally, she felt it dislodge. She poked it again, pushing it further out of the lock mechanism, so that it was hanging halfway out. One final push and it fell – and Terri waited, not breathing, to hear the clank of success.

When she heard the key land on the mirror, she allowed herself to exhale.

Carefully, she started to pull the mirror back toward her, back underneath the door. It slid through the gap with barely a hair's width to spare, carrying its precious cargo through the slim gap. When she was finally united with the key, she grasped it in a sweaty palm and sat back, panting several breaths of relief. She'd done it. Except she hadn't of course. She was still only at the beginning. And still with no plan to get home even if she did manage to make her escape.

Forgetting about her bloodied fingers, Terri pushed them into her hairline, trying to clear her vision from the wispy waves that had fallen in front of her eyes, and winced as the cuts screamed at her. Clutching the key, she kneeled back up to the keyhole and slotted it easily into place. It turned with a satisfying click, and Terri used the handle to hoist herself upright. She pulled the door toward her and hobbled back as it opened inward.

And then she froze as she saw a figure on the other side.

Twenty-Eight

Don
Friday

Don's colleagues buzzed around, filling out forms and taking photographs. An ambulance was now parked up and preparing to extract the still technically unidentified remains from their previously final resting place. He blew out a sigh. Tracking down the car registration was at least a step in the right direction, but it wouldn't stand as a conclusive identification of whoever that skeleton had been in life. They would become possession of the police department, added to the lengthy box of cold case files. Even Don's recollection about the missing person report from years ago wouldn't hold much water. Who's to say Annabel Hackton hadn't got herself caught up in something she regretted, and knew of an easy access, abandoned plot of land to dispose of a body?

They came to say goodbye. Mrs Miller taunted him through the years.

Victim or culprit – the question he'd been asking since the beginning. There were over ten years between the last evidence of Mrs Hackton's contact with Audrey Lloyd, when she took stewardship over her on her release from the sanatorium in 1937, and her disappearance in the late

Forties. And how did any of this connect to Audrey's death, and a beaten Theresa Nicholls sitting in hospital?

It didn't, most likely. Don knew that, and yet he couldn't help but stand by what he'd told Sterne earlier. You never did know what might come back to haunt you.

Don made his next plan of action — direct a couple of spare officers to help him with the search of the house when they'd finished dealing with the unidentified remains. Check if Annabel Hackton was still alive, some-where. Check on a connection between Theresa Nicholls and Annabel Hackton. He'd have to send someone to City Hall and then down to the basement archives of the station. It wouldn't be so simple to track down informa-tion about a woman who might well have left the state, or even the country, decades ago. But that's what keen young rookies were for.

As he'd been thinking about his mental to-do list, he'd turned to face the direction of the house again, gazing up the steep slope tangled in weeds and hardy desert plants, the top of the house just visible, peering down at them all. He twisted back around to the clearing, looking for a victim to spend the rest of the day poring through dusty old files. He spotted a young officer standing awkwardly off to one edge of the clearing, staring into the tangle of bracken at the base of the hill.

'Officer,' Don said with natural authority, walking over and coming to a stop just behind her shoulder. 'I need help down at the archives and City Hall today, if you're up for it?'

She seemed distracted for a moment, staring still down into the bracken, but after a beat turned toward him and nodded.

'Yes, Detective.' She paused before gesturing to herself. 'Officer Sinclair.'

'Good to meet you.' Don nodded, before taking in her slight frown of curiosity and adding, 'What have you seen?'

He stepped forward so he was next to her, shoulders in line. He peered out in the direction she had just been looking, into the tangled plants that filled the small gulley between the lawn above them that held the obelisk and the dusty clearing in which they stood.

'I don't know,' she said, turning her attention back in that direction. 'I think I saw something glint in those plants. But it's gone now.'

Don's eyebrows furrowed in an expression that matched the young officer's and he peered closer into the sharp brambles. He tilted his head from one side to the other and took a side-step off to the right, before moving slowly back, scanning the bracken all the while.

'There!' he said, raising a finger out toward the bright glint as the sun caught whatever it was at the right angle.

Sinclair followed his point. 'Yes! There it is – I *knew* I saw something.'

Don surveyed the tangle of hardy plants and blew out a deep exhale. 'Well, there's only one way in.' He took a step toward the edge of the clearing, which dropped down dramatically, in mirror of the steep path he'd followed Chen up when they'd first found the car.

'I can go, Detective?' Sinclair offered, stepping forward eagerly.

Don surveyed her and then looked back to the unruly gulley reluctantly. 'No,' he said. 'You stay up here and keep an eye on that glint – if I'm going off course, direct me back where I need to be.'

'OK.' She nodded but looked sceptical about this assignment of roles. But if this glint was anything of interest, Don wanted to have the first eyes on it. His adrenaline was surging now as it always had in the hunt for clues.

He tentatively approached the rocky slope and lowered himself down so his butt rested on the ground, feet scrabbling in front of him in the dusty soil. Slowly he made his way down, gravel cutting into his palms and red clay coating his suit pants. The slope levelled where the plants started, and Don pushed himself upright, steadying his balance on a spiky bush. Dusting his hands free of the small stones that had embedded themselves in his palms, he carefully reached forward and moved the first of the branches out of his way. The brambles dug into his already smarting hands, and scratched at his legs, but he progressed through, wincing with every scrape.

'More to the left!' Sinclair called from her post above, and he ploughed on, following her direction, his eyes scanning the dead land beneath the thicket. Something caught the corner of his eye – a glint from just up ahead and toward the right, flashing through the spindly branches. It was just what they'd seen from the clearing, the kind of glint his watch made when the sun caught it at the right angle, that the dog would stare and bark at. He took another few steps forward, not caring now as the branches scratched against his body, seemingly thicker than before. Its source came into focus, and Don bent low for a closer look, a branch catching him on his cheek as he did.

'What the—' he breathed, batting the branch out of the way and focusing his gaze on the glinting item. He bent lower, breaking the branches as he moved them out of his way so he could get a clearer view of the shining object.

He picked it up and held it high above the bushes, directly into the bright sunlight. In his hand was a glittering gold statue of an Oscar, streaks of congealing blood clinging to his bald head and shoulders.

Twenty-Nine

Audrey
Thursday

That was her patient tended to, Audrey thought, if reluctant for help. But she was confident Terri would come around. She took the elevator at the end of the corridor outside her parents' old room and rode it to the top floor, where Irina was waiting for her, looking healthy and young. The things Audrey sometimes believed she saw of herself in her mirrored reflection, but then the filter would fade, and she'd be left staring at an unfamiliar roadmap of wrinkles cut around her face. Time had come for her in the way it hadn't for so many that she'd loved. Sometimes she could not decide if that was a blessing or a curse. At least Irina and Mama remained forever in their prime, while Audrey withered.

'How is she?' Irina asked in Russian. Audrey smiled at that. She really did like the opportunity to practise her languages.

'She's feeling better thanks to the...' Audrey paused and realised she did not know the word for laudanum. '...medicine,' she settled on.

They walked together back to the living room, the conversation slipping easily into Spanish before Audrey corrected it back to Russian. 'Russian is better practice for my brain,' she admonished to a laugh from Irina. 'She'll be fine.' She nodded with firm determination. 'I knew she was special. Special enough to survive.' She looked into Irina's young, open face. 'Just like you did.'

Audrey was a survivor herself, and she recognised the trait in others.

1937

Dr Schofield's facility was a whitewashed villa in the heart of the desert. Audrey sat in the sun-dappled day room, gazing out over the orange vista that crawled away from the window. She was poring over the pages in front of her, neatly inputting blocky numbers in the assigned spots, checking details with the stacks of invoices and receipts that came via courier each week.

Nurse Anna pushed through the glass door with Audrey's tray of lunch and set it down on the small table next to her chair.

'Working through lunch again, Miss Lloyd?' Anna smiled.

'I've got a lot to do,' Audrey said, glancing at the tray and the two large green capsules she'd be forced to choke down with her water. They calmed her. So everyone said. But it wasn't Nurse Anna's fault – Audrey knew that much after three years. Anna was just one of a stream of jolly nurses who fluffed Audrey's pillows, brought her food and encouraged her to socialise with the other 'guests' in the facility.

'Well, it's good to see you busy,' Anna said with the bright, saccharine smile Audrey was sure would fade from her face the moment the doors shut behind her. Audrey didn't look up but finished inputting the details from an invoice from Gerritsen Equipment before she heard the smallest of coughs clear Nurse Anna's throat. Audrey bit her bottom lip, feeling the taste of iron spill into her mouth.

'I can't concentrate on my work afterwards,' she said quietly, staring down at the papers in her lap, and hearing only a small child's desperate pleading.

'I'm sorry, Miss Lloyd,' Anna said. 'But it's for the best.'

Audrey nodded. For the best. She put down her pen and grabbed the pills, knocking them to the back of her throat and swallowing them painfully down her oesophagus. She looked up at Nurse Anna, who smiled gratefully.

'Would you like me to move you to the sun for the afternoon?' Anna asked.

Audrey looked back to her work and knew she had about twenty minutes before the pills' fuzz would lap at her concentration. 'Come back for me after I've eaten,' she said, and moved on to the next invoice.

Things had got better since her first year at the Desert Palm Sanatorium. She no longer had to dread the thick cold needle plunged into her arm that would convulse her body to the point of screaming agony until she passed out, awaking delirious and forgetful, her jaw exhausted from shattering her teeth together.

'It's experimental,' she'd heard the doctor tell her father confidently, 'but we are seeing some wonderful results with these metrazol shock injections.'

Audrey had had to revisit her childhood survival techniques back in those early days. Learning what the grown-ups wanted from her so she could avoid their punishments. She learned what to say to the doctor, how to lie just the right amount. If she proclaimed herself too cured, they would grow suspicious, and another seizure would be induced. But things had settled over the last year. She'd agreed to a programme of daily tranquilisers, and last month Nurse Anna had arranged with Daddy for Audrey to take over the bookkeeping for the company when Frederick, Lloyd Productions' octogenarian accountant, had finally decided to retire.

'It'll be good for her to have something to do with her days,' Anna had said. 'A useful, sound distraction.' The doctors had been suspicious at first, worried that an active mind might well cause trouble, but Audrey knew enough to keep herself as dulled as they wanted.

And her daily green capsules did most of the work for her.

Arnold would drive into the desert every Sunday to see her, and every Sunday she would beg the nurses to give her her pills later, so she could concentrate on at least one chess game with her father. If she'd behaved that week, then they would oblige. Sometimes he would stay late into the evening, to sit on the veranda and watch the sun pool from orange to pink to purple to navy. The desert night would press thick around them, the ticks of bugs and screams of Audrey's fellow 'guests' filling the would-be silence.

'It's a beautiful night, Daddy,' Audrey had said softly on one of these visits.

He'd grabbed her hand and squeezed it tightly. 'That it is, my precious girl.' He'd tilted his head to look at her.

'I want to go home,' she said.

'I know, my dear,' he'd replied. 'It won't be for much longer now.'

'I miss the house.'

'It's quiet without you,' he admitted before looking at her earnestly. 'You know that you and Mama will always be the loves of my life, don't you, Audrey?' Audrey nodded. 'Good. I need you to remember that.'

Anna came back in just as Audrey was finishing her lunchtime salad and closing the book of accounts for the day.

'Ready for some sun, Miss Lloyd?'

Audrey nodded. 'But first,' she said, 'can I use the phone? I need to speak with Daddy.'

'Of course, Miss Lloyd,' Nurse Anna said and stood back while Audrey got to her feet and re-packed the box of pay checks and invoices and picked it up, sliding her accounts book on top. Audrey settled into the high-backed wicker chair on the veranda and waited as Nurse Anna carried the heavy phone over to her. Audrey dialled the operator and waited to be connected, now soothed by the sounds of the cicadas that accompanied her every day.

'Lloyd residence, Mrs Hackton speaking.'

'I need to speak to Daddy,' Audrey snapped, feeling black tar-like anger at the sound of that woman's voice.

There was a hesitation on the other end before a small sigh escaped. 'I'll get him.'

Arnold came on the phone, delighted as ever to hear from his daughter.

'Daddy, you seem to be paying Mrs Hackton twice each month,' Audrey said hurriedly, knowing that soon her pills would take effect and she'd be unable to have this conversation until tomorrow morning, when she might well have forgotten all about it. The pills did that some-times, causing confusion each morning as she attempted to pick up where she'd left off the previous day. 'I'll need you to send over the last few years of accounts so I can see how long this has been going on for, but I think Frederick must have been losing his touch near the end.' She ran a hand over her forehead – partly in frustration, partly in satisfaction – as she imagined the mammoth job of untangling the senile old accountant's mistakes for the last however many years. Daddy could have lost thousands of dollars because of this.

'What's that, dear?' Arnold said in his pleasant, absent-minded way.

'The accounts, Daddy. They're a mess. You've been overpaying Mrs Hackton, by a *lot*. Each month there's her salary payment, and then two weeks later an additional payment for twice that amount. Did the woman not say anything to you when it started?' Audrey felt her hackles rise as they always did when she thought of her father's assistant. She'd just been quietly taking the money, taking advantage of the old accountant's mistake. What kind of loyalty was that?

'Oh, don't worry about that, dear,' Arnold said. But something in his voice told Audrey he was forcing his usual lightness.

'No, Daddy, I will worry about it. I've nothing else to worry about these days.' Audrey sighed. 'I just wanted to tell you urgently that I don't think you can trust Mrs Hackton, although I've been saying that for years.'

'Audrey.' Arnold's voice was suddenly lower and sterner as it came across the line, as if his previous lightness had been removed by a syringe with a particularly sharp needle. 'I've told you not to worry about it.'

'And I've told you I think something needs to be done. I can call the lawyers in the morning. Pass on what I've found – I'm sure we can get to the bottom of this.'

'No,' Arnold snapped suddenly. But Audrey found that she actually didn't quite have the energy to worry about why her father was taking that tone with her. She stared into the desert garden in front of her, the lush green grass tended to each day by a team of gardeners. Towering cacti with sprouting purple blooms.

'Audrey?' She heard her father's voice drift further away, her muscles relaxing, her focus fogging.

The pills.

'Audrey, are you alright?' her father asked. Perhaps he sounded more urgent. She could not tell. 'Audrey? Do you promise you will leave these accounts alone. Don't call—'

But she had dropped the phone back down onto the receiver. It was easier, for now, not to worry about the thieving old witch. Easier not to worry about why Daddy wouldn't deal with it.

But the next day, her memory was still intact despite the drugs she'd swallowed down the day before. This pleased Audrey, evidence that, in some way, when it really mattered, her brilliant mind could fight back against those awful green pills. She called her father first thing, before her lunchtime dose would get the chance to dull her again. But he was adamant. He would not send over any more paperwork.

'Perhaps doing this job is taking its toll on you,' he sighed.

'No,' she cried, 'please *trust me*, Daddy, it's not. Mrs Hackton is stealing from you. She is!'

'She is doing no such thing, Audrey!' Arnold raised his voice again, and this time Audrey was clear-headed enough to recognise the change.

'Alright, Daddy,' Audrey said calmly. Too calmly, if anyone had been bothered to listen closely. 'I'll speak to you tomorrow.' They hung up and she immediately called the operator again and asked to be connected with Jonathon North, Lloyd Productions' new lawyer.

'Hello, Mr North, it's Audrey Lloyd here.'

He sounded hesitant to greet her. 'Oh, um, hello, Miss Lloyd.'

'We've corresponded of course,' she oozed, feeling her old power flicker back to life. Mama nodded her approval from the corner of the day room. 'And you're aware I've been doing the accounts for Lloyd Productions since Frederick retired?'

'Yes, yes of course. And it's a business matter you wish to discuss?'

'Of course.' Audrey smiled silkily and requested that North ask Arnold for the backdated accounts. 'There's something strange I've spotted,' she said.

'OK, Miss Lloyd,' he replied, 'I suppose I can look into it. Thank you for bringing it to my attention.'

Audrey hung up the phone and sat back in her chair. She hadn't had this feeling in a long time. The feeling that she was doing something. That she was useful.

The next day Arnold arrived unexpectedly at the door to her room, first thing in the morning. She was doing her morning toilet – washing her face with the good lotion she'd requested from Daddy, fluffing her lashes with a black mascara wand. It wouldn't do for her to let herself go, she'd decided. Not now she had a purpose again. The knock took her by surprise, and her hand jerked the mascara into her eyebrow, leaving a scratch of black on her forehead.

'Shit,' she muttered, reaching for her flannel to correct the mistake, as her father pushed the door open without waiting for her to respond.

'Audrey,' he sighed heavily, 'why can you not just leave things alone?'

She turned in surprise at the sound of her father's voice. 'Daddy, what are you doing here?' He looked drained and weary, as if he'd been up all night.

'I had North on the phone yesterday,' he said by way of an answer. 'He said you'd asked him to look through our back accounts.'

'Well, you won't listen to me.' Audrey got to her feet and stood, legs apart, facing her father. 'And I won't let that woman get away with ripping you – ripping *us* off.'

'She's been a loyal employee,' he replied. 'She's earned that money.'

'Horseshit,' Audrey spat. 'She already gets paid well enough for that.'

'Audrey – please. Can you not just trust me? You know' – he dragged in a deep inhale – 'you know what happens when you start to get these ideas. I knew I should never have let you do the accounts.'

He had not said it explicitly. He didn't need to. They both knew where getting ideas, what keeping busy, had led Audrey to in the past. But this time was different. She could feel it and, despite everything that had happened, she trusted her instincts. Mrs Hackton was bad news, and Audrey couldn't let it drop.

'No, Daddy,' she replied stubbornly. 'I can't trust you. Not when it comes to that woman. She's done nothing but drive a wedge between us since you hired her. She's done nothing but berate and taunt me. It's no wonder I've ended up in a place like this!'

Arnold looked like he'd been slapped. 'Do – do you really think that?' His voice was choked, and Audrey saw a glisten in his eye. Not since Mama had died had she seen her father cry.

Good.

She wanted him to suffer. She wanted to him to feel as wretched as she did, trapped in her prison every day.

'Yes,' she spat determinedly. 'And you let it happen. All of it is your fault. Mama and I would have been better off without you.'

Thirty

Terri
Thursday

Her heart hurtled into her throat, and she felt adrenaline pulse through her veins as she adjusted her sight to the dark, windowless corridor lined with mannequins. There was one right by the door, facing slightly away from her so the sweep of its long black ball gown was the first thing that had greeted her as she'd pulled the door open. It had taken a moment of panic before she'd realised it didn't have a head.

Like the mannequin on the way to the bathroom upstairs, they were all dressed in a finery Terri could never afford even on her planned wedding day. There was a hollow sadness as she thought about the wedding dress she'd picked out with her mom from a boutique in New York. They'd gone last spring, when wedding plans and her future in LA still seemed exciting and realistic. She'd lost the deposit on the dress, when she'd called months later to let them know she wouldn't be able to make any more of the payments. She'd had to lie to her mom, tell her that she'd changed her mind about the dress. That Ethan was so wrapped up in work they were postponing the wedding for a little while anyway. She couldn't tell them the truth. They'd only want to help, and Terri knew her

218

troubles were far beyond the realms of the few hundred bucks they'd be able to afford to give. Her dad still ran the family restaurant, her brothers well entrenched in it now too. The restaurant had always done OK, but it had three families to support now – the income it created was the only thing keeping food in the mouths of her nieces and nephews. Besides, something like pride had stopped her from turning to them. She was the one who'd made it out of Connecticut after all. College in New York, a new life in LA.

Tentatively she took a step out into her headless audience and gave a strained grunt as she began to drag her busted ankle along the soiled carpet. She could just about see a spiral staircase at the far end of the darkened corridor, which she dragged herself toward, occasionally clinging to the dust-covered silk that adorned the mannequins, intricate beading sanding against her already injured hands.

Finally, she reached the staircase and leaned against the bannister in relief – trying to summon more strength than she thought she had left to not succumb to the desire to sit down. She gazed up the hollow of the staircase winding up above her and wondered how on earth Audrey had got her down it.

Then she remembered. There was an elevator.

To the right of the staircase was a small enclave, which Terri hobbled over to and found the golden grille of an old-fashioned elevator. There was a large mother-of-pearl button inlaid to a brass holder, and she instinctively reached to push it – before her own survival instinct pulled back her hand just in time.

Audrey.

If Terri called that elevator, Audrey would hear it. She knew just from looking at it how much noise the ancient machinery would make. Terri had no idea where the old woman was in the house – she had no idea even where *she* was in the house. For all Terri knew, Audrey was standing directly by the elevator one, two, three floors up. And Terri did not want to alert Audrey to the fact that she was up and about.

She turned with an inward sludge of dread back to the spiral stairs and began the process of hobbling toward them. She managed to make her way up, relatively quietly, on all fours, the wooden steps digging painfully into her kneecaps, bloodied hands leaving tell-tale smears. Just as she was about to turn the final bend in the stairs, she hesitated, listening out for sounds of life on the landing above her. All seemed quiet, and so she continued her ascent, dragging herself onto the landing before pushing herself up to sit against the wall and take stock of where she was in this warren of a house.

Terri was on a small, circular landing crowded with shelves displaying various sculptures. The sculpture display was interrupted only by another golden grille for the elevator. How she longed to able to use it. To ride easily up and wander out, telling Audrey, 'I feel much better now, thank you for your hospitality, but don't worry about selling the house to Thornton Kendal anymore, I think I've changed my mind.' Then she would get the fuck out of there, back to the office to whatever dogsbody duties Glenn and Mr Thornton would find to punish her for being ill. She gave a snort of a desperate laugh to herself. The thought of filling out Glenn's expense reports and typing out Thornton's correspondence seemed like a welcome trade for where she actually was.

She allowed herself to breathe for a moment before pulling herself upright and recommencing her lolloping hobble down the corridor. There were what seemed like endless doors to she didn't how many rooms, and she wished she still had the energy to care about what treasures might be hiding in any of them. One hand went to her right pocket – pen, earrings, mirror were still safely inside. Then her hand moved to her left pocket and curled itself in a tight fist around her saviour, gripping it with desperate thanks. Forget about a week with Audrey, Terri could have spent months searching this house and still never have made it to that hidden bedroom if Audrey hadn't put her there herself.

Something like gratefulness surged in her mind toward the old woman then, though her survival instinct balked at the thought. She'd locked Terri in. She'd drugged her. She could never have known she'd delivered her prisoner exactly to what she'd sought all along.

Pushing herself on, Terri staggered along the dark corridor, eyes now easily adjusted to the lack of light – so much so she thought she must be imagining it when she saw a soft greyish glow spill out onto the floor ahead. Breathing a literal sigh of relief, she hurried forward and found the bottom of the curved staircase, leaning for a moment against its elaborate bannister and staring out of the giant windows into the moonlit silver-tinged woodland.

She used her good leg to lead the way up the stairs in a disjointed, uneven climb. By the time she crawled up to the very top landing, she could feel the agony from her ankle grit into her stomach. Combined with her pounding head, exhaustion and cloudy mind, Terri wanted nothing more than for this to be over.

With one final draw of determination, she limped on toward the living room.

Thirty-One

Audrey
Thursday

Audrey was outside at the same table she'd once sat at while watching men perform military drills across her beloved home. Dusk had long since fallen across the hills, but Audrey had no appetite for food, and she had not taken Terri dinner; the girl would probably still be unconscious for a little while yet. Audrey was undoubtedly distracted; she could not quite recall the dosage she'd administered into the glass of water. Perhaps Terri was already awake down there, stomach churning with hunger. Audrey shook her head; Terri could wait a little longer. She gazed out at Mama's memorial, cast pale blue in the late summer night, and felt her beside her.

'You're taking care of her well, *mi amor*,' she said kindly. 'Just like Daddy did for me.'

Audrey frowned at that, a tight swallow suddenly constricting her throat. She turned toward her, but Mama had gone. Why would Mama have said a thing like that?

1937

The gates to the Lloyd Estate were pushed open by Carl, while Audrey waited in the back seat. She gazed up at the

223

dogwood-shaded driveway that would lead her home after all this time. But would it really be her home without her mother or her father?

Audrey had been called into Dr Schofield's office just after lunch, green pills in her bloodstream, not yet having taken effect.

'I'm so sorry to be the one to tell you this, Miss Lloyd,' he said, his thick, dark moustache trembling a little as he did so. 'But I'm afraid we've had word from a Mrs Hackton? Your father's secretary I believe.'

'What does she want?' Audrey had snapped, already disinterested.

'Well, I'm afraid it's your father. He's dead.'

Audrey didn't hear the rest of the doctor's sympathies. Her old companion, grief, had taken hold of her, slipping into every crevice of her being. She felt the dizzy feeling of falling wildly that she remembered so clearly from when she'd lost Mama. Through her fug of shock and the green pills now surging through her veins, Audrey only vaguely took note as Dr Schofield continued speaking.

'The good news is that it seems there is a fund available of immediate capital in order to continue your treatment here, uninterrupted.' Audrey did not have the energy to take in this supposed good news – the thought of her life bound to that place now an absolute certainty, without even Daddy to visit. 'His funeral is next week, and it has been agreed that, subject to certain behavioural assessments over the intervening days, you will be given temporary discharge into the care of Mrs Hackton so that you may attend. Now this is on the understanding Mrs Hackton has of your condition, and the assurance that you will continue on your course of medication for the three days you are absent from our care.'

Audrey had nodded vaguely, and Dr Schofield had arranged for her temporary discharge form. Before she'd even fully begun to reconcile with what had happened, Carl had come to pick her up and Audrey's back finally faced the whitewashed villa prison that had been her home for three long years.

But Daddy was dead. Audrey realised as they pulled up the winding driveway that she didn't even know how he'd died.

When they reached the house, Carl opened her door, before fetching her bags from the trunk and placing them on the top terracotta step. Audrey had packed hardly anything when Carl had first driven into the desert, but as time had gone on, she'd asked for Daddy to bring or send her some of her favourite outfits, the decision to drape herself in beauty something she could at least control. The rose bushes next to the door bloomed with heavy flowers, ranging in colour from soft flesh to deep blood. Her mother had enjoyed tending to her roses for the brief time she'd lived at the house, and Arnold had considered it a tribute to Estella's memory to keep them alive.

'Is that everything, Miss Lloyd?' Carl asked.

She blinked away from the rose bush. 'Hmm? Oh yes, thank you, that will be all.' She fished a dollar bill that had been languishing in her purse for several long years and handed it over, which he accepted with a grateful bow of the head before returning to the car. Just before he climbed inside, he smiled at her sadly.

'It's good to see you back at the house, Miss Lloyd.' Audrey thought she saw him blink away a tear. 'Place hasn't been the same without you.'

Audrey remembered her father sharing a similar senti-ment with her on one thick desert night.

'Thank you, Carl,' she replied softly.

The wide marbled corridor she'd come so used to signalling home gave her the shaded chill it was designed to. The car ride had been hot and stuffy, and her silk blouse was patchy with unsightly damp stains, her dark green skirt sticking uncomfortably to the back of her legs. But as Audrey had dressed in the outfit in her small desert bedroom, Mama had smiled her approval from the corner. The heels of her shoes clipped down the corridor, but as she walked into the bright, sunlit space of the lounge, she realised the place was deserted. There were no sounds of the cook in the kitchen, no bustling housekeepers carrying piles of freshly folded linen. There was only Mrs Hackton, who stood up stiffly from her seat on the couch.

'Where is everyone?'

Mrs Hackton took a preparative breath. 'I sent them home for the time being. They are…' She paused, searching for her words. '…quite distressed.'

'Distressed?'

'I think you should sit down, Audrey.'

'This is my house,' Audrey snapped. 'Don't tell me what to do.'

Mrs Hackton's face softened, her jaw slackened, and her lips pressed together in sympathy.

'Of course,' Mrs Hackton relented. 'But we need to speak, and I think you would like to be seated for it.'

'What happened to Daddy?' Audrey asked.

'That is what I would like to speak to you about.'

'You never told them.'

'I thought it might be best to do it in person. I'm…' She stopped to swallow thickly, and Audrey knew she didn't mean the words she said next. 'I'm glad you've finally come home.'

Audrey narrowed her eyes. 'What happened to Daddy?'

Mrs Hackton took a deep breath and Audrey noticed her hands were trembling where they were clasped around each other in front of her stomach. The woman exhaled slowly and then sat back down on the sofa and reached forward for a glass of clear liquid, which she gulped before scrunching her face up.

'Your father has been…' She paused again, and Audrey was infuriated. Why was this woman struggling to get her words out so? Normally you couldn't shut her up. 'He hasn't been well. These last few months.'

Audrey narrowed her eyes again. 'He hasn't mentioned that.'

'Well, no, I imagine he wouldn't. I'm not sure he realised quite how unwell he was.'

'Ridiculous,' Audrey breathed. 'How can a person not realise how unwell they are?'

'The mind tries to protect itself.'

Audrey shook her head and walked toward the gold drinks trolley. The bottle of gin was out of place and the top barely screwed back on. Audrey bent low to fetch a martini glass and mixed herself a proper cocktail. For her first drink in three years, she wouldn't be joining Mrs Hackton in gulping neat liquor with shaking hands and pulling faces after it. Mrs Hackton remained quiet while Audrey worked, and only when Audrey turned around, dropping an olive from between her thumb and forefinger into the viscous liquid, did Mrs Hackton start to speak again.

'The mind tries to protect itself,' she repeated. 'He would claim he was fine, nothing to worry about – but I knew. I could see it.'

'So you're a doctor now, are you?'

'Audrey, sit down.' Mrs Hackton could never help herself; commands were second nature to her.

Audrey remained standing and took a deliberate sip of her drink.

Mrs Hackton watched her closely, an expression on her face Audrey couldn't quite read.

'I tried with you,' Mrs Hackton said after a moment. 'I really did. With your mother gone, I knew your father would fail you in so many ways.'

'Daddy never failed me,' Audrey snapped.

'Not in ways you would recognise, no. But you've always been an – odd – girl.'

'Odd to you I take as the highest compliment.'

'I'm sure you do. Audrey, I know you've never liked me – I tried to help but I could never understand you. It made it difficult.' She tilted her head to one side. 'And to be frank I never much cared for you either. A precocious child and an even more difficult adult. I learned many years ago that Arnold handled you in the best way he knew how.'

'What happened to my father?' Audrey asked the question for a third time, each word landing in the room like a boulder.

Mrs Hackton took another gulp of gin. 'He wasn't well.'

'I don't believe you.'

'His *mind* wasn't well.'

This stopped Audrey's drink midway to her lips. 'His *mind*?'

'He has been struggling lately, Audrey. Brightest light in the days, but I heard his blackness at night. The wails and shouts, the self-mutilation.'

'Self-mutilation?' Audrey spluttered.

'He would scratch sores into his forearms,' Mrs Hackton said. 'He would sit at his desk and scratch and scratch, until his nails were filled with skin and blood ran down his arms.'

Audrey felt sick. 'I don't believe you.' She refused to let her eyes drift down to her own forearms where, underneath her layer of silk, she knew there were similar scars. Mrs Hackton knew it too.

'You don't need to,' she replied simply. 'But I was there, and I tended to him. I had to dismiss the evening staff, so disturbed they were by his night-time terrors. For the last four months *I* have barely spent a night away from this house.'

Something fluttered awake in Audrey. 'Four months ago? That was when I alerted North to your illicit little payments.' A white-hot fury threaded through her veins, and she advanced toward the old assistant. 'What did you do? Refuse to leave so you could keep control over him? Demand he kept cutting you those checks? You probably put something in his food to weaken him.'

Mrs Hackton shook her head softly. 'I understand why you need someone to blame. When my Eddie died, I was driven to mania because I would never know the name of the man who'd put that bullet in his lung.' She breathed out softly. 'But even if I had known there would be nothing to do. He was probably just a lad, following orders the way Eddie had. And how many grieving widows were looking for Eddie's identity because of the bullets he'd put in their husbands?'

'What are you talking about?' Audrey snapped.

'Sometimes blame doesn't land where you think it should.'

'Don't try to distract me. I'll get a post-mortem on Daddy. I'll prove you were drugging him. I'll put you in prison.'

'Oh, Audrey.' Mrs Hackton shook her head softly. 'There'll be no post-mortem.'

'You might have disguised it as a heart attack or a stroke, but I'll pay the best damned people—'

'Audrey, please listen to me.' Mrs Hackton got to her feet and paced toward Audrey, who was now moving from foot to foot, agitation sloshing her drink from her glass. Audrey hadn't realised she was crying, sobbing, in fact, with great rattling breaths, until she tried to take a gulp of her drink, but the hard, sharp liquor was mixed with the salt of tears.

'Audrey, Audrey.' Mrs Hackton placed her hands on Audrey's shoulders, holding her still.

'Don't touch me!' Audrey whirled away and, with her back to Mrs Hackton, bent double over a chair and groaned loudly, allowing her glass to drop onto the floor.

'Audrey, please!' Mrs Hackton raised her voice to a loud shout. 'Calm down!'

'You're a thief!' Audrey screamed, and when Mrs Hackton replied her voice was as loud and terrifying as Audrey's own.

'I am no such thing!'

It shocked them both into a heavy silence, only Audrey's racking breaths filling the cavernous living space. Eventually she pulled herself upright and turned to face Mrs Hackton, knowing that her cheeks must surely be painted black from her mascara.

'What happened to Daddy?' she asked for the fourth time. And this time she got her answer.

Mrs Hackton watched her for a moment before tears spilled from her eyes as she opened her mouth and said, 'He put a shotgun in his mouth.'

Audrey felt like she'd been whipped. Her oldest wounds split open at once and agony gushed through her. She saw Mama and Irina flicker at the corners of her vision, but she pushed them away. Mrs Hackton was all she needed to concentrate on now.

'You put that shotgun in his mouth,' Audrey said with a surprisingly steady voice that took more energy than she thought she had left.

Mrs Hackton swallowed thickly and took a moment to compose herself, straightening her shoulders and firming up her stance. She looked Audrey dead in the eye and inhaled.

'Audrey, I know we have had our troubles, but you must recognise I was a loyal and devoted employee of your father for twenty years. Dare I say it, a *friend*.' Audrey scoffed but Mrs Hackton ploughed on. 'I was young when I came to work here – you won't realise because you were even younger yourself – but I was just twenty years old, and already a widow.' She gave a shake of her head.

'And yet you still drove him to suicide – a fine way to show your thanks.'

Mrs Hackton's top lip quivered almost imperceptibly into a snarl. 'Actually,' she said, her voice terrifyingly steady while her eyes blazed, 'I didn't drive your father to suicide.' There was a heavy beat before she finished the sentence. 'You did.'

Audrey stepped back, winded. The *cheek* of this woman, to accuse her of such a thing. But before Audrey could gather herself enough to speak, Mrs Hackton bent to the coffee table by her knees and picked up a folded

231

sheet of paper Audrey recognised from Daddy's correspondence pad.

'Here.' She held it out. 'I think you should read this.'

Instinct told Audrey that on that single sheet of correspondence paper was a final message from her father that she did not want to read. She took a step back, a determined ignorance flexing the muscles in her jaw. Mrs Hackton gestured with it again and Audrey averted her gaze, so it landed on the polished golden statue of Daddy's first Oscar. From the corner of her eye, she saw Mrs Hackton shake her head sadly and put the paper back on the table.

'One day you'll want to read it. And when you do, you'll want to speak to me.'

'Another reason never to then.'

Mrs Hackton blew out a small sigh. 'If you don't want to understand from Arnold himself, then let me just say this. The money your father was paying me, that you believe I stole from him. It was because he felt he owed me a debt.' She cocked her head and reconsidered her word choice. 'No, he *did* owe me a debt. He owed me for many things, and let me tell you I deserved that money.' She leaned forward and took another sip of her gin, but it wasn't quite the desperate grab of before. 'I never wanted to tell you this about your father.' Her eyes met Audrey's. 'Remember that. But I will not be accused of being responsible for Arnold's death. Especially when that accusation lies far more at your feet than mine.'

'I didn't even see Daddy before he died – I haven't been here for three years! How can you suggest—'

Mrs Hackton raised a palm and Audrey found herself falling to silence. Despite everything, Audrey wanted to know. She wanted to hear what the old crone would say.

'Those payments you were so adamant on investigating – in discovering them you awakened your father's guilt. He carried so much guilt, Audrey – so much guilt from *your* mistake. Your treacherous, stupid, egotistical mistake. Forced down and never tended to' – she paused and inhaled – 'so that when he had his own guilt to pile on top – well, he could barely cling on. The checks to me were one way of him dealing with that. They were cut silently, and I took my payment with no further discussion. But you kicked up *such* a fuss about them.' She rolled her eyes theatrically. 'And your poor father's mind couldn't take it. That's when the night-time terrors started. He would send himself crazy in that study of his, trying to punish himself as best he could. Only I could give him the reassurance he needed, because only *I* knew the truth.'

'What truth? What could he possibly be so ashamed of *me* finding out? I was his *daughter* – we were closer than he ever was to his *staff*.' She spat the final word as an insult, but it failed to land. Mrs Hackton got up from the couch and paced in an arc around the room.

'Oh, Audrey.' Mrs Hackton shook her head sadly. 'The truth about everything. The truth about your mother.'

Thirty-Two

Don
Friday

'That's fresh blood,' Don told Sinclair, having scrambled hurriedly back up to the clearing, his suit pants ripped from where he'd rushed through the bushes, his forearms covered with tiny nicks. 'Well, no more than a day old.'

'That could kill someone,' Officer Sinclair said with a nod toward it. 'A blow with a heavy object like that.'

'It could,' Don agreed, trying to mentally match this weapon with the body that had been shipped off earlier that morning. They didn't have the post-mortem results yet, which he now expected to show that the death had been caused by an intentional blow. Did Theresa Nicholls murder Audrey Lloyd and pose her body at the bottom of the stairs? But then Theresa herself had taken a pretty hefty blow to the back of her own head. Don surveyed the Oscar in his hand again, trying to imagine both scenarios. It was feasible that if the weapon was wielded by the old woman, it would not be a fatal blow, and if it was wielded by the younger it surely would be.

He considered for a moment before deciding. It was time to go back to Theresa Nicholls and press for the answers she'd failed to give earlier.

'Right,' Don said with a nod, 'come with me, Officer Sinclair.' He fished an evidence bag from inside his suit jacket pocket and secured the Oscar inside it as they moved around the car, where the skeleton was now being carefully removed from the back seat. He led Sinclair back up to the house and to his car parked outside. He unlocked it and bent across the centre console to the bagged discharge form on his passenger seat and handed it to her along with the Oscar.

'Take these back to the station and get them processed and checked in. I want prints from that statue, if there are any, and then I need you to call the coroner's office and do whatever you can to get the results from the body found this morning. If they've not got to it yet, make them.' The young officer looked wide-eyed but determined at his instructions, giving a jerked nod of confirmation. 'And then,' Don continued, 'I need a check on an Annabel Hackton. Spelled as it sounds. If she has a record, last known whereabouts, that sort of thing. If there's nothing on our end,' he added, thinking of the dusty archive basement at the station, 'then get down to City Hall. I want birth certificate, wedding, death – anything you can find. And especially,' he began climbing into the car, 'let me know pronto if you find *any* relationship between her and Theresa Nicholls.'

'OK.' Sinclair nodded again, obviously distracted as she tried to take in all of her instructions. 'Who is Annabel Hackton?'

Don sat down in the driver's seat and pulled his seat belt across him. 'She might be nothing to do with this. But that car down there is hers, and her name is on one of those pieces of evidence in your hand.' Sinclair looked down at the plastic bags in her hand and nodded in understanding. 'And years ago, I investigated a report of her disappearance.' Sinclair's eyebrows went up and Don saw her instinctively glance over her shoulder in the direction of the car and skeleton. 'Might not be her in there,' he said steadily, drawing the young officer's attention back to him. 'The report never went anywhere. But keep me updated if you find anything.' He gestured down to his car phone. 'One of the guys on my floor will give you the number. But I'll call to check in, too.'

'OK, Detective,' she said again, and turned back in the direction of the clearing where her squad car was presumably parked.

Don put his car into reverse and performed a painful several-point turn to extract himself from the turning circle. He raced dangerously down the winding driveway and saw a car behind him, seemingly appearing out of the wilderness all around. That must have been the track from the driveway to the clearing that had allowed the full team to assemble with ease. Sinclair was in his rearview mirror, watching out of her windscreen, that same determined frown she'd worn while taking her instructions still furrowed between her brows.

At the bottom of the driveway, they both turned onto the main road, but soon separated as she turned off toward the station, Don toward the hospital.

While he drove, his mind wandered, trying to tie past to present, to build a case the DA would want to see. Did that include Don's rookie notes from decades ago? Don knew the answer was no, but his mind wandered to them all the same. To the person who'd told him to look for Annabel Hackton. To the one other avenue of identification for the body in the car.

It was the end of the Forties. He'd been out of the academy less than a year and was covering a shift for a desk sergeant at the Beverly Hills Police Department. It had been a quiet afternoon, not much in the way of interest for the young Don who was so hungry for action. Don had been flipping through the paper, sipping on a mug of coffee and whiling away the hours until the night shift when he would be back on patrol. He'd only agreed to go on the desk as a favour he'd hoped would start building him credit for his new career.

There had been a commotion when a man had stumbled in. He looked at least seventy, perhaps older, but with dark wavy hair that seemed to be putting up a good fight against the few strands of grey. He was well turned out in a double-breasted navy suit that fit so well Don recognised it must have been tailored. The tie at his throat shone like real silk. There was a trickle of blood down the side of his face, and one hand was cupped over the small wound above his temple.

'Oh, sir!' Don exclaimed, straightening up from where he'd been leaning on the desk. 'Are you alright?'

'*Nyet!*' The man shrieked, distress pinching at his features. He blinked in surprise at his own hysteria, and then took a moment to visibly calm himself. When he spoke again it was in English, with an indecipherable accent Don could have placed as equal parts German, Russian and American.

'What's happened?' Don asked, coming around the side of the desk and gesturing for the man to sit down on the wooden bench that lined one wall. He picked up a pen and pad and joined the man on the bench.

'My daughter,' he gasped, 'she is being held hostage. I was attacked.' Don had felt a little leap of excitement at the action. 'I need to speak to a detective.'

'I'll get you a detective,' Don reassured him. 'But first I need to know what happened.' The man looked visibly annoyed and strained his neck to look behind Don at the double doors that led into the station. 'Can you start by telling me your name?' Don had his pen ready, hovering over his pad.

The man gave a strained roll of his eyes but answered. 'Lev Popov. And my daughter is being held against her will.'

'Right, OK,' Don said slowly. 'And how are you spelling that?'

He thought the man might hit him, but he did diligently spell out his name.

'And your daughter – did you say your daughter?' Don looked up to double check, and Mr Popov gave a terse nod. 'And what's her name?' He'd been taught to get the details first, something which Don later recognised he'd taken far too seriously in his first over-enthusiastic years. Soon he'd learned which details were less important to get immediately, and when to dive into the meat of a case.

'Irina Popova,' Mr Popov said. 'And she's being held at Lloyd House! Up on the hill!' He had grown more irate with Don's methodical questioning, and flung out the hand that had been cradling his wounded head to gesture in a vague direction. Don pulled a face at the gaping cut, the skin split to show pressed white flesh beneath it. 'You!' Popov got to his feet and ran toward Detective Brooker, who was just coming out of the double doors reading a file. 'Are you a detective?'

Brooker blinked in surprise. 'I am.' His eyes went to the cut, and then to Don, who was still sitting down. 'What's going on?'

'My daughter!' Popov wailed. 'She's being held hostage.'

'Now then, Mr—' Brooker looked between Popov and Don, searching for his last name.

'Popov,' Don supplied, getting up to join them on his feet. He watched as Brooker's face responded to the name, a dark frown descending between his brows.

'Popov?' Brooker asked Don, as if to double check. Don nodded. 'And where do you think your daughter is?'

'Lloyd House!' Lev flung out his arm again.

'The movie producer's home?'

'He's dead,' Don supplied helpfully.

'It's his daughter, his daughter is holding—' Popov tried to explain, but was getting caught up in his own breath and his words were stumbling over one another.

Brooker eyed him suspiciously before turning to Don. 'Officer Vernon, isn't it?' Don nodded in confirmation. 'Can you take Mr Popov here' – as he said the name it sounded like a struggle to get it out – 'to an interview room.' He flashed a glance toward Mr Popov. 'I have a quick call to make, and then I'll meet you outside it.'

Don was surprised; this wasn't the usual course of events for taking a report of a kidnapping. But he did as he was told and led the apparently equally perplexed Mr Popov to a vacant interview room. As he closed the door Popov turned and stopped him.

'Your colleague doesn't believe me,' he said, having managed to calm himself on the way. 'I was a lawyer for many years; I know when someone thinks me a liar. But

239

find Annabel Hackton – she'll back me up. She knows what his daughter is like.'

Don nodded and closed the door on Mr Popov while he waited outside for Brooker to come hurrying back down the corridor.

'What else did he tell you?' Brooker said urgently.

'That his daughter was being held captive up at the Lloyd Estate,' Don rattled off. 'And to find someone called Annabel Hackton who can back him up.'

'Doesn't sound right, that, does it?' Brooker said with narrowed eyes.

'Well, I know Arnold Lloyd died about ten years ago. I've no idea who lives there now, but' – Don jerked his head to the closed door behind him – 'well, he said it was Lloyd's daughter.'

'And why would the heiress to a movie fortune want to kidnap a Russian girl?'

Don shook his head. 'I don't know.'

'Exactly,' Brooker said with some satisfaction. 'It's a ploy. I don't know what it is he's playing at, but we've been hearing rumours of a Soviet cell in LA for the last year. The Feds want us to keep an eye on it, report anything unusual.'

'The Feds?' Don had breathed. The Feds and the Lloyds. This case was certainly going to make the journal he'd started keeping.

'I've just called them,' Brooker confirmed with a nod. 'I'll take it from here with him. You go back and finish your desk shift.'

It was something like youthful ambition that had prompted Don to push.

'Are you sure you don't want me to go check it out?' he asked, jerking his head back toward the closed door of the interrogation room that held Lev Popov.

Brooker frowned. 'What for?'

Don thought. 'Due diligence. So you can tell the Feds we're absolutely sure.'

Brooker's eyes drifted from one side to the other while he contemplated this. 'No, let them handle it. They won't want us stepping on their toes.'

But Don hadn't quite been able to get Lev Popov's pleas out of his memory and, on the way home, in his parents' borrowed Chevrolet, he'd turned off at the junction he needed and headed up a winding hill toward two half-hidden wrought iron-gates, framed by a canopy of overgrown branches. He'd got home, Audrey Lloyd's laugh still ringing unnervingly in his ears, and written up his journal. A few days later there was an article in the *LA Times*.

> A Russian man has caused a furore, stumbling into the Beverly Hills Police Department with a significant head wound and outlandish claims. The man caused quite a stir when he burst into the police department based at City Hall on Thursday and demanded to speak to a detective about a property in the hills once owned by illustrious film producer the late Arnold Lloyd.
>
> 'He was quite clearly distressed,' a spokesperson for the police department has said, 'with an obvious head wound. He made an allegation about a property in the hills, an allegation that has been dismissed.'

Concerns have arisen about the man's heritage, with the curious case striking rumours of a Soviet intelligence cell right here in our very city.

'We do not know what pressures are put on intelligence officers of the Soviet Union and what effect that pressure might have on their psyche,' says political commentator and city councilman Carter Ellroy. 'This incident has proved quite concerning. The man in question has been detained and we are sparing no expense to investigate any leads that might help protect our great nation.'

After the recent implication of Alger Hiss in un–American activities we cannot be too careful with the threat of traitors within our borders. We remind our readers that our tip line is always open with any information.

Neither Brooker nor anyone else in the department had been willing to engage Don further on any discussion of the matter, and eventually, after an evening lost to Annabel Hackton's busybody neighbour, Don had moved on.

But now, as he drove toward the hospital, Don considered all he knew. Two women apparently missing, connected to Lloyd House. One of them almost certainly the skeleton found by accident in the back seat of a stuffy car. And now, thirty-five years later, another woman who might only have survived through a fatal act of self-defence – or revenge.

Thirty-Three

Audrey
Thursday

The scent of the dogwoods hung on the air, mingling with the faint gasoline undertones of the smog from the city below. The sun was set by now, but still daylight reigned in that way it clung on in summer, the moon forced to glow against a still-light sky. The white shard of Mama's memorial pierced the horizon like a sabre and Audrey gave a small sigh as she gazed out at her parents' final resting place.

Audrey had not had to worry about how to insert Daddy into the ground next to Mama. His body, with half of his head so wretchedly blown off, was in no state to lie in eternity next to Estella's pristine corpse. She would not have wanted to see her husband so afflicted. Her father's funeral service – the one Audrey had been granted temporary discharge in order to attend – was a cremation, attended by old colleagues who offered what seemed like uncertain condolences. Mrs Hackton had attended in silence, leaving after the velvet curtains had closed on Arnold's coffin.

After it was done Audrey had clutched his heavy marble urn while she descended the steep steps toward Mama's grave. It had been cold against her body and the

243

slight breeze in the air had whipped her long black funeral dress around her legs. Her hat had remained in place, though, pinned to her dark hair, its black net draped across her eyes. She upturned the urn and trod a circle around the small lawn that held the obelisk, pouring her father's ashes onto the ground to reunite with his one true love. No matter what Mrs Hackton had told her so poisonously three days earlier when Audrey had returned from the desert.

'Estella had an affair,' Mrs Hackton had said. 'That was why you left Florida. That was why he built this prison for her, all the way on the other side of the country. Your mother wasn't ill. Not in the way everyone believed. She was sorrowful, that much was true. Melancholy and a touch of hysteria, as we used to call it back then. She cried to me a couple of times – she missed her home in Florida, she missed her lover and she felt terribly guilty for betraying Arnold. Love is a complicated thing like that. Arnold couldn't bear to see his precious Estella miserable and lacklustre, and so he took it into his own hands to fix her. Cocaine and laudanum mainly – and, oh, the improvement in her moods at once! But then they'd be followed by even worse bouts of melancholy and depression. And so he had to keep her at the right level at all times – a delicate balance. He had his notebook where he'd keep track of all his prescriptions. He'd note down the times and dosages and her responses to them.' She'd given a small shudder. 'I thought at the time it was akin to human experimentation, but what could I do?

'He paid me well and I was a young widow with nowhere else to go; I certainly had no place to keep him from doing whatever he pleased with his own wife. I did grow fond of him, in the end. I understood he wasn't a well man. Didn't quite know how to show his love properly. When she caught the Spanish flu Arnold was beside himself. Now she had physical ailments to add to her mental ones, and the household staff all believed their beloved Estella was so weak already, on the verge of death. But only I was permitted in her room. Only I spoke to the doctors and took their prescriptions to treat her cough, nodding intently at their detailed descriptions of dosage, knowing full well I would be given alternative instructions once they were gone. By that time, you see, Arnold believed he knew all there was to know about the world of pharmaceuticals and how to help his poor Estella. When Arnold realised I was following not his instructions, but the doctors', he took it into his own hands. Quite surprised the doctors were when Estella took such a turn for the worse. But still Arnold continued to administer his own treatments.' She gave Audrey a small shake of the head and raised her arms out to her sides. 'And as we both know – your father was no doctor.' She dropped her gaze out of Audrey's sightline for a heartbeat, her eyes returning to Audrey's with something like pity.

'It took all of my powers of persuasion,' she continued, 'to convince him to allow *you* to be taken care of by Dr Schofield. It was months before I could make him see his treatments for you were working about as well as they had for Estella. But eventually he saw that I was right.'

Audrey almost gagged. 'Whatever Daddy gave me would only have been for my own good,' she said, almost believing the words, begging the ghost of her father for it to be true. Then she remembered that first year at Desert Palm, the shock injections, the constant threats of lobotomy. Anger sizzled through her. 'They tortured me at that place and *you*' – she advanced with one finger outstretched, spitting the word – 'you sent me there.'

'Better to be tortured by doctors than at the hands of your own father.'

Audrey had thrown her out – she would not go back to that place. And she'd known Mrs Hackton wouldn't make her. As she had left, she'd given Audrey a look of such pity that Audrey knew she'd been telling the truth.

After Mrs Hackton had gone, the first thing Audrey did was pick up the piece of paper from the coffee table, barely touching it between her thumb and forefinger, and taken it down to the safest place in the house. Some instinct inside told her to burn it, but she couldn't quite bring herself to – the last record of Daddy's thoughts. She knew, though, that she would never read it. What if Mrs Hackton was right? What if Daddy blamed her?

'I never would, my darling,' Daddy said from next to her, his face alight.

Audrey smiled warmly and shut the bedside drawer firmly. There was no need to ever open it again.

She thought now of her own patients. Of the women who had taken up residence in the safest room in her grand house. The people Audrey had tried to help. Sometimes, if she were truly honest with herself, she feared what she had learned at her father's hand. *No*, she corrected herself. She would not let Mrs Hackton give her cause to doubt her own brilliant mind. Daddy had done all he could to help Mama, and Audrey had only done the same.

Annabel Hackton, that poisonous witch. Audrey found the past coming for her again, the very last time Mrs Hackton had come to visit the old house on the hill. This memory sent a tremor through her. It soothed her. It energised her.

She always reached for it in her weakest moments.

1948

It had been eleven years since Audrey had returned from the desert. She was in Daddy's old office, where she spent a lot of her time those days, reading her math book and setting puzzles and equations for herself to break. She chatted to Daddy and Mama while she worked, telling them how the nice Christmas ham Mrs Doyle had sent every year for the last decade had failed to arrive that year.

'I think she might be with you now,' Audrey said quietly, getting to her feet off Daddy's old chair, and standing to gaze through the office window, down at the grove of trees she had once helped Mrs Doyle harvest the fruit from. No one had tended to them in ten years and most of the fruit trees had died, their roots strangled by brambles and bracken. A few had grown tall and unruly, unpruned and untended as their fruit dropped and rotted, their overgrown branches cracking and breaking in the occasional winter storms. Audrey smiled. She liked them better this way.

Audrey had ventured into town every now and again during her first years back at the house, calling Carl for his services to take her to the store or out to dinner to eat a lonely meal in lavish surroundings. But then war had come again, and Carl's son had gone off to fight, while Carl himself retired, handing over the card of a younger colleague who he said would be happy to take on the job. But Audrey didn't much fancy a stranger coming up to her house whenever she wanted to go anywhere. No, without Carl, she would just stay put.

She arranged for all her deliveries to come weekly, although her tea was temporarily halted when London failed to prioritise Fortnum and Mason hamper exports while under siege during the Blitz. It was the Nazis after all, Audrey had learned, before turning off the radio and vowing not to listen to the news again. Sickly guilt threatened to bind her if she didn't push it down into the very fractures of her mind. She only found out about peace from the grocery delivery boy slipping a newspaper declaring *Victory!* in bold black letters into her weekly food supplies.

Audrey dragged herself away from the window over-looking the wilding fruit grove, and took herself out of the office to make some tea. She was just passing through the living room on the way to the kitchen when she heard a car pull up at the top of the driveway. She stopped and frowned, turning to stare at the entrance hall where an echoed knock reverberated from the front door. She stalled in indecision, staring down toward the prospect of real company for the first time in six years. It wasn't conscious thought that moved her to open the door, no spark of desire for conversation, just some inbuilt response to answer a door when someone knocked on it. She regretted it almost as soon as the bright daylight spilled into the hallway, the person on the other side tense but smiling – awkward and forced.

'I don't want to see you,' Audrey said, reaching to close the door again.

'Audrey, please,' Mrs Hackton said with a stiff smile, stretching out her thin lips.

The last eleven years had aged her terribly, and wrinkles cut deeper than ever into her face. But Audrey had to admit the woman did at least seem well maintained.

Her hair was nicely coloured and styled, and she wore a muted skirt suit that looked well-tailored. In her hands was an ugly plastic jug.

'I brought you a present,' Mrs Hackton said, holding it out in front of her.

Audrey frowned. 'What is it?'

'It's Tupperware!' Mrs Hackton responded brightly. 'It's my new business. Well, not *my* business, of course' – she gave a strange giggle and her words tumbled over themselves – 'but I discovered them earlier this year and have been selling them ever since. They really are wonderful, everything you need for an organised pantry!' Audrey was startled at this flippant sales pitch and watched her, perplexed. 'This is from our new range. It's perfect for serving cold drinks in the summer; you can keep it right in your fridge. And not so heavy as a glass one...' Her words trailed off then, her sentence juddering to a staccato halt.

'Why are you here?'

'Can I come in? It's been a long time.'

'No,' Audrey said determinedly. 'No, you can't.'

Mrs Hackton seemed to consider her response for a moment before deciding she wasn't going to listen to it. 'I'll be just a moment,' she insisted, stepping toward the door. And before Audrey could stop her Mrs Hackton was in the house, starting down the entrance hall. Audrey blinked at her retreating back and glanced outside again, seeing an ugly red Chevrolet parked inelegantly across the very middle of the turning circle.

Audrey hurried to catch up to Mrs Hackton and felt a small pinch of satisfaction at the woman's wide eyes as she took in the state of the place. The racoons had recently started braving it inside at night, nibbling on the crusts of bread left out on plates for days on end. One particularly lucky beast had devoured an entire plate of cured meats, the edges starting to curl and stiffen in the air. At least someone had enjoyed it, Audrey had thought, watching the little creature from the other side of the room as it picked up piece by piece in its little paws. Mrs Hackton couldn't avoid an obvious wince as she passed by a mound of faeces, black and dry, with metallic green bluebottles feasting away. But she seemed determined not to cause an argument and Audrey watched as she almost visibly stuffed her complaints back down inside and smiled.

'Didn't keep on any of the old staff, then?' she asked, coming to a stop in the living room.

'I don't like to be disturbed.'

Mrs Hackton nodded twice silently and gazed around the room again.

'Why are you here?' Audrey asked again.

Mrs Hackton paused with a thoughtful expression before speaking.

'Audrey, the last time I was here I told you some terrible things about your father. Some terrible *truths* about your father. But I also told you that I stood by him – I was loyal until the very end.' She nodded. 'He took good care of me while he was alive, and I've done well to support myself since his death. However, I now have an opportunity' – she nodded down to the jug again – 'an opportunity to really make something for myself. I've come to ask you – Arnold's daughter – for a small business investment.'

'Money?' Audrey spat. 'You think I'm going to give you *money* so you can sell plastic jugs?'

'It really is a very good business model, and an opportunity has arisen if I could—'

'I don't *care* what opportunity has arisen for you – you thieving old crone!'

'Audrey, please,' Mrs Hackton said, struggling to keep her anger at bay.

'Get out!' Audrey screamed, her arm flying out toward the door. 'Get out and don't come back! You drove my father to suicide, *you* killed him, and now you come here to extort money from his estate?!'

Mrs Hackton closed her eyes for a moment, as if readying herself. 'Audrey, I know how *troubled* you are.' She said the word with not an ounce of care. 'I know you've had some difficult times in your life. I won't lie and say they weren't designed at your very own hand, but still, I watched you struggle. I hoped I could come here today – many years later – and speak with a reasonable woman. A woman who might understand that she has so much, while I have so little. A woman who might see fit to do the right thing herself.' She stopped and gave a bitter, shallow laugh. 'But of course, I was far too optimistic.' She eyed Audrey then, a warning stare, as if giving her a moment to prepare herself.

'I never quite wanted it to come to this,' she said with an air of confession. 'I was happy with my savings. I could build a good life with them. I have never been a greedy woman, Audrey.' Audrey scoffed loudly but Mrs Hackton ignored her. 'No, I really haven't. But now, I have a chance to build something proper, and rather than pass it up I have decided to come here and claim only *part* of what is rightfully mine.' She stopped and nodded before correcting herself. 'What is rightfully Jeanie's.'

Audrey rolled her eyes. 'And who is Jeanie?'

'My daughter.' Mrs Hackton gave Audrey a hard look then, and Audrey knew the answer before she even spoke it. 'Your sister.'

Audrey felt a cold, hard fist pummel right into her stomach. The thought of Daddy and that woman sent disgust curling through her – the thought that Daddy could be with *anyone* other than his beautiful Estella. But, as Audrey gazed at Mrs Hackton's determined face, she knew it was the truth. In the more than three decades Audrey had had the displeasure to know Annabel Hackton, she had, at the very least, never known her to lie. Audrey had seen the payments for herself; an illegitimate child had always been the obvious explanation Audrey had not wanted to dwell on. But now it was confirmed.

Audrey froze, unable to work out what to do next. This child was a threat to everything. A threat to Audrey's life here – her home. Her home that Arnold had built for *them* – for her and Mama, not some illicit love child.

'After you had your *incident*,' Mrs Hackton said pointedly, 'and went to Desert Palm, Arnold and I grew close. He needed someone. He needed support and love and care and all the things his life lacked. It was short, but it was special. We knew each other so well it just felt natural, it felt right.' She spoke wistfully and romantically before her voice hardened. 'But I never quite understood the pressures that were on him. The guilt he carried – not just for what we were doing, but for you and your mother. He felt he'd failed everyone.' She nodded. 'And that was the end of it. The end of us, almost without a word. Until I discovered I was pregnant of course.' She gave a small shrug. 'But he took care of me, he took care of us both, financially speaking.'

Audrey felt sick and brought her hand to her chest to steady the retch that was working its way up her oesophagus.

'He never met her,' Mrs Hackton clarified, breaking for a moment as her mouth pulled into a grimace and she tipped her head upwards, dabbing underneath her eyes in a show of wiping away her sudden onset of tears. 'Refused. Said the whole thing was a betrayal to you. I'll never claim to agree with his decision, but I respected it. Until the day he died I respected it, and in the eleven years since I have not rested a dime on my daughter's Lloyd name.'

Silence thickened between them. Decisions and memories racing through Audrey's head. 'Until today,' Mrs Hackton said after several moments. 'Until it was necessary. I'm asking for a small amount. A fraction of what my daughter is due.'

Audrey stared at her, and then she gave her answer. 'No.'

Mrs Hackton frowned. 'No?' It took a moment for her to comprehend the simple, single-syllable word. 'No?!' she shrieked suddenly, a mania ripping through her. 'You little bitch! Your father would be ashamed of you – he'd be *horrified* at what you are. Reducing his house to squalor, his beautiful, beautiful house.' She looked around at the living room, incredulity and sadness seeping out of her. 'Refusing to help me even after *everything* I've done for that man! Everything I've done for you! The secrets I've kept, the lies I've told. You don't even understand the smallest fraction of what I'm due. Always protecting Audrey, precious disturbed Audrey!'

Audrey's face twisted into a scowl of pure hatred, but Mrs Hackton wasn't finished with her rant, her mouth slack, diatribes and lies flowing like mucky black oil, until suddenly—

—they stopped.

-

The sound of movement behind Audrey brought her back to the darkening evening terrace. She twisted in her seat and saw through the open doors of the kitchen the silhouette of a figure moving unevenly toward her from deep in the living room, one foot dragging behind them in an exaggerated limp. She could see a flurry of dark hair, and Audrey frowned with a smile.

'Reeny?' she asked. 'Have you come back again?'

But it was not Irina.

Thirty-Four

Terri
Thursday

'Reeny?' Terri heard a reedy, faraway voice call to her not just through the house, but through the decades. 'Have you come back again?'

The woman had clearly lost it, and Terri did not have time to be pulled into Audrey's mania. She had traversed this house, battered, drugged and broken, and now she was so close to the end. Her hand went back to her pocket and rubbed the thin old paper between her thumb and forefinger. She'd done it; she'd saved them. Determination took her across the threshold of the kitchen, Audrey's silhouette framed in eerie moonlight through the doors at the other side of the cavernous room.

Terri still didn't know what she was headed toward, what her plan for escape was. She still felt at Audrey's mercy, the blackness from the absence of the warm and happy laudanum seeping through her system, dragging the very centre of her being down like a whirlpool draining a dirty bath.

Instinct suddenly stopped her in her tracks, her mind taking a moment to catch up with what her body had done. She had heard something. Behind her. The shuffle of footsteps?

She twisted back toward the living room. The clutter she knew dominated the room in daylight now threw ominous shadowed figures across the space. She blinked into the dark, eyes adjusted to the gloom, but still unable to pick out details.

She thought she saw a crouched figure at the end of the sofa, almost turned to go back and approach them, when recognition clicked into place and she understood it was just the pile of boxes that contained stacks of books. There was no one there. There never had been – all the times she'd heard the creaks and spectres of this house. Just her and a delusional old woman, a feeble call toward her long-gone friend on the wind. Adrenaline surged suddenly through Terri, killing any visions of ghosts and figures – it was just the two of them, and Audrey had already won so much from Terri.

That thought stopped her again. So many people had won so much from Terri. Ethan perhaps most of all. And this time, when Ethan came to mind, it was that little bit harder to conjure the good times, the glint in his green eyes, the laugh that reverberated around the room. She ached inside, like her muscles used to after a hard-won track meet – but this ache was buried deeper. She realised now how exhausted she was from loving this man. Her hand went to feel the paper in her pocket again. She'd come this far – she could keep going. Keep going for the Ethan who had been easier to love. *But had that Ethan ever even existed?*

The taunt floated up unbidden and unexpected. She pushed it down and forcibly closed the gaping hole within that told her to retreat to the bedroom and beg Audrey for more drugs.

It was time for Terri to take control of this situation. To take back control of her life.

Thirty-Five

Don
Friday

Don arrived at the basement parking lot of Sacred Heart and realised he'd skipped lunch. The day had ticked by and with all the distractions, morning had turned to afternoon and Don felt the shallow growl of hunger in his belly. It had been a long time since a case had kept him this distracted. Somewhere around year ten on the force, he'd seen almost everything – there were no shocks left to behold on a case. And so there was always time, and appetite, for even just a quick bite.

As his hand was on the silver handle of the door, the car filled with a shrill, tinny sound. It took a moment for Don to realise it was the black handset in his centre console, flashing its orange light on and off as it rang. Don had only ever received two calls on this phone before, and one had been a test run from Jill inside the house when he'd first gotten it installed.

'Hello?' he answered.

'Detective Vernon? It's Officer Sinclair.'

'Have you got an update?'

'I've processed the evidence like you asked, and chased up results from the morgue – hoping to have an answer for you on that soon – but I have done the search on Annabel Hackton. I looked in the archives.'

'Yes?' Don sat up a bit straighter.

'There's just the missing person's report you mentioned from spring 1948,' Sinclair told him.

'Nothing else?'

'Not on our end. But I've been to follow up at City Hall like you asked – there's no connection between her and Theresa Nicholls. I called the East Coast and Theresa Nicholls checks out – born in Connecticut in '55, months after both parents and two brothers emigrated from Greece. Definitely no relation between them.'

'Alright, thank you, Sinclair. That's very helpful. Call me if you get anything else, and if you can't get me, call the department and leave a message. I'll check in with them when I can.'

He climbed out the car and took the elevator up to the ward, passing by the nurses' station without even stopping to say hello, stalking straight toward room 18. He burst in, questions ready on his lips, but was confronted by an empty bed. He frowned and spun around, seeing that the bed had been stripped, any evidence of its previous occupant erased.

'Rose,' he said, coming back down the corridor toward the nurses' station and calling to the woman in pink scrubs, who turned around with a file in her hand.

'Back so soon?' She greeted him with a familiar smile.

'Theresa Nicholls,' he said, jerking his head down the corridor. 'Room eighteen. She's gone.'

Rose gave a single nod. 'Discharged herself. Not long after you came by this morning, actually.'

Shit.

'Was she fit enough to?'

259

Rose gave a shrug. 'She had some bad sprains, on her fingers and ankle. But they seemed a few days old, had been strapped up and tended to. Freshest wound was to the back of her head, hell of a lump and a fair few stitches, but didn't seem to have any signs of concussion. Gave her the leaflet though and told her to come back in if she starts to feel dizzy or sick, but…' She held her arms out to one side. 'If a patient wants to discharge themselves, not much else I can do.'

Don nodded, taking it all in. 'Did she go home?'

'That's where she said she was going,' Rose said. 'Called a taxi and gave the address as some place in West Hollywood.'

'125 Slater Drive?' Don remembered.

'That's the one.'

'Alright.' He slapped his hand on the top of the desk in a farewell gesture. 'Thanks, Rose.'

'If it helps,' she said, stopping him as he turned back in the direction of the elevator. 'Urine tests came back after she'd already left.'

'Yeah?'

'She had morphine in her system. *High* levels.'

'An addict?'

Rose shook her head. 'Not for me to say. But there's usually a reason when patients discharge themselves after the police have been round.'

Don said thanks and goodbye and jogged as fast as his bulk would allow back to the elevator, his foot tapping agitatedly as it made its slow descent to the basement parking lot. He got back to his car and sped off, heading straight for West Hollywood.

Theresa Nicholls's street was nice and simple; each condo had its own short driveway next to a square of manicured front lawn with identikit mailboxes out front. *This street must have one hell of a housing association*, Don thought.

He walked up the porch steps and rapped his knuckles against the door, waiting the few slow minutes for the sound of a bolt to be drawn back and unlocked. The door pulled open a crack, Terri's sheepish face appearing in the narrow gap.

'Ms Nicholls?' Don greeted with her his friendliest smile. 'Detective Don Vernon – we met this morning?' He pretended to introduce himself again, as if his presence in her life had been so insignificant, she would surely have forgotten all about him by now.

'Yes,' she said, blinking an expression of greeting onto her previously bewildered features. 'Yes, of course. Hello. What – er…' She glanced briefly back over her shoulder. 'What can I do for you?'

'Well, I went to the hospital and they said you had discharged yourself, and I just have a few more questions about your presence up at Lloyd House this week. We've uncovered a few things in looking at Miss Lloyd's tragic accident that I was wondering if you'd be able to shed some light on?'

'Oh, erm…' She seemed to consider for a moment before hobbling back and holding the door wider. 'I'm not sure what I would know.' She gave an awkward shrug. 'But I'll do my best.' He smiled and stepped into the house, as she continued talking. 'I really was only up there for work.'

'Yes, I did call your firm—' Don stopped in the middle of his sentence and gazed around the condo, which was completely empty, aside from a rickety-looking wooden dining set and an old black and white TV. He turned back to her, suspicion creasing the edges of his eyes, his jaw tightening. 'Are you moving?'

She held his gaze for a beat, a thick swallow rippling her throat. And then she surprised him by turning away in evident embarrassment and wiping away a stream of tears that had just erupted down her pink cheeks.

'I – I'm sorry,' she gasped, limping away from him toward the dining table, where she pulled out a chair and buried her face in her hands, shoulders shaking.

'Ms Nicholls?' he asked, following her in confusion. Was this some kind of ploy? But Don was adept at reading people, he'd had nearly forty years of practice at doing it for a living, and this breakdown seemed as unexpected to her as it was to him. She kept her face averted from his, hand held up against her temple as a shield. He went into the kitchen, found a glass, and filled it with water from the spluttering tap.

'Here,' he said, placing it down in front of her and taking a seat opposite. 'Drink this and take some deep breaths.'

She did as she was told and, after a few minutes, the tears seemed to subside, and her voice levelled as she sipped the water.

'I'm sorry, Detective,' she said, swallowing a gulp. 'It's just been quite a week. We – we've had some money troubles. Bailiffs,' she finished weakly with an embarrassed glance around her empty home. 'That's why I was so determined to work on the Lloyd Estate acquisition,' she added, but something in her voice wavered and she shifted her sightline away from his eyes. 'Hoped there would be a bonus check if I managed to seal the deal.'

And there was the unreliability he'd sensed from her that morning. Perhaps just shy of outright deceit, but there was more to this story that she was not telling him. He fished out his notebook. Don was well-seasoned at this. He could eke answers out of even the most reluctant victim or culprit – and now was the time to find out which Terri Nicholls truly was. He made a show of moving the notebook to one side, just an afterthought she needn't worry about, and focused sincerely on her face, still mottled from tears.

'You've clearly had a lot going on,' he gestured kindly to her injuries, 'and have been through something. But I really could do with having a few more details confirmed, just to help me wrap up this case, and then I can be on my way and shut the file.' He gave her a weary smile – just some old timer keen to file his report and clock off. There was no danger in letting her guard down. 'Would you be up to answering some questions for me?'

It took another moment, but eventually, she nodded.

Don exhaled and pulled his notebook back toward him, opening it up and clicking his pen. 'How did you get up to the Lloyd Estate every day? It's quite a way from here. Did you drive?'

Theresa nodded. 'I did. Until…' She paused and looked sheepishly down again. 'Until I had some car trouble. On Wednesday morning I had to get a couple of buses.'

'Interesting,' Don said casually, looking up from the note he'd made at the very start of the day when he'd called in a basic background check on her. 'Because apparently your car has an outstanding speeding ticket. From earlier this morning. When, according to you, you were walking down from Lloyd House trying to get help for Audrey Lloyd?'

Terri closed her eyes and her shoulders sagged. When she opened them again, she gave Don a resigned look before answering. 'The bailiffs took it. I haven't had the car since Tuesday.'

'So, not car trouble?' One lie already.

'The trouble was it was taken.'

'And these bailiffs went joyriding in the early hours of this morning?'

She blew out a sigh but looked back at him determinedly. 'Seems that way. And I don't see what that has to do with anything.'

'Well,' Don said slowly. 'If of course you *were* lying about this detail, it would raise a few questions about what else I might need to verify about your description of the course of events.'

He saw a thick swallow ripple down her throat, and her knuckles whitened as she unconsciously gripped the edge of her chair.

'So,' Don ploughed on, changing the subject away from the mysterious speeding ticket. Keep her on her toes. 'You went up there every day – why?'

Terri looked visibly relieved that he'd abandoned the issue of the car. Don made a mental note. 'She asked me to spend the week with her. She said she'd sell the house if I went up there to keep her company.' She gave a shrug. 'Guess she was lonely.'

Don made a note in his book, before looking back up, his eyes on hers. 'So what went wrong?'

She seemed momentarily speechless, her bottom lip parting ever so slightly from her top. 'H-how do you mean?'

'Well.' He adjusted his sit bones and leaned forward a little more. 'Your hostess is now dead. And you,' he held out a hand in gesture, 'have sustained several injuries yourself. That, to me, sounds like things have gone wrong. How did you hurt your ankle?'

'I slipped,' she answered and took a deep inhale. 'Down the steps in the garden.'

'The same steps Audrey fell down?'

She nodded. 'I slipped on Wednesday afternoon. I must have not been concentrating, I don't know. But we were having lunch on the terraced garden, and I just lost my footing down the stairs.'

'How did you get home on Wednesday evening?' Don frowned, thinking of navigating that long, winding driveway on foot with a busted ankle.

'I – well, I didn't. I must have hit my head too, because I was faint. I lost consciousness for a little while. And when I woke up, I was in bed, my ankle all wrapped up.'

'Audrey took care of you?'

Terri gave an awkward nod of agreement.

'So how did she end up at the bottom of her garden stairs?'

'I've told you.'

'No,' Don shook his head, 'you've told me she fell, and you tried to reach out to stop her, but she knocked you off balance and you hit your head. Help me understand how you both got to the *top* of those stairs in the first place.'

'I was feeling better,' she answered slowly. 'I wanted to go home. I was coming out into the garden to tell Audrey that, to... to ask if she had a phone I could call a taxi from. She was standing at the top of the steps. I must have startled her – she thought I was still in bed. She started to fall, and I tried to catch her. But with my ankle I was slow, and then... then when she reached out for me she knocked me. I must have stumbled onto my bad ankle, and it just crumbled. I hit the patio, and she – well, she fell down the stairs.' Terri shrugged and gestured to him as if to suggest he knew the rest.

That was her story, and she was sticking to it.

Don thought for a moment. 'Can I use your phone?'

'Um, sure,' Terri answered after a confused beat. She held out her hand toward the kitchen. 'Phone's on the wall by the refrigerator.'

'Thanks,' Don said and got to his feet.

He left her on her own at the dining table and considered the conversation they'd just had in light of everything he'd found out earlier that day. Terri had been up there for work. Her colleagues had confirmed that she'd been asking about the project. The speeding ticket was not hers – her car had been taken.

There was still something Don didn't like about her story concerning these apparent bailiffs, but he couldn't argue that the house did seem to have been stripped of anything valuable. He checked inside the kitchen cupboard, plates and bowls and cups all still there – if she was planning a move, surely those would have been boxed up as well. Her sprained ankle had been caused by a simple fall down the same steps that had proved fatal to Audrey.

Don tried to work out the sequence of events in his head. After hurting her ankle, Terri had stayed the night at the house. Strange, but perhaps understandable given her lack of transport and injuries. She'd woken up, surprising Audrey, who then tumbled to her death. Terri then made the long journey down to the payphone at the Double Tree mall. It did fit together. There was nothing to the hoofbeats of Audrey Lloyd's death other than plain old horses.

Except for a bloodied Oscar.

Except for a car with human remains.

Except, except, except.

He hoped Sinclair had uncovered some more answers for him as he picked up the receiver.

Thirty-Six

Audrey

Thursday

Audrey watched with a vacant smile as Irina limped closer, her progress through the kitchen cast only in darkening blue dusk, awkward and slow.

Audrey's vision glimmered. No. It was not Irina.

Audrey frowned and got to her feet, hoping that perhaps the movement would help jolt her mind. She'd been so confused lately. Not just lately – for many years. A brilliant mind left to its own devices survives in the only way it knows how. She had kept herself occupied over the years, kept herself stimulated with company. She'd always known they were figment, but it didn't matter – her mind was dazzling enough to make them as real as the racoons that visited.

Memory faltered into reality. Audrey took a step forward. It *was* Irina.

'Reeny,' she said softly. 'You came home to me.'

But the figure didn't reply – only continued its slow, determined limp toward her. Audrey shook her head. *Concentrate.* She moved back, back toward the edge of the terrace, to the first dead flowerbed of the hanging garden. The last vestiges of daylight blanketed the blonde stone and the figure's shadow stretched long and spindly across the terrace as it stepped out from the kitchen.

'Reeny?' Audrey asked once again as past flickered into the present with the juddering unease of her father changing film rolls.

1948

Audrey wiped down Daddy's old Oscar with a rag from the kitchen, the murky grey cloth barely soaking up the ruby red as she smeared it across the tarnished gold. It wasn't a perfect job and already the blood was tacky and starting to dry across the golden man's feet. She put it back on the sideboard before turning to Mrs Hackton, who was sprawled across the living room floor, scarlet spreading through her chignoned grey hair. Audrey gazed at her a little while, thinking about all their years together, their shared history, and how she supposed it must always have been leading here. She tried to feel grief for the woman, perhaps even guilt, but found she couldn't. She felt only distracting hope.

Audrey found Mrs Hackton's car keys in her handbag and manhandled the woman awkwardly into the back seat, before going to change out of her blood-soaked clothes. She returned to the Chevrolet and enjoyed feeling it vibrate to life in her hands before she careered off down the driveway and onto the old dusty tracks that had been cut through the grounds for the filming of *Sunset Over the Desert*. The tracks were overgrown now, and branches slapped against the car windows with long scratches. Eventually she pulled up to a spot with a small, flat clearing. She had decided not to bother burying Mrs Hackton – no one would be coming onto her property anyway. Audrey gazed down at her father's old secretary, and then she rolled her carefully off the back seat and onto the dusty ground. An offering to the coyotes Audrey heard howling at night. It wouldn't be long before they sniffed out the mangled meat at the back of her head.

Audrey climbed back into the car, filled now with the fresh smell of death, and drove down toward the gate, leaving her sanctuary for the first time in years. But this was a journey worth taking. She was going to get Reeny back. Her Reeny. After all this time.

She turned right into town and then followed the signs to the freeway, stopping at a gas station long enough to fill up the tank and buy a road map. It was a long, straight drive up to San Francisco and Audrey stared determinedly ahead for the full six hours, knuckles pressed white on the steering wheel. All she could hear were Mrs Hackton's parting words. A parting lie perhaps – but Audrey needed to know.

'Refusing to help me even after *everything* I've done for that man!' the old secretary had spat. 'Everything I've done for you! The secrets I've kept, the lies I've told. You don't even understand the smallest fraction of what I'm due. Always protecting Audrey, precious disturbed Audrey!' Audrey had seethed, but Mrs Hackton wasn't done. 'But we weren't protecting *you* really, were we? We were protecting the world *from* you.' She had inhaled through a grimace, her teeth bared in battle. 'From you and your strange, dangerous head. Causing destruction wherever you go – you could never be trusted! There is so much you will never know.'

'Daddy told me everything!' Audrey had screamed in defence, already edging subconsciously toward the side-board. Audrey knew that what she was claiming wasn't true, but she was riled and desperate. This woman was crashing down every structure Audrey had ever been able to cling to.

'He was scared of you! Scared of what you were capable of!'

'No he wasn't! He knew it was all an accident, a terrible, terrible accident.'

'It was no such thing! You put those bullets in those guns and gave them to those fucking Nazis!' Audrey had never heard Mrs Hackton curse before.

'I didn't mean to kill her,' Audrey had whimpered, hearing and hating how pathetic her own insistence was.

Mrs Hackton had stilled then, a look of curious surprise creasing an arrogant smirk into her mouth. 'You still don't know?' she asked, a poisonous laugh rippling the words. 'Do you mean to tell me you *still* don't know? They never told you at that godforsaken desert hospital?' Audrey didn't answer, but she didn't need to. Her blank expression said everything, and Mrs Hackton cackled. 'She isn't *dead!* Irina survived, you foolish, self-centred little girl. Two bullets grazed superficial flesh wounds into her sides, one straight through into her spine. She will never walk again, but she is alive.' Mrs Hackton watched the news settle on Audrey and then laughed again. 'My, my, Arnold really did like to keep his secrets from you, didn't he? He promised me he would tell you, when he could trust that you would leave them in peace.' She cocked one eyebrow. 'Perhaps he never believed your little obsession with that girl would let you do that.'

It was an animalistic rage that had cut Mrs Hackton down. After the first blow had connected with the side of her head, a loud, crunching crack echoing into the living room, Mrs Hackton had fallen to the floor, but she was not done. Her eyes darted and Audrey knew her vision must be confused, disorientated. She blinked and squinted, desperately trying to force her beaten brain back together. Audrey raised the Oscar above her own head again just as Mrs Hackton seemed to give up, lolling back onto the floor, one last whispered sentence before the golden man crashed back down.

'I always knew you were dangerous.'

Audrey savoured the memory on the drive to rescue her only friend, over and over again, feeling life course through her own veins as she remembered Mrs Hackton's still, dead ones.

Outside of San Francisco Audrey stopped at a diner, ordered a tea and rolled her eyes when told they only had coffee. 'Water will be fine,' she muttered before going into the back, securing herself inside the phone booth and tearing through the phone book until she found the Popovs' address. There was only one Popov family listed.

She pulled up outside a large Victorian-era house, with straight wood panelling and intricate brackets and railings carved into scrolls and winding patterns. It was in the centre of a large plot of land and Audrey stared down the concrete path through the manicured front lawn that led to the porch steps up to the front door. The short distance felt suddenly like a mammoth journey, one she didn't know if she had the energy to complete. But the thought of Irina surged adrenaline through her, and she climbed from the car, racing up the porch steps to tug heavily on the bell rope that dangled by the front door. A young maid answered, a handful of dusters stuffed hurriedly into the pocket of her apron.

Audrey opened her mouth to try to find the words and felt a small gurgle escape instead. After a moment of concerted effort, she found her voice. 'Is this the Popov residence?'

The maid nodded. 'They're away I'm afraid. On a trip to Canada.'

Audrey felt her mouth round into an O of disappointment, unable to process that she won't get to see Reeny again after all. 'Irina,' she said quietly, a longing call for her old friend.

'Oh... Irina?' the maid said. 'Yes, she's here.' She blinked and then smiled. 'Sorry, she doesn't usually get visitors.'

Audrey felt her insides turn to sludge and her head swam for the briefest of moments before she nodded vigorously. 'Can I see her?' she breathed.

The maid nodded and stepped aside. 'She's in the orangery. I'll take you through.'

Audrey stepped into the house and waited for the maid to close the door behind her, before following her through wood-panelled halls and out into a brightly lit orangery with a potted olive tree in one corner. There was a set of high-backed wicker chairs around a low coffee table, a wheelchair pushed in next to them. Audrey could see the mess of flyaway dark curls of her friend.

'Ms Irina?' the maid said, moving around to the side of the chair, leaving Audrey to stand alone, staring at its back. 'You have a visitor.'

Audrey could do nothing but stand and stare as she heard the effort it took for her friend to turn in her chair and lean over the side to peer behind her. She felt the tears on her cheeks as she saw Irina's dour, round features for the first time in fourteen years – her bulbous eyes pulled wide in shock, mouth opening into a choked gasp.

The maid glanced between them for a moment before dismissing herself with a small bow of her head. 'I'll leave you to it, miss,' she muttered as she exited the orangery's open door and closed it behind her.

'Reeny,' Audrey choked, stepping forward and falling to her knees at the arm of her friend's chair. 'I'm so, so, sorry.' She sobbed and wailed and felt a rush of emotion she couldn't untangle. She lowered her neck and rested her head on the arm and felt Irina's firm hand cradle the nape of her neck. Audrey did not know how long they stayed like that, but eventually Irina moved her hand to Audrey's shoulder and used her other to gently lift her chin with a crooked index finger.

'What took you so long?' she asked.

Audrey didn't know how to say the words and she swallowed a thick lump before answering. 'I thought you were dead,' she whispered.

Irina paused for a moment before nodding and sitting back, gesturing for Audrey to take the seat opposite. Audrey complied and smiled a wet smile at the sight of a chessboard on the low table between them.

Irina caught her gaze and gave her own tearful smile. 'I've still never found anyone to challenge me like you.' Audrey stared at her then, feeling hollowed out from within, a howl of internal anguish at the years they'd been robbed of together. Irina swallowed. 'I asked about you. All the time. I asked why you weren't coming to visit me in the hospital. I wanted to play.'

'Did they tell you it was my fault?'

Irina averted her eyes away from Audrey's face to her lap, where her fingers fidgeted together, winding and writhing over one another. She nodded. 'Papa told me.'

'I'm sorry,' Audrey said again, weakly.

'I understand, in a way,' Irina said, her voice quiet, barely audible. She looked up, her expression suddenly hard. 'I can't say I would have done the same thing. But you'd never had reason to bother yourself with the politics of other people.' There was something in the way she said it that flared with an old anger. She closed her eyes and turned her head, opening them on the knobbled trunk of the olive tree in one corner of the room, its grey-green leaves brushing the glass ceiling. 'At first I was angry you didn't tell me. Furious in fact. I thought I'd finally found a... a sister of sorts in you. Someone else who under-stood me, understood what it's like.' A hand rose vaguely to gesture at her head. 'I thought we shared everything. There was nothing I didn't tell you. But you kept this from me, and that told me everything I needed to know.' She blinked slowly and gave a small shrug. 'You knew what you were doing would hurt me in some way.'

'No!' Audrey wailed, the old burn of guilt flooding her. 'No! I didn't, I could never have expected—'

Irina turned her gaze back to her and raised a hand, quietening her.

'But over the years,' she continued, 'especially watching the war, watching every horror imaginable pummelled against my people...' She stopped and gave Audrey a grave nod. 'Pummelled against *your* people. I understand the secrecy. I understand the confusion. Back then we could never have had any idea what people could be capable of. I knew Papa and Arnold were working with Leon Lewis, investigating the anti-Semitism. I thought it was the small stuff – Jews getting fired, property damage, dirty looks in the street.' She paused and gave a little sad laugh. 'How strange that those things that once drove us from our home in Berlin now seem like such small inconveniences in comparison.' She looked back at Audrey. 'None of us could have ever imagined, ever *believed*, what they could do.'

'I should have told you,' Audrey whispered.

'You were afraid you'd have to choose a side,' Irina answered for her. 'You knew they didn't like us, whether you wanted to understand the reason for it or not. And you needed that work.' She stared at Audrey then, a clear, scrutinising gaze. 'I would have jumped at the chance to be put to use myself.' She gave a one-shouldered shrug. 'I like to think I would have been a little more discerning about *who* I worked for, though.'

'I regret it every day.'

'Of course you do.' Irina shook her head then and leaned toward the box lying next to the chessboard. She unpacked it and handed Audrey a white pawn. 'I think you need to be white today.'

Audrey smiled and accepted the gesture, placing her pawn on the board. 'How have you been?' she asked as they set up.

'Bored,' Irina said. 'So very, very bored. It's impossible to explain.' She caught Audrey's eye. 'To anyone other than you. Some days I think I can feel my very lifeblood seeping out of me. I feel myself shut down, so only a facsimile is left. Just a shop's mannequin staring out of these four walls.'

'You still live with your family?'

'The boys have all moved out. Sascha is the only one still nearby. He's a lawyer now, like Papa. Comes by for Friday night dinner every week. The others have spread their wings.' She shrugged. 'And I'm just the spinster daughter with nowhere to go and nothing to do.' She waited for Audrey to open the game and then said, 'I was sorry to hear about your father.'

'Thank you,' Audrey said softly. 'I've been alone all these years since.'

They played on, at first in silence, and then conversation trickled slowly in through the crack in their quiet. Irina filled her in on her other brothers, spread across the country, one returned to Berlin to help with the increasingly tense situation between the Americans and Soviets in the capital. 'They're all doing things,' Irina said with a sad smile, and Audrey marvelled at the wasted brainpower that was being channelled into thirty-two wooden pieces in a game.

The maid came in halfway through and asked if they would like afternoon tea bringing in, and as Audrey bit into the soft white bread sandwich from the platter the girl put down, she felt herself drift back in time. The food relaxed them, the game relaxed them, and by the time Irina trounced her in victory, it felt as if the last fourteen years had been nothing more than a mere blink of the eye. They played again, and again, until at last dusk began to fall around the windows of the orangery and both women stared out into the gathering dark.

'How long are you in town?' Irina asked.

'I'm not,' Audrey replied. 'Not really. I just drove.'

Irina frowned. 'You just drove?'

'I found out you were still alive and I just started driving. I didn't really plan it.'

'How *did* you find out I hadn't died?'

'Ah,' Audrey said, 'now that is a long story.' An idea struck her. 'I can tell you on the way back to LA.'

'Back to LA?' Irina asked, placing her half-eaten sandwich back on her plate and brushing her hands free of crumbs.

'Come back with me,' Audrey said, the idea now cementing into place. It was the only thing that made sense. The world had no use for them, but they had use for each other. 'We will never be bored again. We can play chess and set puzzles. I can practise my Russian again. I fear I will be rusty by now. As must your Spanish be. We can fill our days as we please – keeping ourselves busy and stimulated and—'

But Irina was shaking her head. 'Audrey,' she said, her voice quiet but firm. 'I will never return to LA. Not...' She fumbled over the next sentiment and Audrey could see it pained her to speak it out loud. 'Not with you.'

Audrey blinked, processing it slowly, carefully. 'It's the best thing for us both,' she said. 'Trust me. I'll make it up to you. You'll see... I'll look after you, now.'

The maid did not hear Irina's protests through the closed kitchen door, the radio playing loudly over the sound. Audrey wheeled her out to the car, apologising loudly as she bumped the chair down the porch steps, ignoring Irina's pleas to just leave her be.

Irina seemed to calm once she was seated in the car, her chair left on the sidewalk, waiting for someone to find. She turned to Audrey with heavy, wet eyes and shook her head.

'What have you become?' she asked in Russian.

Audrey laughed gaily, too gaily. 'I told you – I need to brush up on my Russian lessons!'

And then the car pulled away.

–

Audrey watched her approaching companion again. Of course Irina had come home to her. She and Irina had been back together so long – thirty-four years, if her math was right. She smiled to herself at the thought – of course her math was right. Mama and Daddy had kept them company too of course. The odd person had come to visit her over the years – to try to persuade her to sell up, or ask if they could photograph the house, and even one optimistic young man asking her to donate her land to Greenpeace. These visitors had always provided a good excuse to get out Mama's tea set. But no one had ever stayed long. Not when they understood she would not give them what they'd come for.

The figure limped closer. Audrey understood, now, that this was not Irina.

Terri. That was who it was.

'But you're not well,' Audrey said. 'You should be in your room.'

No one ever stayed long, she remembered with a small frown. But Terri – Terri had. And Audrey had realised how much use she could be to other people.

She could care for them, keep them safe, make them well.

Thirty-Seven

Terri
Thursday

The pain in Terri's ankle had been killed by adrenaline. Somewhere on the journey through the living room and kitchen, spectres running through her head, Terri had found the will to confront her captor. Terri needed her. She did not have it in her to search this damned house any more in the hope of finding a phone, and she did not relish the thought of sneaking out and down the long, dark driveway on an injured ankle with the fear of Audrey appearing behind her at any moment. No, that was not how this would end. Anger pooled through her broken body – anger at Audrey, at Jason, at Glenn. At Ethan. Anger that people just kept taking from her whatever they wanted. That she never stood up and said no. That she never demanded what *she* needed. Well, now that would change. She was going to demand Audrey call her a cab, and then she was going to get home, call Ethan and tell him she'd done it, she'd succeeded where he'd failed, and she was going to finish it with Jason – her way.

She stumbled through the kitchen toward Audrey, who seemed to be waiting patiently for her, framed in the eerie glow of dusk beside the broken kitchen doors.

Audrey's face seemed to clear, as if she was only just seeing Terri for the first time. The sharpness that Terri had become accustomed to, the formidable woman tweaking puppet strings as she saw fit, returned to the old, lined face.

'But you're not well,' Audrey said, her voice strong, wilful in pure contrast to her expression just a moment ago. 'You should be in your room.'

Terri didn't have the luxury to be distracted – she would not let it happen again. Audrey was standing at the edge of the dead raised flower bed, just at the top of the lethal stone steps that had crumbled Terri's ankle.

Terri continued her slow hobble forward and came to a stop just in front of Audrey, about a foot away. She could see the wrinkled vision of Estella Lloyd in her face, finally reaching the age the famous muse had never had the chance to see. Large amber eyes, still lined in messy dark kohl Terri was sure had not been changed since her first day there. A satin scarf returned to her head, diligently hiding those greys that betrayed her years.

'You should be in your room,' Audrey repeated, eyes falling to Terri's blood-streaked hands before creasing in what Terri thought she recognised as concern.

'No. I need to go home.' The words did not come out as forcefully as she'd wanted. They sounded more like a plea – like she was asking Audrey's permission.

'No, you need to be in your room.' Audrey refused the request. She took a step forward and placed her surprisingly strong grip on Terri's upper arm, trying to guide her back inside.

'No,' Terri tried again, her voice still breaking over the simple command. 'I need to go home.' She needed to be stronger. Needed to remind herself what she was going home to. Why she had come here at all. She pushed her hand into her right pocket and squeezed her fingers around the thing that would save them. 'I'm going home, Audrey. You need to call me—'

But Audrey was shaking her head, gripping her harder, speaking over her, louder than Terri was. Terri tried to step away, but Audrey pulled her back, closer. Terri's feet stumbled and she brought her right hand out to the side to steady herself. They were precariously close to the top of the steps – if Audrey continued this struggle, one or both of them would surely end up at the bottom, likely with worse than a broken ankle.

Audrey seemed to recognise this too because in that moment she relaxed her grip on Terri's arm, her body stilling, her beautiful, enigmatic face creasing into a confused frown as she stared at Terri's right hand, still outstretched in balance and still gripping the thing that had given her her power. Audrey's expression cleared and she turned her face toward Terri. Where Terri had expected to see fury and aggression there was only betrayal.

'Of course,' Audrey said softly. 'I should have known.'

Terri felt an apology bubble to her lips, but somehow, she kept it from bursting.

'I need to go home,' Terri repeated one final time, feeling hot, inexplicably guilty tears spill down her cheeks. This woman had locked her up, Terri reminded herself. *She was only trying to help*, the coward in her whispered back. 'Please, Audrey, I need to call a cab.'

It was then she realised Audrey was still holding her, because her grip relaxed even more for just a moment as Audrey decided what to do.

Suddenly Audrey's face split into a bright, inappropriate smile. Her hand tightened again. 'No, no,' she said loudly. 'Much better if you stay here with me. Much better for us all.'

Terri tried to take a step back, trying to yank her arm out of Audrey's grasp. She lost her footing, twisting backwards as Audrey herself was knocked off balance. She felt the hands of the house's ghosts on her hair, pulling, yanking her back—

—and then Terri was on the ground, her head screaming with agony where it had slammed against the stone tiles for the second time, yesterday's injury radiating an explosion of fresh pain and confusion. Her eyes swam, but she forced them open, looking upward into the silver of the encroaching night that sang with Audrey's scream before blackness took her once again.

Thirty-Eight

Don
Friday

'Officer Sinclair's not here,' Mitchell told Don, the bustle of the station coming down the line into Terri Nicholls's kitchen. 'She tried your car phone but there was no answer, so she left a message if you rang. I'm not a secretary you know, Don; just because I'm stuck here chasing a stolen car doesn't mean I'm at everyone's beck and—'

Don laughed, interrupting him. 'And how is the great case of the Quick Stop Motel car theft? Working with San Bernadino's finest minds, I assume?'

'Shut up,' Mitchell answered gruffly. 'Do you want your message or not?'

'I'd appreciate it.'

'Alright, it's a long one. You got your notebook?'

'Yep.'

'She's managed to get an answer from the coroner about the post-mortem on your body from Lloyd House.' Don's pen hovered excitably above the page. 'Death caused by a blow to the side of the head, most likely from a blunt object.' *Gotcha.* 'Skull is caved around one contact site. She's given me all the details from the docs – do you want them now?'

284

'No, no,' Don said, 'that's fine for now; I'll look at the report when I get back to the station. But the blow is definitely not consistent with the fall down the stairs?'

'Doesn't look that way.'

'And the Oscar?'

'I don't know who she's sleeping with' – Mitchell paused to snort at the joke at his female colleague's expense – 'but she managed to get that hurried up at the lab too. Nothing on it. Except for blood. Techs say the base has been wiped down.' Don made some more fevered notes. 'Last point says she looked into Annabel Hackton and a connection to Theresa Nicholls.'

'That's alright, I've spoken to her about that already,' Don said, finishing off his notes with a determined period. 'Thanks for the message, Mitchell. If Sinclair calls with any other news, try my car phone immediately and let me know.'

'I'm not your fucking answering serv—' but Don hung up before he could begin his rant again.

Don considered what the post-mortem confirmed as he made his way back through the kitchen to re-join Theresa Nicholls, still sitting awkwardly at her own dining table in the middle of her tragically empty home, brow furrowed as if she was working out a complicated problem.

The Oscar had been used in a deliberate attack. Wiped down and thrown over the edge of the garden into the brambles below. It would have seemed like the perfect hiding place for a murder weapon. And it would have been, if a skeleton hadn't also been found and the circus hadn't come to town.

'Everything OK?' she asked, as he sat down.

He considered for a moment, deciding on his best tack.

'After Audrey had fallen,' he said carefully. 'You went down to her, to see if she was alright?'

Terri nodded. 'She was in a bad way. But she was still alive – I think.' She paused and shook her head, distress creeping back into her features. 'I don't know, I've been going over and over it. I was in pain, I was disorientated. I thought she was still alive when I left to get help. But maybe – maybe I was wrong?' She stopped and wiped away her tears, which did, at least, seem genuine.

'Theresa, I think it's time you told me the truth. The more honest you are with me now, the better things will go for you.'

She stared at him, the whirring of her internal decision-making visible on her face for several protracted seconds. And then she crumbled. Full, rich sobs burst out of her, a dam of emotion she'd spent so long holding in. Don waited patiently for her to find her breath, but this time he did not offer her a refill of water, or hand over his old handkerchief to wipe away the tears. He waited until she steadied, finally looking up at him with large, doleful eyes of regret.

'I – I ki—' she whispered before stammering to a stop, hands flying to her mouth as if to catch the words before they escaped.

'It's OK, Theresa,' Don said. 'You should tell me now.'

Thirty-Nine

Audrey
Thursday

Audrey had been holding on to Terri. The young woman had been her stability in so many ways these past few days, but in those last few moments it was in its most basic, physical sense. She had been the one thing keeping Audrey anchored to the top of those steps, as her heels had drifted precariously off the edge of the stone in their struggle.

But suddenly Terri was gone. Seemingly yanked from Audrey's grasp, on the ground with a loud cry of pain. Audrey's first instinct was to help her. To take her back down to the bedroom where things were kept safe and treat her as well as she could. But it was too late for such projects. Audrey's hand now grasped at thin air, her balance thrown backwards. Her body held for what seemed like an endless moment, on the cusp of life and death, unsupported and unbalanced in the crisp night. Time seemed to rush back to her all at once, gravity re-enacting its deadly mission.

As she fell, she felt Irina by her side, falling with her. *We'll be reunited now.* The words came in every language and no language at once. Audrey connected with the stone steps, her body tumbling gracelessly over them.

Why didn't I think of this sooner? she thought.

1948

After they'd returned from San Francisco, Audrey had set Irina up in Mama's old chair, smiling in tender reminiscence at how Daddy had pushed her sleeping mama so gently along the corridors of their home. And now it was Audrey's job to do the same.

Over the first few days Irina had begged to go home, and it had hurt Audrey's feelings to see Irina's face curl at the sight of the house in the same way Mrs Hackton's had.

'You need staff, Audrey,' she'd said, staring at a mound of racoon faeces.

'Nonsense,' Audrey had retorted with a laugh, 'they'd only get in my way.'

After nearly a week of Irina's palpable distress, refusing to play chess, refusing to play cards, refusing to speak in any language other than English, Audrey grew quite worried about her friend. She tore desperately through her brilliant mind for any solution she could find to ease Irina's troubles, until, at last, it caught on the memory of Mrs Hackton, of all people.

'He had his notebook where he'd keep track of all his prescriptions.'

Perhaps Daddy would have some answers to how to cheer Irina up. It had taken her the best part of a day in Daddy's office before she found the notebook she needed, smiling in recognition at Daddy's neat handwriting filling in each page, divided into four columns with diligent notes in each of them.

Date / Time – Substance – Dosage – Response

She pored through it all, reading her mother's last years of life.

Buoyant for most of the day, took Audrey shopping and to tea. Returned with matching hats.

Audrey remembered that day. Mama had been in such good spirits. They'd gone to the milliner on a whim on the way back from afternoon tea, giggling together while they tried on the designs. She did not want to acknowledge the next entry, did not want to tarnish that day.

Too high yesterday. Terrible melancholy today. Begging to end it all. Must revise dosage.

Daddy had not perfected his method. But Audrey was far cleverer than Daddy had ever been. If anyone could do this right, it would be her.

She'd long ago found the old stash of drugs in the bathroom cabinet, and so carefully embarked on her own regime, designed to keep Irina in the best spirits possible. But she never got her chance to perfect her process. Her experiments were still too early in their journey for her to know if she was bringing Irina true peace. With laudanum Irina had proved more willing to join in with a few chess games, but no longer played with the same brilliance she once had. She broke off in distraction at the sound of a rustling bush or stared into the sky as a bird flew overhead. Sometimes she would just sit and laugh, while Audrey had no idea what the joke was.

Irina had only been back at Lloyd House for about two weeks when four loud bangs reverberated through the living room from the front door. Irina was blank with melancholy, flipping through *Directions for Knowing All*

Dark Things with little interest. Audrey had her pencil to a pad, creating a ciphered code like she used to, but this time for a puzzle to keep Irina occupied. She'd explained cheerfully over dinner the previous night how the Vigenère square worked, not noticing Irina's dulled flinch at the topic of conversation. Audrey had a great plan to hide a quote from *Anna Karenina* in code, the type of mental agility both of them needed to keep sharp.

'I wonder who that could be,' Audrey said, getting to her feet just as a loud, shouting voice accompanied the renewed pounding announcing their visitor.

'Irina!' an accented voice boomed through the door. 'Irina, are you there?'

Irina turned in her chair, eyebrows pulled high on her head. 'Papa?' she asked, but her voice was quiet.

'Audrey! I know you came to our house!' Lev called. 'The staff told me. And now Irina has gone!'

'Papa!' Irina said again, this time crying out with a strained voice.

Panic consumed Audrey. She would not lose Irina again. Not now, not now she was so close to making her happy. She spun away from the door and grasped the handles of Mama's old chair, thrusting the creaking old contraption out of the living room and down the corridor.

'Papa!' Irina called out again, over her shoulder, and Audrey heard only the cries of a desperate child.

'I'll look after you, Reeny,' she said. 'You just need to trust me and let me help. We're better together.'

Audrey didn't have time to take Irina back down to her usual room, and so she pushed her into Daddy's old office. She ran quickly back to the living room to collect Irina's glass of water, upturning another large, unmeasured dose of laudanum into the glass. 'Drink this,' she said, thrusting it into Irina's now frantically shaking hands as she called out over and over again for her father. 'Drink it!' she screeched when Irina failed to comply. The tone of her voice cut through Irina's distress and with a slow, reluctant movement she brought the glass to her lips. 'There,' Audrey said with a relieved smile, 'that will make you feel better. I'll go and deal with—' She stopped before identifying the person they both knew was on the other side of the door.

Audrey locked the door hurriedly behind her, dropping the key into the pocket of her slacks. Lev was beating the door now with a frenzy, calling for his daughter, threatening the police.

'Mr Popov,' Audrey said with an air of falsified calm. 'How can I help you?' She pulled her bottom lip into an attempt at a smile. 'It has been many years.'

'Where is Irina?' he asked, his voice breaking desperately over the question. He had aged a lot since Audrey had last seen him. His hair had thinned practically to the point of baldness, while his once-lean frame had filled out with heavy jowls and belly. 'I know you came to our house. It could only have been you. Irina has no other old friends. And you took her—' He shook his head. 'I don't know why, Audrey. I heard you had some – troubles – after everything that happened. But you need to let Irina come home.'

Audrey's face hardened and her bottom jaw gurned in rising fury. Who did this man think he was to talk about her *troubles*?

'Who's to say she wants to come home?'

Lev blinked at the question. 'Then let her tell me that herself. Let me see her. It is not like her – not to write, not to even say goodbye to the staff. She was very close to Chloe – she would have told her if she had plans to move away with you. There was no need for secrecy if she wanted to leave.'

'She doesn't need anyone else!' Audrey's voice rose. 'Not *Chloe*' – she sneered the name – 'not you – or anyone. We are perfectly happy with just each other!'

'Let me see her.' Lev's tone became steely, and Audrey saw the hard-lined lawyer underneath the ageing face.

'She doesn't want to see you.'

'Irina!' Lev called again, loudly and more determined. He pushed his way into the house, knocking Audrey back with his forearm. She staggered back a couple of steps, by which time he'd stridden through the entrance hall and into the living room. 'Irina!' he called again, scanning around the empty room and making for the corridor.

As it had been with Mrs Hackton, it was almost a surprise to find Daddy's old Oscar back in her hands. It felt comfortable there. Heavy. Solid. Protective.

But Lev Popov did not go down as easily as the old crone.

He dodged out of the way at the last minute, so she caught only a glancing blow above his brow – splitting the thin flesh across his forehead easily. Blood streamed down his face, and he stared at her, framed in the corridor's entrance, horror descending on his features.

'You're mad,' he whispered. He looked over his shoulder back into the large, unending cavern of a house and seemed to make a decision. He moved quickly for a man in his late sixties and dodged around Audrey, heading back for the front door. As it slammed shut behind him, Audrey blinked in surprise.

That had been much easier than she'd thought.

She went back down the corridor and unlocked the door to the office again, and found Irina sleeping, as she'd hoped, in her chair. She left Irina unconscious and returned to the living room to finish her puzzle. Irina would be thrilled when she woke from a restful sleep with something challenging to set her mind to.

The second knock on the door had come a few hours after Lev had fled. Audrey approached it cautiously and found a young, uniformed policeman on her doorstep.

'Can I help you?' she asked, her gaze skating over to the non-uniform car parked across her turning circle. Interesting.

'I'm here regarding a report we've received,' the young man had replied, his voice wavering, fingers fidgeting with the shirt of his uniform, tugging it down in small, nervous increments. Audrey watched him a moment longer, a slight pink flush painting the tops of his cheeks. This boy had not been sent by the police — at least not in any capacity that suggested they really cared for him to find the truth. He was sweet and young, a rookie, as easy to read as Daniel Bowen had been all those years ago. Audrey considered for a moment. Irina was sleeping, and Audrey had finished her puzzle. She had time for a bit of fun. And she was sure Irina would love to hear the tale of the young police officer; she was only sad Irina was not awake to witness it for herself.

'Well of course,' she said, stepping back from the door. 'You must come in and ask me whatever you wish.'

Afterwards, she watched the poor boy flee back to his non-regulation car, and she planned to call the station and tell them all about how Officer Donald Vernon had trespassed on her property, with no warrant or concrete reason for suspicion. She smiled to herself, thinking of his young face covered in grime, working the same factory she had always imagined she'd sent Daniel Bowen back to. It was a small thrill, but a thrill nonetheless. One that kept her feeling alive, which she had not felt in so long. But first, she would wake Irina. Let her listen in on the conversation. They would laugh together like old times. She would understand. If anyone would understand, it would be Reeny. Audrey walked back to the office and opened the door, a smile and her tale ready on her mouth.

But it was too late.

The stench of vomit rushed her as soon as she opened the door. Yellow bile mixed with last night's stew was splattered on the carpet, thick dribbles down Irina's still chin. Her head was thrust up to the ceiling, mouth still agape from where she must have struggled and gasped, choking as her oesophagus filled and filled with Audrey's carefully slow-cooked beef shin.

As with Mama, the tears did not come. Even without Daddy using them all up.

'Take her out to the land,' Daddy said from beside her. 'Leave her with Annabel.'

And so, using all of her strength, Audrey carried her friend to the back of Mrs Hackton's car and laid her down across the back seat. She drove back to the clearing where she had left Mrs Hackton's body. It had now been dragged away, leaving only darkened, dried entrails to suggest she was ever there. Audrey would not let Irina face the same fate. She closed the doors firmly, keeping her friend forever safe from wild dogs, and then took the key from the ignition and tossed it far into the land. And then she began the walk back home. It was best if she didn't have a car after all.

Best if she just stayed all alone.

Company wasn't good for her.

—

She had been right, of course. Company was not good for her. She had tried it again, one last time with Terri. She'd thought she was better now. She'd played no games. She'd wanted only to care for the girl, the way she'd tried to care for Reeny. The way Daddy had tried to care for Mama. But now she was lying at the base of the steps in her own garden, Mama's white memorial pricking the night sky above her head, upside down and disorientating. Audrey blinked, trying to focus her swimming head on the white marble. Her body was agony; her limbs screamed. But her mind, as it always had, kept her company. Her brilliant, brilliant mind could not be quieted by a few stone stairs.

She heard footsteps. Uneven and soft, coming down the steps, following her in the wake of her fall.

Perhaps now it was Terri's turn to take care of her. Audrey would tell her where everything was, maybe even show her the notebook so Terri could keep track of Audrey's medications. It would finally be the opportunity she needed to teach Audrey Greek.

She murmured weakly as she felt Terri pick up her wrist, pressing deep, searching for a pulse.

'Audrey?' Terri said, her voice raspy.

Audrey tried to speak again, tried to tell her about Mama's chair, about the medicine, about how she would be fine if only Terri would care for her. But the words didn't come, soft murmurs were all she could manage.

'You're alive,' Terri confirmed, seemingly to herself. 'Stay there.'

Audrey would have laughed at the pointless instruction if she had the strength. Terri rose again, her footsteps carrying her back up the steps. Perhaps she already knew where Mama's chair was; she would get it and place it on the top patio and then she would return to carry Audrey up to it. And then Audrey would be taken back into the bowels of her home, into the room that kept precious things safe. Audrey blinked again at the white marble of Mama's memorial and waited patiently for Terri to return, her fantasy as real as if she were already tucked into the pistachio bed. She heard the footsteps return, more hurried this time, desperate, heavier. And as Audrey gazed only upward into the night-drenched sky, a shining gold statue appeared above her.

Now perhaps you'll understand what you did to me, Mrs Hackton said from somewhere that was both next to her and inside her all at once.

Shut up, Mrs Hackton, Audrey thought as the glinting bald head rushed down toward her, white knuckles gripping its base in desperate fury.

It's time for us to be together again, Audrey, Irina said as Mama and Daddy nodded encouragingly along.

You're right. And for the second time that night Audrey thought, *Why didn't I think of this sooner?*

The blow came with a crack of agony that Audrey swam away from. She swam toward her loved ones.

They were together again.

Forty

Terri
Friday & Saturday

Terri threw some balled-up sweaters into the leather holdall, a pair of pants, a few pairs of underwear. She didn't have the energy to plan any outfits; all she needed was clothes.

The detective had finally gone, long after sunset. He hadn't been what she'd expected – the old grandfatherly policeman, close to retirement, his edge sanded down by age and apathy. There had been a spark in his dull brown eyes that she'd missed until it was nearly too late.

I killed her. That's what Terri had nearly confessed. Nearly blurted out, the guilt that had torn her apart all day winding itself up inside her like a screw. But she'd gathered it back in, withdrawing the words at the very tip of her tongue, just as they readied themselves to leap forth toward Detective Don Vernon.

It had taken time, a lot of probing, many, many more questions she mostly had not wanted to answer, but she had finally absolved herself of suspicion. For now, at least. Her name was not quite clear, not yet anyway, but finally she'd been left alone, tears of relief flooding out of her as she heard his car roar off down the street. Planning for the next day had started immediately – she couldn't just sit there in an empty condo that had a target on its back. Now not just from Jason's gasoline canister, but from the LAPD too.

She pulled up the zip on the holdall and dropped it on the floor by her bed. It landed next to her handbag, which she stooped toward, prising the leather edges apart, checking the contents were still there. Her treasure was another confession she'd managed to keep from Detective Vernon. When she'd discharged herself from hospital, unable to lie for another moment at the mercy of yet more people trying to take care of her, the nurse had handed her a plastic bag of clothes she'd been wearing when brought in, along with a small paper pouch containing the personal effects that had been found in her pockets.

'Fountain pen, pair of earrings, compact mirror and a folded piece of paper?' the nurse had said with a smile, handing them over, before giving a reassuring small laugh. 'Don't worry, we don't read anything! Is that everything you expected?'

Having spent most of her hospital stay churned up by guilt and memories from the night before, half-mad from pain or dulled by painkillers, Terri had completely forgotten about her treasure. She'd nodded and forced herself to remain calm, accepting the paper pouch and stowing it immediately in her nightstand once she'd returned home. She'd retrieved it only after the detective had left and slipped it into her handbag. It would be her first stop tomorrow.

Terri pulled back the covers and climbed into bed fully dressed. She didn't have the energy to brush her teeth or shower, and so she just rolled over in her old college sweatshirt, positioning her head at an awkward angle on the side to avoid lying on her injured skull. She expected she would have trouble sleeping, that nightmares from her week at Lloyd House would stand upright over her, taunting her whenever she closed her eyes. But, instead, she found that back here, back home, back in her own bed, all she wanted to do was settle into her fluffy pillow and shut out the world.

Ethan filled her mind. Ethan as she'd thought he had been. The image of him she'd clung so hard to for so many years – out of love, out of loyalty, out of fear of loneliness. Long haired and bright twinkling eyes reflecting the Coney Island illuminations. An image she now understood was as real as the ghosts that had stalked the hallways of Lloyd House.

She felt herself dozing off and as she lost her grasp on consciousness the happy memories turned sour, doused by reality. The nightmares did come for her in the end, just not the ones she expected.

Ethan throwing a glass at the wall in frustration for losing yet another client. Ethan drunk and slurring and begging her to leave work early to come and pick him up from a bar on a Wednesday afternoon. Ethan grabbing her roughly by the arm and shoving her back against the kitchen counter, so she'd cried out where it pressed a blue striped bruise across her back for the next week. He'd sobbed and apologised, and she'd forgiven him as she always had.

Because they were a team.

She opened her eyes widely and suddenly into her darkened bedroom – the realisation that that could never be true again jeering her awake.

Squeezing her eyes shut again, she focused on the physical relief of her body being still and comfortable, the mattress cradling her battered bones. Eventually her mind emptied, and she let herself tumble into the depths of slumber.

The next morning Terri woke not feeling particularly refreshed. She'd slept long and deeply but felt no benefits of rest. Smelling the damp stench on her, she finally dragged herself into the shower, lathering herself tentatively and wincing as the soap stung the cuts on her fingers. She dressed in her most comfortable, baggiest outfit – jeans and an oversized sweatshirt with the sleeves rolled up. At one time it had belonged to Ethan, but had made its way to her side of the wardrobe over the years. She used to feel him when she wore it, but now felt only stiff, starchy cotton.

She called a taxi from the phone in the kitchen and, while she waited for it to arrive, hopped from the bedroom with the holdall and her handbag looped awkwardly over one shoulder. A horn blared from the street outside and Terri limped outside.

'There are two stops,' she instructed the driver as she slid cumbersomely onto the long bench back seat, shoving her bags next to her. 'The first is Cline and Co on West 11th and Oakfield.'

'The pawn shop?'

'Yep.'

'Alright, I know it,' the driver confirmed lazily. 'And the second?'

'The second is a bit further out of town,' she confirmed. 'But it's OK, I can pay.'

Forty-One

Terri stepped out of the car into the motel parking lot, feeling awkward and uncomfortable, pulling at her jeans and sweatshirt self-consciously. With her weight balanced on her good foot, she bent to collect her bags from the back seat, her handbag now zipped firmly up, its contents hidden from the driver.

Six thousand dollars. That's what the overly excitable pawn broker had handed over in uneven wads of old bills, gathered together in worn rubber bands. He had grinned too much, which told Terri she was getting royally ripped off for her troubles up at Lloyd House, but he'd asked no questions.

As she limped, weighed down by her baggage, she considered the potential of that money. Two roads diverged ahead of her. One looped back round to the past: hand it over to Ethan – a small but significant enough sum to get Jason off their back for the time they needed to wrap up everything else.

The second veered straight into a future on her own: pack up what little she had left in LA and buy a plane ticket back to Connecticut. Get an apartment. Join the family business maybe. Move somewhere else. She'd always wanted to visit Europe; perhaps this was her chance. Solo, for the first time since she was a nervous sophomore at a college mixer. This path glowed with the golden hue of hope tinged only slightly with a dark edge of the unknown. The other path was well-trodden and familiar, but, she now recognised, had become a quagmire of regret and pain.

She made it across the motel parking lot toward room 4, and raised her hand to the door, knocking firmly.

'It's me,' she called softly, 'Terri.'

As Ethan pulled the door open, face furrowed, glancing over her shoulder into the empty parking lot behind, she felt herself weaken. She yearned for the familiar path, found herself believing, however briefly, that maybe if they just sorted this out, just paid Jason off, it could lead to a new future for them both.

'Get in, quickly,' he said urgently, pulling her inside so she stumbled on her bad ankle and winced with the pain that shot through it. He slammed the door behind them and turned to face her, taking in her appearance for the first time. His face softened, eyes darting from the bandage on her head, the yellowing shiner from Jason across her cheek, her bound and scabbed fingers. 'What happened?' He stepped forward and gathered her in his arms and for a moment she couldn't speak. He smelled of cheap shampoo and body wash, not the favourite cologne she was used to – but still it was Ethan, strong and steady, holding her close like he hadn't in a long time.

The embrace was brief.

He stepped away from her again, holding her out at arm's length, his previous concern about her injuries forgotten. 'Did you get it?'

She had made her decision, had done before she'd even knocked on the door. She dropped the holdall on the floor, her handbag with it. The zip stayed closed.

Terri stepped away from him and nodded, pulling out the envelope from her back jean pocket. 'I found it,' she said, handing it over.

He tore open the envelope, a greedy child on Christmas Day, and unfolded the ancient sheet of paper, hungry eyes reading the elegant slanting hand that swooped across the page. Terri knew what it said. She'd read the short note down in that musty old basement bedroom, but had not looked at it again. Not even when she'd sealed it carefully in the envelope last night after the detective had gone, scared of tearing or ruining it in some way.

So much hinged on this one old note.

Revived Last Will and Testament of Arnold Lloyd. 13 October 1937.

I wish my estate to be divided equally between both my daughters. Audrey by my beloved Estella. Jeanie by my loyal Annabel.

I am sorry for all I have done. I hope in death I can make amends for the wrongs I've done in life.

Audrey, you are strong, and you are right.

You would both have been better off without me.

Terri thought those few lines the saddest thing she had ever read. But Ethan's face shone only with victory.

'You did it,' he said, breathless with adrenaline. 'You beautiful, beautiful woman, I knew you could do it.' He rushed toward her then with a quick, hungry kiss that pressed her lips painfully against her teeth.

'Ethan,' Terri said slowly. 'Audrey Lloyd is dead. Everything is yours.'

Ethan's face split open again with a wide, toothy grin, a howl of satisfaction filling the small, dingy motel room.

Four weeks ago

The situation with the business had been escalating for the better part of the year. The arguments, Ethan's drinking – it had all finally reached its apex. Terri was nearing her limit. She'd even called a travel agent to get the flight schedule from LAX to Bradley International in Connecticut, stuffing the torn sheet with the scribbled information into the pocket of her handbag. She wasn't ready for it. Not yet. The thought of life without Ethan terrified her. In adulthood he was all she'd ever known – the comfort, the familiarity were enough. Happiness was not owed to everybody. But lately she had started to wonder if perhaps she could be so bold as to want it for herself.

It was a Saturday and Ethan had taken off in the car, not saying goodbye, not telling her where he was going. Terri had been out in the garden, drinking wine under the canopy of the rich dark vine leaves, when he burst out onto the patio, shaking and shell-shocked.

His sunglasses were broken across his face, shards of glass from the left lens embedded into the skin around his eye.

'Ethan!' Terri shrieked. 'What the hell happened?' Her first thought had been a car accident. He'd been driving drunk and had hit something – or worse, someone.

'She's mad,' was all he said, his voice quiet and dazed.

'Who's mad?' Terri asked, bewildered. 'Where have you been?'

Ethan blinked and held his hand up to the side of his face where Terri could see a large bruise starting to blossom around his injured eye. He staggered forward and collapsed in one of the patio chairs, blinking disorientated around the garden.

'Wait there,' she said, jumping to her feet. 'Just wait there, I'm going to get the first aid kit and then you can tell me everything.'

She fetched the kit and a large glass of water along with two aspirin. Carefully, she removed the sunglasses frame and then set about painstakingly removing each shard of glass from his perfect face with a pair of tweezers.

'Ethan,' she said in a low voice. 'We're a team. You have to tell me what's been going on.'

'Jason has been on my back. Turning up the pressure, he wants his money back. The interest alone is...' He broke off and shook his head jerkily. 'I don't know what he'll do if he doesn't get it, Terri. So – so I went to Pops.'

'You went to *Pops*?'

'I don't know, I thought he might have some savings, something stashed away from the sale of the farm,' Ethan said, flinching as she dug out a particularly large shard of black glass. 'But he didn't.' Terri was not surprised. Ethan's grandfather, Pops, had sold the farm when his nana had died, and now, having lost both his daughter and his wife, had no impetus to do anything other than sit in his one-bedroom apartment and complain about the state of the world. Terri had met him only once. He'd called her a foreigner and not engaged her in much more conversation.

'Did I ever tell you they weren't my real grandparents?' Ethan said, and Terri blinked in surprise.

'No,' she said slowly, wondering where this was going.

'I've always known; they'd told me how Mom had gone to live with them when she was a teenager. But I never knew anything else, and I didn't really care. They treated me like I was all theirs, so what did it matter to me?'

'OK,' Terri said carefully.

'Pops told me more today. Mom's real mom was Nana's cousin, Annabel. Annabel Hackton.' He paused over the name, as if saying it might connect him to his lost family somehow. 'This woman, my other grandma I guess, dropped my mom off to stay with them for a weekend. And then she just disappeared.'

'Disappeared?'

'That's what Pops said. Never came back.'

'She just abandoned your poor mom?'

Ethan nodded while Terri dropped the final shard of glass onto the table. She picked up the bottle of antiseptic and tipped it onto a cotton wool bud. 'This is going to sting.'

'Well,' Ethan continued, flinching as Terri pressed the cotton wool to his head, 'well, there might be more to it. Pops always reckoned dumping Mom with them had been this cousin's plan all along. But Nana' – he paused and considered – 'Nana always thought there might be something to Annabel's story.'

'And what was her story?'

Ethan didn't answer immediately, as if he was still getting it straight in his own head. 'She gave them an envelope when she dropped Mom off, said it was insurance if they ever needed it. It was Mom's birth certificate.'

'Why is that insurance?'

Ethan sighed. 'Because the man listed as my mom's dad is Arnold Lloyd. The film producer.' Terri's eyes widened and she sat back in her chair, stunned. 'Apparently this Annabel said there was a note, a suicide note that was also his will, saying he left everything equally to both his daughters. She'd never felt quite right about taking half of the fortune and she'd had enough money to live well off. But, well, she'd got some new business venture she wanted to invest in. She was going to ask Arnold's other daughter, his legitimate daughter, for the money. But she didn't expect it to go so well; they didn't get on or something. The will was her back-up plan.'

'OK,' Terri said slowly, trying to tie this story of Ethan's heritage to their current situation.

'Pops had never believed her, thought it was too far-fetched a story. This cousin had worked for Lloyd and Nana had always said she'd had some kind of big crush on him, but it never sounded like it had been reciprocated. When Annabel didn't come back, Nana called the police, but they said there wasn't much for them to do. She'd driven off on her own, she was a capable adult, a resident in a different state and there was no evidence to suggest she was in danger.'

'She'd left her daughter behind?'

Ethan shrugged. 'I guess back then they just assumed hysterical women did shit like that. Hell, even Pops thought that. Maybe she did get some money from Lloyd's daughter and decided to set out on her own, leave the baggage back at the farm.'

'And they never wanted to track down your mom's apparent fortune?'

'Nah.' He shook his head. 'Not Pops's style, is it? He's a farmer.' He put on a gruff impression of his grandfather.

'*Don't need to go harassing a bunch of Hollywood types for money based on somethin' that's prolly not even true.* They never even told Mom.'

'But he told you.'

'Said if I needed money, there might be a hell of an inheritance due my way.'

'You believe it?'

'I do now.'

'Why now?'

'I went up there.'

'Went up where?'

'To Lloyd House. Arnold Lloyd's daughter – my aunt, I guess – she still lives there, some kind of shut-in. From the state of the place, I wouldn't say anyone's been up there in years. But it's a *big* old house. Lots of land, must be worth a fortune. I asked her for help, told her who I was.'

'And?'

'And her reaction told me that everything my real grandma had claimed was true.'

'So she'll help?' In the whirlwind of the crazy story, Terri had momentarily forgotten the state Ethan had come home in. She wanted to believe so badly that it could all be solved that easily.

Ethan scoffed. 'She could more than afford it if she wanted to.' His face twisted into a caustic scowl, an expression that made Terri's instincts stand alert. It was an expression she'd seen only a handful of times during their relationship, but when she had it had made her want to flee for cover.

'But she said no?' Her voice fell limply over the words.

'She didn't just say no,' Ethan said, shaking his head again. 'I told you – she's mad. She flew off the handle. Called me a liar and cheat, just like my grandmother had been. Trying to get my hands on what was hers, grabbing money from her, that was all we cared about. She – she got *violent*.' He seemed as surprised to say the word as Terri had been to hear it. 'She must be in her seventies by now, but she just came at me. Smashed a great big hardback book into my face.' He gestured at his injuries. 'So I just got the hell out of there.'

Terri deflated. 'It's not fair,' she said, hearing how pathetic it sounded.

'Terri, we don't need her.' Ethan sat forward, green eyes glittering now. 'I have Mom's birth certificate. Half that place is mine – we just need to call a lawyer!' A desperate cackle of laughter broke through his words, and Terri wanted nothing more than to let him have this victory. Let him think he'd solved their problems. But she couldn't. She shook her head.

'Ethan, it's not that simple.' His face darkened, but she continued. They'd had similar complications come through the office before; she wasn't an expert in probate law, but she knew enough. 'An illegitimate offspring can't just turn up and demand half an inheritance. There's no evidence. A name on a birth certificate isn't enough – the courts will need to see an acknowledgement from Arnold Lloyd himself that he accepted your mom as his daughter. And how the hell are we supposed to get that?'

'The will – his suicide note – it's up at the house.' Ethan had turned defensive.

'You're going to go back up and ask for it? That easy?' She gestured vaguely to his injured eye.

'No,' Ethan said steadily. 'You are.'

'And why would she give it to me?'

'She won't *give* it to you, but you can go up there and find it.'

'And why would she let me in? You said she's some kind of recluse.'

'I don't know!' Ethan threw his hands up in frustration. He cast about for a moment before settling back on her. 'Go up there for work. Try to buy the place or something. It'll get you through the front fucking door without a book in your face at least.'

'OK,' Terri said slowly, thinking hard. 'I'll ask around at work, see if I can float the idea.'

'Terri.' His voice softened, the annoyance falling from his face. He leaned forward and grabbed her hands. 'Please, Terri. You have to make this work. This is our last chance. It's all we have left.'

And that had been all she'd needed to discard the flight information from her handbag. They had a hope now, a plan. And when it was all sorted Ethan could start writing again. Stop worrying about the business. They could get back to how they had been.

She didn't stop to question whether you could build a future by trying to recreate the past.

Forty-Two

Terri
Saturday

Terri had done everything Ethan had asked of her. She'd even started to get carried away with the idea of actually acquiring the Lloyd Estate for Thornton Kendal, for the added bonus of a boost to her career. If she did find the will, she'd guessed the easiest option would be for Audrey Lloyd to rid herself of some of her three hundred acres in order to pay Ethan his share. And Terri would have a buyer ready and waiting, most likely securing herself a promotion and bonus check to boot. It was a win–win. That was how she'd seen it. The old woman could live out the rest of her days in her house, isolating herself as she pleased on her remaining half of the land. Presumably, when the time came, Ethan would come to inherit that as well. It was meant to be simple. It was meant to be the answer.

But Audrey had been a force she had not expected. And now the woman, who just days ago had been so vibrant and full of life, lay in a cold morgue.

'All of it,' Ethan breathed, staring at the suicide note. 'All of it's mine?'

Ours, Terri wanted to correct.

'I – I think I killed her.' Terri had not known she was going to say it. Hadn't known exactly what she was going to say when she came to this moment, but she'd known the moment was coming. Unavoidable. 'I'd slipped down the stairs, hurt my ankle.' She launched into her explanation. Her defence perhaps, even if she knew it was not strong enough.

But Ethan wasn't listening; he hadn't even responded to her confession. He was reading and re-reading the note that granted him a fortune.

'She kept me hostage, Ethan!' Terri's frustration combusted inside of her in the face of her fiancé's disinterest. She stepped forward and grabbed the will from his hand, tearing a slight nick in the old paper as she did.

'Hey!' He reared up, eyes following only the precious note.

'You don't even care what she put me through! She *drugged* me!' He blinked in surprise, but she carried on before he could respond. 'She locked me in a room; she wouldn't let me go. And Jason' – she threw her injured hand in the air, broken fingers now bound properly at the hospital, gesturing to her bruising cheekbone – 'this is what Jason did to me! All of this' – her voice faltered; she fell back – 'all of this. I did it all for you.'

'I—' Ethan looked momentarily dumbfounded. 'I know you did, Terri. You did amazingly.' His voice softened, eyes landing on hers briefly before flickering back to the will in her hand.

'I didn't, though,' she said, shaking her head. 'I think I killed her.'

Ethan swallowed thickly, jaw muscles tensed. He didn't know how to respond.

'I was in pain; I was scared. I don't remember it; it was all such a blur.' She shook her head, dropped her hands to her sides. 'We were arguing – she saw I had the will, and I think, I think she understood I was there for you. The look on her face.' Terri would never forget that look. Total betrayal. 'Somehow I fell over, I don't know how, and Audrey fell down the stairs.'

'There you go then,' Ethan said warily. 'It was an accident, just an accident.'

'I – I think I pushed her.' Terri welled up, real tears that choked. 'Murdered her.'

'No.' Ethan shook his head. 'No one could think that. After what she did to you.' He held a hand up toward her. 'Like you said, drugging you, holding you hostage. No one would blame you for self-defence.'

'She was also kind to me,' Terri gasped. 'She listened to me; she was interested in what I had to say.' Terri felt a wave of warm, sickly guilt as she remembered the first time Audrey had looked at her with that sparkle of intrigue in her kohl-ringed eyes. She shook her head. 'She was confused, just a confused old woman. You know she thought her best friend was still there, her friend who must have died years ago. She was a genius too.' As Terri spoke, she thought of the life, the vibrant, brilliant life that had been extinguished at the bottom of those stairs. 'And all those years alone, I think she just didn't know how to cope.'

'She was a mad old lady who wouldn't help us when we needed it,' Ethan spat. 'Her time was coming – her time has *passed*. Now it's our turn.'

'I don't know, Ethan.' Terri lifted the will in front of her again, inspecting it closely through tear-blurred eyes. 'If I killed her, if I *killed* someone, just for this – for a

313

piece of paper with desperate man's promise made decades ago.' Terri shook her head and moved her other hand into position. 'I don't think I want it like this, Ethan. I don't think I can live with the reminder of it.' Her fingers met at the top of the page, tensing, readying themselves to make that first tear. The first tear that would lead to a second, that would lead to a third, until Ethan's last hope of salvation was nothing more than confetti. Because, she had realised, it was *his* debt with Jason, not hers. Just as he had not once staked the claim on Lloyd House as *theirs* – it was his alone.

'Terri, stop!' Ethan's voice was pure panic, eyes wide and staring, focused only on the paper in her hand. 'Don't – whatever you think you're going to do, don't.'

'I don't want it like this, Ethan,' she repeated. 'Not if I killed someone.'

'Jason will come for me; he'll come for you too. We can't pay him off without it.'

Terri shook her head, no longer worried about Jason. 'I *killed* someone, Ethan!' she screamed, spittle flying desperately out with the words, her fingers making the beginning of a rip with the words.

'No, you didn't – I did!' Ethan roared in response.

Terri stared, her arms dropping a little as her shoulders sagged, shock coursing through her body. The man she'd loved, the man she was going to spend her life with. The man she *had* spent her life with.

'H-how?' she stammered. 'You weren't there.'

'I was calling and calling the house on Wednesday, but you didn't answer. I tried again on Thursday, and you still didn't answer. I stole a car' – he gestured vaguely out toward the motel's parking lot – 'hotwired it like Jason had taught me when were kids.' He stopped and gave a gruff attempt at a laugh at the irony. 'I came home, but you weren't there – the bed wasn't slept in. I didn't know where else you could be, so I went up to Lloyd House. I – I was worried.'

'About me?' Terri realised with a deep sadness that she did not believe it. 'Or about the will?'

'About both, alright?' Ethan threw his arms up in exasperation. 'Yes, I was worried about the will – it's all we have left, for fuck's sake! The last thing standing between me and Jason's goons.' Terri didn't point out that she had already been subjected to Jason's goons. 'You'd fucked it up so far – *four* days you'd been going up there and had nothing to show for it.' She heard the venom in his voice. 'I didn't know what was going on! I thought maybe I needed to take things into my own hands, that you might have left me, run out on me or something.'

'No, you did that to me,' she said quietly.

His top lip curled a touch upward. 'I had no choice, Terri. You know that. I have tried *everything*.'

'No, *I've* tried everything!' she screamed. 'You've just got drunk and wallowed.'

'I've sorted this, haven't I?!' he responded, pointing to the will. 'I killed that bitch and saved us a hell of a lot of hassle. Now *everything* is mine, no contest.' He shook his head, blonde hair rippling under the shitty orange bulb. 'You were so naive to think it could ever end any other way.'

Terri sagged. She stared at the man her fiancé had become. Perhaps the man he always had been, the signs wilfully ignored over the years. Love truly did blind. And she had loved him – still did love him – with a raw intensity that agonised deep in her soul. But sometimes, maybe, love just wasn't enough.

Then the knock came at the door, and Terri dropped her head. She could not look at him anymore. Not after this.

'Who the fuck—?' Ethan glanced over his shoulder.

'I think you should get it,' she said quietly, rubbing the tears from her cheek with the palm of her hand.

Ethan moved to the motel door and pulled it wide. On the other side was Detective Don Vernon, the flickering blue lights of a squad car dancing around the parking lot behind him.

Forty-Three

Don
Saturday

Ethan Archer was in the back of the marked car driven by Sinclair, who had met them outside the motel that morning with the wire equipment signed out of the station. Terri had come exactly as he'd asked – jeans with a heavy seam to hide the thin, rectangular device, and a baggy sweater to conceal the wires snaking up her body to just underneath the collar. A bag to suggest she was joining Ethan in hiding.

Terri sat next to Don in the passenger seat of his car, stoic and dry-eyed as they began the hour drive back to LA.

Yesterday he'd thought he was getting a confession from her. '*I ki—*' could only have ended one way. But she'd re-thought her words and said instead, more softly, 'I think I pushed her.'

Don had looked at her in interest. With a body bludgeoned to death, this was an odd point to admit.

'How do you mean, you think you pushed her?' Don prompted, eyes narrowing.

'I don't remember entirely; it was all such a blur.' She shook her head, eyes lowered. 'But I know I was angry, and I was scared. We argued at the top of the steps. She wouldn't order me a cab to get home; she wanted me to stay. She was gripping me tightly and, and then—' Terri stopped abruptly, a line creasing between her two dark brows, thinking hard.

'Then what, Terri?'

'Then I fell back on the ground. And I think I pushed her as I fell.'

'How did you fall back?'

She blew out a sigh, a deep frown of thought still twisted into her brow. 'I must have just tripped – but, that house. God, it does things to you if you spend too long there. I…' She paused as if trying to work out the words. 'I thought I felt hands on my head, buried in my hair, pulling me back.' Terri gave a small shudder at the thought, before looking back up at Don with an air of final confirmation. 'But there was no one else there. I don't know if I did it out of self-defence, or revenge… or just plain anger.'

'OK,' Don said slowly. 'So, you think you pushed her. Then what happened?'

She looked momentarily confused. 'Well, like I said, when I woke up, I went to check on her. She was murmuring but she was alive. I guess it just took me too long to get help.'

Don had taken this half-confession in carefully. 'And what about the Oscar?'

In that moment Don knew she was innocent. Terri blinked with genuine confusion.

'What Oscar?'

And Don had filled her in on Audrey Lloyd's violent end.

Her reaction had begun as shock, before an understanding had dawned on her, hands coming to her face as she stretched a silent groan into her palms. When she pulled them away her eyes glistened with tears again.

'I overheard you on the phone before,' she said sadly. 'The stolen car from the Quick Stop Motel. Where was it found?'

This had not been the response Don had expected. 'Oh. Down on Sycamore.'

She gave a small, bitter smile. 'The same Sycamore that meets with Elm, on the corner of which is the Double Tree mall? The nearest civilisation to the Lloyd Estate?'

Don pulled his notebook toward him, ready for business. 'Alright, Terri. Maybe it's time you tell me everything you know.'

He'd seen it had been a battle for her, a momentous decision that she had taken a long, silent minute to consider before nodding her agreement and beginning to speak.

She did not speak now though, not one word for the whole journey back, only the radio tuned to a Sixties station playing the hits from Don's past crackling between them. She waited patiently in the station too while he got the final confession from Ethan. On a moulded plastic chair, untouched cup of coffee next to her — handbag clasped desperately against her body.

–

In the interview room, Ethan gave his version of events up easier than Don expected.

Ethan had driven up to the bottom of the driveway and parked on the side of the road, tucked into the darkened moon-shadow of the trees, and walked from there. He claimed he didn't know what he planned to do, but instinct told him he needed the option of sneaking in and out without the roar of a car attracting attention at an all but abandoned house. He snuck in through the unlocked front door, desperate and addled with only thoughts of the promise of the old will – an obsession that had gripped him since he'd first heard about it.

'Desperation does funny things to a person,' he said with a melancholy shake of the head. 'Breaks your bones and warps you from inside out till you don't even recognise yourself anymore. The not knowing, the solitude in that motel room' – he paused and shook his head – 'it did something to me. I stopped caring about anything except getting that will. Getting what was mine.' His left hand jittered nervously open and closed as he talked. 'I got there, and I saw the place, and I thought – I just didn't care anymore. If I just killed the old bitch, I would get everything – and plenty of time to search the house for the will. I didn't think about all my careful plans before – for Terri to be there for work, to have a legitimate reason to be there and just happen to find the will. What luck.' He gave a scratched, sarcastic laugh. 'In that moment I didn't think that questions would be asked, didn't worry that suspicion could land only at my feet. I'd forgotten all of that. I thought Terri had abandoned me and with it…' He stopped and sought a word. 'I guess my sanity did too, I guess.

'I'd only just got into the living room. There was someone walking through in the dark. I waited for them to leave and was looking for a light when I heard voices outside on the terrace. It was Terri and Audrey. Terri looked—' He stopped, and Don was satisfied to see at least a scratch of sympathy for his fiancée carve his expression. 'She looked fucking awful. I didn't know what had happened, but she was limping, beaten. I knew Jason had hit her, but, man, I hadn't thought it had been that bad. But – but in that moment, I thought she must have chosen Audrey. That she'd stayed with Audrey to escape Jason – to escape me. I was furious, I wasn't listening to what they were saying, but as I got closer, nearly outside, I saw them tussle. Terri was holding something out – a piece of paper – and from the look on Audrey's face I knew what it was. Terri had done it. But Audrey wouldn't let go of her, and she was standing so precariously at the top of those steps. She was going to fall, and she was going to take Terri with her – so I rushed forward and pulled Terri back. I just grabbed her, by her hair, and she fell back to the ground.' He shook his head then, guilt drooping his eyes. 'I know it must have hurt her, but she would have gone down those steps with Audrey if I hadn't!'

Don let this defence sit in the air, untouched, until Ethan continued.

'Anyway, I thought it was all done. Audrey was dead, and we had the will. It was exactly what we wanted. But then Terri got up – I hid back in the kitchen; I didn't want her to see me – I wanted everything to be clean. But I saw her go down and check on Audrey. It was clear the old woman was still alive; she came back through, babbling to herself about calling an ambulance. So, when she'd gone, I – I took care of it myself.'

'You dumped the car at the nearest place you could get a bus from and were back in San Bernadino for breakfast,' Don finished for him.

Ethan nodded sadly. 'Something like that.'

–

When they were done Don found Terri exactly as he'd left her, hunched over her handbag gripped with white knuckles, coffee still undrunk on the side.

'You can leave if you want. We have everything we need for now.'

She nodded silently and stood, moving her bag carefully onto her shoulder. 'Can I leave the state?' she asked.

'As long as you leave forwarding details and come back willingly for the trial.'

'OK.' She accepted the conditions. 'I'm going to go back to Connecticut for a while.'

Don nodded and watched her leave, one hand raised in gentle farewell.

'Don, what are you still doing here?' Ray bustled through from the offices. 'I don't want Jill on the phone chewing my ear off about you working weekends again. Not worth my head.'

Don laughed. 'Heading home now, boss. Just wrapping up the Lloyd case.'

Ray gave him a knowing smile and a nod. He clapped his hand on Don's shoulder, a silent acknowledgement of a job well done.

Don accepted the praise and turned toward the cloakroom. It was done now. He'd be home in time for Saturday lunch with the grandkids. He thought about his old journal, no doubt hidden somewhere in the depths of a drawer. Maybe he would dig it out. Round out the Lloyd case.

And round out his career.

Forty-Four

Terri
Saturday

Terri clutched the handbag containing her future close to her body, the prop holdall of clothes down by her feet as she waited for her taxi. In her hand was the impound slip from the lot where her Maverick was waiting for her to collect it. Overnight there had been a raid on Jason's club, her car picked up from outside and immediately impounded thanks to the technicality of Thursday's early morning speeding ticket. Some of Don's colleagues had been close to arresting both Jason and the man he worked for for some time now – various drug and RICO charges – but with the guarantee of Terri's cooperation and testimony they finally had enough to move in and seal the deal.

She climbed out of the taxi at a dusty lot surrounded by a chain-link fence and trailed the attendant through rows of abandoned cars, her ankle aching as she struggled to keep up with his pace. She saw the familiar red before the attendant could point it out, and hobbled up to the car, placing her hands on its now dented bonnet. She didn't care; she was sure her brother could knock that out for her. Touch up the scrapes of silver where the paint had been scratched off from Jason's careless driving.

323

The attendant handed her the key and she signed the paperwork, throwing her bags into the passenger seat before sliding into the driver's. The ignition roared to life, and she closed her eyes for just a moment, feeling the car's vibration shudder through her. She glanced down at her handbag with a smile, the cash from the pawn shop still inside, and pulled out of the parking space. She exited the impound lot and stared out at the road spearing into the distance ahead of her. The road into her gold-tinged future. She was going home.

And then who knew where?

Author's Note

While everyone else in this book is a work of fiction, Leon Lewis was a real man – dubbed by the Nazis as 'the most dangerous Jew in Los Angeles'. He was indeed a Jewish lawyer in Hollywood in the Thirties, who worked tirelessly to build his network of spies against the encroaching threat of Nazism within the American border. Hitler's administration did have their eyes on Hollywood as the epicentre of the country to spread their fascist, anti-Semitic message, and the power of the German film market at the time meant that many producers indulged the whims of the German consulate. Isolated patches of the Hollywood Hills were used as training grounds for disgruntled veterans, or sons of veterans, for fighting and rifle practice in Nazi-style uniforms, and rogue naval employees in San Diego did illegally sell US military arms to fascist organisations.

While Audrey's role and the incident at Laurel Bryce are purely fictional, in 1934 Leon Lewis invited forty powerful studio heads, producers and directors to a secret meeting at Hillcrest (the real Jewish country club at the time), to raise funds to continue his spy ring. Together they pledged $24,000 (almost $500,000 today) and Lewis and his spies' continued work resulted in prosecutions of American Nazis and the prevention of many acts of sabotage and assassinations, including a plot to kidnap twenty major Jewish figures in Hollywood and execute them in a public parking lot.

Thank you to Clare for putting me on to this little pocket of history. And for a full account, including a million fascinating and heroic tales I couldn't quite fit into Audrey's story, *Hitler in Los Angeles: How Jews Foiled Nazi Plots Against Hollywood and America* by Steven J. Ross is an excellent read.

Acknowledgements

My first thanks for this book have to go to my editor, Russel McLean, without whose patience, vision and encouragement I'm not sure there would be a book to read at all! It was a difficult beast and one I lost faith with many times, but Russel saw the wood for Audrey's tangled trees for me and got it across the finish line. I am genuinely so thankful for all your support, ideas, and not-so-silly questions. Thanks to the wider Canelo team for your patience and hard work. Thanks to Miranda Ward for your eagle-eyed copy edits, and to Lisa Brewster at The Brewster Project for the beautiful, haunting cover.

Thanks to Clare at the Liverpool Literary Agency for taking me on as a debut, and for always championing my writing.

Huge thanks to my Writing Chats girls (and all excellent authors in their own right) Dani, Sarah and Meera for the endless podcast voice notes, advice, support and therapising.

Last but never least, thanks to my friends and family – Mum and Dad for buying up half of Waterstones' stock for my debut, which I have no doubt you'll both end up doing again for this one – your support in everything I've ever done is so appreciated and I love you both very much. To Hannah, Steve, Tim, Sarah, Theo, Ruby, Steph, Shaz and Katie for just always being there and championing my career so far. And finally, to Dave and Butter for making my everyday just brilliant and putting up with me – you definitely get the brunt of my writing stresses so really this, and every book, should be dedicated to you.

CANELOCRIME

Do you love crime fiction and are always on the lookout
for brilliant authors?

Canelo Crime is home to some of the most exciting
novels around. Thousands of readers are already enjoying
our compulsive stories. Are you ready to find your new
favourite writer?

Find out more and sign up to our newsletter at
canelocrime.com